HANDLED BY OFFICER

BY
KYM ROBERTS

Cover Art by
Susan Coils of Custom Covers
www.coverkicks.com
Edited by
Blue Otter Editing
www.blueotterediting.com

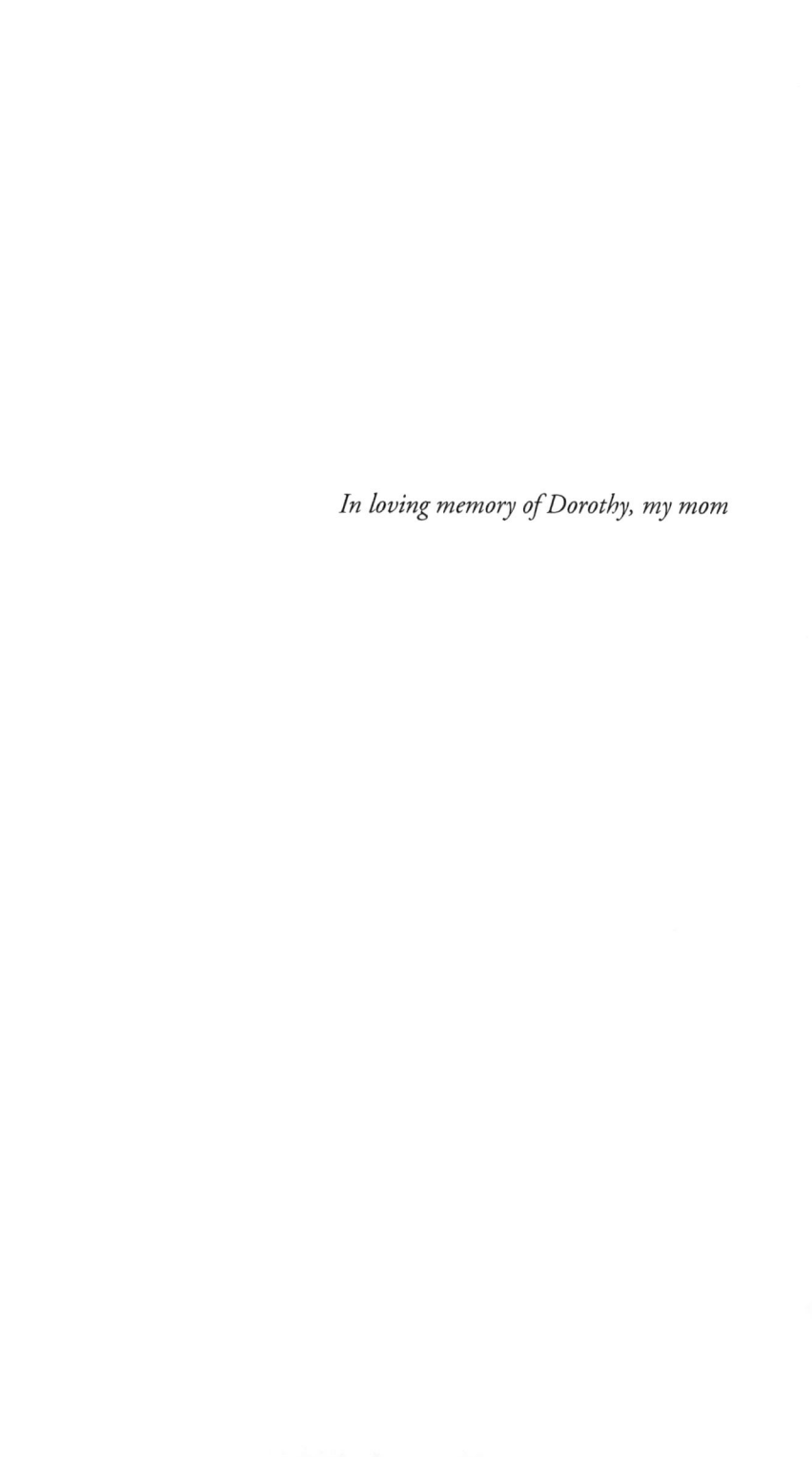

In loving memory of Dorothy, my mom

SPECIAL THANKS

There are so many people who took part in the creation of this book, to my very first critique partner: Angi Morgan, who taught me so much, to The Lit Girls: Jessica Davidson, Mary Duncanson, Kimberly Quinton, Misa Ramirez, Rebekah Reed, Beatriz Terrazas, Marty Tidwell, Tracy Ward, and Wendy Watson who have helped me in countless ways, to the women of Chick Swagger who accept me and all my non-girly ways, to Jerrie Alexander who made this book possible, and to all the members of NTRWA for your continued support —

Thank you!

But most of all thank you to my family, the reason every officer wants to go home:

HBO.

CHAPTER ONE

Mistake number one thousand, six hundred and eleven.

That's what this was, and there was no turning back. She'd screwed up royally this time.

"From this moment on, you will address every man or woman you pass in the hallways of any facility with, 'Hello, sir,' or 'Hello, ma'am.' I don't care if they're an officer, the chief of police, or your mother."

Gone was the friendly, rounded face with a quick smile and laughing eyes. Sgt. Joe McCain's voice bellowed through the auditorium as his brow cocked, and his eyes shot holes into every member of the police academy's eighty-second class.

Sgt. Jekyll was in the house ... and Kiley Gibbons longed to turn into Recruit Hyde.

"What have you gotten me into now?" she whispered to her sister. The complete opposite of Kiley, her twin was tall and lean, with long, silky brown hair and chocolate eyes that glistened with excitement. Her excitement confirmed Kiley's suspicions. She was nuts.

"Shhh." Her sister, Kay Lee who preferred to be called Lee, smiled with amusement.

Sgt. McCain's sights zeroed in on the pair.

Holy crap.

Kiley knew she looked like a startled cat in the middle of a roadway — big green eyes glistening in fear, her heart thudded to a sudden splat. She'd be road kill in a matter of seconds, and her fellow recruits would be scattered in the wind. Not literally, but if they leaned any farther away from her, Sgt. McCain would look like Moses parting the red sea. The only thing that kept Kiley in place was the recruit sitting next to her — her twin had enough spine to absorb Sgt. McCain's wrath.

God, it'd be nice to have half that spine.

Kiley tried to emulate her sister's straight back and lifted chin. She lost the battle with every purposeful step the sergeant took in their direction. By the time he reached the front row, she'd nearly disappeared into her padded seat.

"Did one of you ladies have something you wanted to add?" He leaned in for added effect.

His question was simple enough in context; too bad his tone cut Kiley off at the knees. She tried to swallow the fear. It went down with a loud gulp that hitched in her throat.

"Excuse me, sir. She has the hiccups, and I told her to be quiet. It was my fault." Big sis to the rescue as usual.

As if on command, Kiley hiccupped. Her hand flew to her mouth. *God, she was such a loser.*

Sgt. McCain gave the sisters one last look before addressing the entire group. "Starting tomorrow, your hair will be above your shirt collars. If that means you have to cut it ... cut it. You don't want me to cut it for you. Is that clear?"

His eyes returned to Kiley, taking in her wild curls. Slowly. Deliberately. Images of Army recruits getting their heads buzzed flashed through her mind. She hiccupped again, just to add to her humiliation.

Some recruits nodded. Others whispered, "Yes, sir." The majority responded with silence.

"I said, *Is* that clear!" The sergeant's voice bellowed off the walls, smacking each recruit in the face with his demand.

"Yes, sir!" Louder and stronger as a whole, their voices almost matched that of the man standing in front of them shaking his head in disgust.

Kiley wasn't sure who dreaded the next six months of training more. Her or Sgt. McCain.

Welcome to the world of the Kansas City Police Department, Kiley girl.

***

Walt Raynham looked over the room of recruits and couldn't help but smile as Sgt. McCain set his expectations. They were fresh-faced and naïve, some with stars in their eyes, others with pure terror radiating off every last inch of their stiff bodies. Like the doe-eyed blond with curls gone wild cascading over her shoulders. She'd caught his eye immediately. She was the exact opposite of the tall, willowy, athletic brunette sitting next to her.

In Walt's book, that was all good.

"She won't make it through the week." His partner smirked.

Something deep inside him stirred with Bret's contempt. Walt rubbed his jaw and cooled his expression before addressing the cynical cop he spent most of his life with. "You're wrong," he whispered over his shoulder. "If she wants to make it, there's nothing stopping her."

"How much you want to bet on that?"

Walt tried to shut his partner down. He left the blond behind and walked toward the exit. "I'm not betting on any of the recruits. We don't do that."

Right on his heel, Bret kept his voice low. "This won't tarnish your reputation. You won't be an instructor much longer."

Walt rolled his eyes, sensing the direction his partner was going. If history was any indicator, Bret Dugan would hound him throughout the morning, continue over lunch, and end in the locker room at the end of the day. Then he'd throw out one final comment as they got in their cars to go home. But it wouldn't end there. The process would repeat itself tomorrow. And the next day. And the day after that. Until finally, on the verge of insanity, Walt would give in.

Or he could just give in now, make the bet, and forget about it.

He stopped in his tracks and turned. Bret came up short, nearly running into his chest. But when he caught sight of Walt's extended hand, the anticipation of triumph was written all over his face.

Walt set his terms, "Fifty bucks says she makes it," and waited for Bret to balk at the amount. With two ex-wives and a kid by each, his partner was working every off-duty job he could find just to pay for the kids he couldn't afford to see. The hole in his wallet sucked, almost as much as Bret's life.

Bret hesitated before his eyes lit up with mischief. "I've got a better bet."

Warning crept up Walt's spine as his partner, standing more than eight inches shorter, tried to drape his arm around Walt's shoulder and steer him for the door.

"She quits—you have to ask her to marry you."

Walt choked on Bret's last words, which weren't in his vocabulary. His career path and family didn't mix. He knew what it was like to lose a father to the job. No kid, or wife should suffer that fate. And with two failed marriages, Bret, of all people, should at least value the process of getting married. Walt tried to pull away from his crazy partner, but Bret held tight to the epaulet on the shoulder of his shirt. Unless he wanted to tear his uniform, Walt would have to listen to Bret's half-baked plan.

Or break Bret's hand. (Somehow, that idea held a little too much appeal.)

"If she stays, you're free and clear. But if she leaves," Bret wore the smile of a snake, "you have to ask her to marry you."

Walt pulled away, not caring if his shirt tore. His partner had finally lost it. The sooner Walt received his transfer to the tactical unit, the better off he'd be. And the longer Bret would live.

"Unless, of course, you know she's going to break down in tears before the end of the day. It's kind of hard to propose to a *complete* stranger." Bret's eyebrows did a freaky dance above his eyes.

And this was the way the rest of the month would go. Walt should have let it lie. Instead, he'd taken the bait and stuck himself with this stupid shit for … for God only knew how long before his transfer finally came through the chain of command.

Pulling his sunglasses off his forehead, Walt put them in place before turning to Bret. "You're crazy. Marriage isn't in my future and it shouldn't be in yours, either."

Bret's grin got bigger. "Then put your future where your mouth is."

"When you grow up, maybe you can ask a *third* woman to marry you. I won't take that risk, no matter what the odds. She'll make it through the academy … if she wants to." Walt turned to walk away, but Bret's hand on his bicep stopped him. He looked over the top of his sunglasses at the man who was pushing all his buttons in the wrong direction.

"I saw the look in your eyes. You won't be able to resist her."

"You're wrong." Walt wasn't going to propose to anyone, and he damn well planned to stay as far away as possible from Recruit Kiley Gibbons.

Images of her naked underneath him with her hair sprawled across his pillow identified the real threat he was feeling. The real danger wasn't asking her to marry him or taking her to bed once she graduated from the academy and became a police officer. The real threat was his desire *not* to wait for graduation. For the student to become a lover.

Now.

A smile slid over Bret's face. Walt got the distinct impression his partner had read his thoughts — had seen his weakness at the exact moment Walt identified it.

"Who are you trying to kid. That was a love at first sight moment. I should know, I've experienced it twice." The creases in Bret's forehead smoothed with his smile, he was enjoying the moment too much.

"Yeah, how'd that work out for you?" Walt didn't wait for a response, he yanked his arm free and strode out the door with Bret following close behind, apparently unfazed by Walt's hit below the belt.

"Mark my words, you'll be proposing to that one."

Bret's prediction made his chest ache. Blood pounded at his skull. His mind rebelled and refused to keep the images of Kiley Gibbons out of his head. Halfway across the courtyard to the physical training section, his partner added to his frustration by whistling a melodic tune from hell. It floated on the breeze like a curse of doom, twisting and turning in his psyche, leaving a gaping flesh wound that refused to be ignored.

By the time they reached the workout mats in the gym, Walt had little doubt he was going to cram the fucking tune, *Here Comes the Bride* right down Bret's throat.

***

The two officers standing at the entrance to the auditorium had been the only thing to keep Kiley from bolting out the door when Sgt. McCain had finished his tirade. Not really, but it helped if she imagined them as the fallen angels. One sinfully sexy, the other treacherously sneaky. It was a double one-two punch that kept her butt planted.

"Where'd Bruiser go? Do you think he's still standing guard outside in case one of us tries to escape?" Kiley whispered to her twin.

Again, she got shushed. But this time it came from the over-weight recruit named Allen on her right. Her sister just smiled briefly and continued taking notes about the rules and regulations they were going to face.

God, it was boring.

She let her mind wander to the more interesting pair who'd left the auditorium. The larger man commanded attention. Demanded to be acknowledged whether she wanted to or not. She told herself the only reason she even noticed they were gone was due to the lack of inflection in the current speaker's voice, a monotone that could turn a double espresso into melatonin.

But *that* man, the officer with the flaxen hair and broad chest, looked like a Norseman standing at the bow of a boat, ready to conquer a new world. He was the perfect distraction from the hell she'd have to endure in order to wear the uniform. And to collect a paycheck, that's exactly what she was going to have to do. Focus on the man she couldn't possibly touch.

Wouldn't her boyfriend just love to hear that?

CHAPTER TWO

They looked like penguins. Some tall. Some short. Some carrying more fat under their downy white shirts as they gathered in the parking lot of the Regional Police Academy. Day two left the recruits divided into four sections of twelve, and labeled Form A through Form D. Which left one female in each group. Kiley's twin was at the opposite end of the nesting ground, rounding up the members of her form like a dominant king penguin.

A hiccup escaped.

Not now.

Just the thought of the instructors eyeing their uniforms for a hint of a flaw, sent her nerves into overdrive. Kiley wanted to tell them the whole stupid uniform was flawed — it was made for a man's body, not a woman's.

She swallowed the lump of apprehension forming in her throat and tried to focus on what they'd learned yesterday about role call formation.

Another hiccup escaped. Accompanied by a chirp.

Wonderful.

A couple of the guys looked in her direction, smirks marring their good looks. She knew they were counting down her days. If not hours. To make matters worse, the waves of heat rolling off the blacktop from yesterday's summer bake fest threatened to turn her complexion to the color of a beet.

Deep bright red, bordering on purple.

Unless the top button of her stiff shirt and her beautiful, black clip-on tie strangled her to death before then. Either way, it was all bad.

Another hiccup escaped.

"Did you see our form leader?" Allen asked, his red hair newly cut and making the baby fat still hugging his cheeks even more prominent.

"No, why?" Kiley couldn't imagine what difference it could possibly make. The instructors were all hard-nosed with a spit polish on their shoes and unbreakable creases in their uniforms. Their voices could drone even the most attentive recruit into oblivion.

She caught the next hiccup before it embarrassed her further.

"We got the big guy, Officer Raynham. I hear he's on the list to go to the TAC unit, and he's the main guy for Defense Tactics." Allen's eyes glistened with something akin to hero worship.

Kiley's heart flipped. Then flopped. Another hiccup brought her hand to her mouth. This was getting old fast.

The back door to the building swung open, negating Kiley's need to respond to Allen's assessment of their luck. The instructors walked out the back door as a team of neatly groomed officers, each member with a role and a purpose. Their macho camaraderie told all of the recruits to shut up and suck it up. Or get out now. The thin blue line was driven into the sand.

In complete contrast, the recruits scattered like penguins waddling double-time to their formations — the weak were sheltered, for now, in the midst of the four groups, three rows deep.

"Attehhhnnn-hut!" A loud, deep voice pierced the air.

She had no idea which officer had issued the command, but it really didn't matter. All the recruits stiffened their backs, shoved their semi-closed fists down to their sides, and notched their chins upward with eyes glued straight ahead to the new concrete-and-brick building. Her joints locked into the ridiculous position she'd been taught, her position in the front row made her feel vulnerable. Exposed. Especially when another hiccup squeaked out of her mouth.

Ugh.

She took a deep breath and let the air expel quietly from her nose. *Please, dear God, let them stop.*

Taking a second breath, Kiley's nostrils filled with the scent of Officer Raynham before she saw him. Clean. Fresh. Masculinity to the extreme. Her body reacted as if he'd touched her, caressed her and it took every ounce of her control not to melt into a puddle of desire at his feet.

Jeez.

Maybe she needed to go back to that Einstein-looking freak of a department psychologist. Somehow in the last twenty-four hours, instincts based on primal needs had taken over her body. Fight. Flight. And … procreate.

His shadow blocked the sun, shading her and the ginger-haired recruit standing next to her who worshiped the ground he walked on. She slid a sideways glance in Officer Raynham's direction. Everything about him demanded attention. His broad chest puffed out, ready for battle. His strong, squared-off jaw and straight nose spoke of a family lineage of Viking warriors. The small notch at the bridge of his nose, just below his eyes, hinted at a previous injury and gave credence to his battle experience.

"Your shoes need polished," he told the recruit two positions to her left.

His voice was everything she'd thought it would be — deep, smooth, and powerful. It floated through the air on a whisper. It did everything *but* drone her to sleep.

She wouldn't doze off in his classes. If anything, she'd be squirming in her seat trying not to imagine his hot breath traveling down the length of her naked flesh. And how was that possible?

She caught the next hiccup.

All she wanted was to be in control of her body — a body she was quickly learning wasn't hers to control. From the ramrod stiffness demanded by Sgt. McCain, to the arousal forming below her gun belt and the hiccups shaking her shoulders, outside influences were in charge and making her feet itch to walk away. Back to the life of day care, where she could at least swipe away a blond curl when it slipped from its tight restraint. Back where dirty diapers and snotty noses didn't assault her senses the way one man's presence did. Back to a world that wasn't a foreign country.

That was her flight instinct talking. Now she at least had two of the three covered.

"Do you want me to cut your hair with a knife, Recruit Gibbons?"

Kiley jumped at the question that wasn't a question at all. While she daydreamed of Mr. Viking, Sgt. McCain had snuck up from the opposite side to stand, red-faced, in front of her. His breath was clean, but in a sterile antiseptic way that assaulted her face with a warm surgical cut. Her straying ringlet of hair slid across her forehead to rest at the tip of her nose, tickling and teasing as it swayed in the hot summer breeze.

"No, sir," she said with more bravado than she felt.

"Then take care of it, or I will!" He turned and walked down the row toward B Squad.

Kiley quickly tucked her hair behind her ear.

"Do you think another recruit getting yelled at is funny, Mr. Tibbs?" Sgt. McCain's question rocketed through the ranks as each recruit flattened his or her expression and tried to melt into the sea of black-and-white uniforms.

The soft response Tibbs muttered faded into oblivion. Obviously, he hadn't learned, being soft-spoken was a forbidden escape route.

"Form B!"

Every recruit straightened. It didn't matter that Sgt. McCain wasn't addressing the entire class. They listened, held their breath and waited for the ball to drop. Because what happened to Form B, would no doubt happen to all of them in the upcoming weeks.

Several times over.

"Drop and give me fifty! Your first lesson of the day — help and assist your fellow classmates."

Bodies dropped.

Some faster and more agile than others. But the entire group of twelve did as instructed. Because to ignore it… Well, that could be classified as suicide.

They rose and fell in an awkward dance that lacked precision and rhythm. Their form leader counted off and walked among them, berating those who couldn't keep up. Tibbs received a particularly brutal amount of criticism for his crime against Kiley, who'd missed his dig while caught up in her own personal hell.

No doubt, she'd hear about it later. From *all* the members of B Squad.

"Step forward, Recruit Gibbons." Tinged with disappointment, Officer Raynham's voice was still sexy and smooth as he watched B Squad's mediocre performance.

Kiley fought the urge to run in the opposite direction and quickly stepped forward while biting her bottom lip.

She was not going to hiccup.

Nor was she going to think about the dream she'd had the previous night of Officer Raynham's strong thighs and rippled abdomen. Or all of the wonderful parts of his anatomy in between. She was in a relationship that made her happy.

Very happy, and a dream was a far cry from everyday life.

Stepping closer than she wanted, Kiley tried not to visualize him naked as her body stiffened at attention. She steeled her emotions and her hiccups, ready for the private ass-chewing headed her way.

She must've been crazy to let Lee talk her into applying for a job with this type of torture. Certifiably insane. Just because her day care job had closed its doors, didn't mean she couldn't get a job at another one. Going to the police academy proved she'd lost more than a few screws in her head somewhere along the way.

Her sister was supposed to be the nut case, not Kiley.

She stared at the black plastic name tag and the colorful ribbons adorning his tailor-fitted shirt. It was the complete opposite of the puckered and pulled version she wore, and it made her grateful for the brim of her uniform ball cap blocking her view of his eyes. The last thing she needed to see was disapproval written all over his face.

That would definitely take a toll on her ego, it would be nice if one man in her life was betting for her to succeed.

CHAPTER THREE

Shit, Gibbons.

Walt knew Bret was pissed. At her.

The glares he was throwing her direction while yelling at his recruits in B Squad told the tale of where Bret placed the blame. Tibbs snickering during her confrontation with Sarge couldn't possibly have anything to do with the discipline handed down two minutes into their day.

Walt waited a couple extra beats as her body swayed with rigidity within inches of his chest. He wanted to touch her. Steady her. Hell, who was he kidding? He wanted to hold her.

When Kiley Gibbons had shown up on Walt's roster list the previous afternoon, his partner had whooped and started planning Walt's bachelor party. Walt had silently cursed the powers that be. He would not take the bet, and he refused to let Bret know she was under his skin. Yet somehow, Bret knew.

What had he done to deserve her? Granted, he'd had a one-in-four chance of Gibbons being placed under his supervision, but why couldn't the *other* Gibbons be assigned to his squad — the one who didn't tempt his body, his sanity, or his job?

Steeling himself against her feminine features and alluring scent, he looked down to the top of her navy neoprene ball cap with the letters KCPD embroidered on the front. Her curls were invisible. Along with her eyes.

Shit, she was beyond short.

He refused to let his mind wander to thoughts of her breasts brushing up against his dick. That was *not* going to happen.

Taking a deep breath, he bent down to peer into emerald-green eyes that looked straight through his own. Her mouth was tightly drawn with stress or determination, maybe both.

Then she hiccupped. A little bird noise that could be described as adorable. If you used words like adorable. Which he didn't.

"Recruit Gibbons?"

"Yes, sir!" Her breath hit his cheeks as she yelled with more force than he'd expected.

Walt denied the smile tugging at his mouth. "This is a private conversation between the two of us. Is that understood?"

"Ye—" Her voice faltered. Her eyes focused, perused his entire face as she tried to decide how to answer his question.

He lowered his voice even further. "I called you forward so that your entire squad couldn't hear us. Okay?"

She nodded, her expression lost in uncertainty.

"Good." He tried to remain focused on her eyes, but when she bit her lip with apprehension, he couldn't help but let his gaze stray to the pink, delicate mouth he wanted to devour.

She cleared her throat and forcefully swallowed, bringing Walt back to the present. "No matter what Sgt. McCain says, *do not* cut your hair," he ordered.

"But—"

Walt didn't let her finish. "It's a test of your personal strength. Don't buckle. Is that understood?"

"Yes … yes, sir," she stammered as she looked for his lack of sincerity.

Walt made sure all she saw was the serious expression of an officer looking out for her best interest.

"Thank you, sir."

"I'm counting on you to show these guys what you're made of." He didn't tell her an instructor had wanted to bet against her.

Then, for a moment, Walt forgot everything. Lost himself in the green depths bordered with a turquoise sea that sparkled in the center. Her eyes could mesmerize him for days. They were beautiful. If you used words like that. Which he didn't.

"Yes, sir. I won't let you down." She nodded imperceptibly to everyone but him, as the sea twinkled and surged in her eyes.

He held her gaze, as painful as it was, and barked out an order the first row of recruits could hear. "Get back in formation, Curls."

She hesitated with the nickname that fit her curls gone wild. Caught his smile and then followed his lead perfectly. "Yes, sir!"

Somehow they felt in tune. Like friends or lovers who'd known each other for years.

Friends. Definitely friends.

If they'd been lovers, she wouldn't have tried to bring him out of his fantasy when she'd caught him staring at her mouth. If they'd been lovers, he would have teased her about her hiccups. Instead, he wondered if she recognized his desire to pull her into his arms and crush all of her apprehensions to dust.

He turned away. Strolled through the rest of inspection acting more relaxed than his clenched gut would allow. Inside, he was anything but calm and composed—he ached. If he was honest with himself, he'd admit it had nothing to do with his stomach and everything to do with her soft curls.

Fuck honesty.

He focused on the job at hand. Crooked ties, lackluster gun belts, and missing creases. Gig lines that looked like zigzag patterns from their neckline to the zipper of their pants instead of the perfectly straight line of a professional. All topped off with unpolished shoes needing a little spit and elbow grease.

Walt flat-out ignored the flashed images of tossing off Gibbons' hat, pulling her ponytail loose, and running his hands through her hair — that was not something to think about. Because that would lead to tearing off her tie, ripping buttons from her uniform, and exposing the soft, firm mounds of her breasts.

He barked something stupid to the last recruit and suspected his cut direct had been unintelligible. Which left him irritated and annoyed and cussing his boss for putting Gibbons in his squad. For enticing him every minute of the day for the next six months with a woman who technically should be *just another boot*. A boot with a cute ass — yes. But not a boot to tempt him into self-destruction.

No. He wouldn't let that happen.

His eyes closed as he turned away from his form. He struggled to get his brain back on track. Back to the training, back to the order of inspection and morning roll call, back to his comfort zone, where sanity prevailed. Because in one moment, he would be standing in front of her, giving his team the commands to stand at parade rest.

While his dick wanted to raise the flag to glory.

Walt made it to the front of his three-line formation and stood facing her, his back to the state-of-the-art building where he'd be stuck with her every day until his transfer came through. He stared, over her head, at a lone runner making his way around the track across the parking lot, while Sgt. McCain finished dressing down a recruit in D Squad for a pathetic attempt at facial hair.

That's what he needed. A good, fast-paced run to excise her from his brain. Sweat pouring off his body…

He did everything to ignore her, yet still found his senses memorizing her. He felt her presence. Smelt her cologne, and heard her sigh. Maybe it was a hiccup, he wasn't sure, but he should've missed the slight breathy noise she made. If she was like the rest of the recruits.

Their eyes met. And locked.

Sgt. McCain was ranting about something as he walked back and forth. If Walt looked, he'd see Sarge's hands firmly placed in the small of his back. Chin tucked in. His stare piercing any recruit brave enough to catch his eye. The fear of humiliation was nearly palpable. But looking into Gibbons' eyes, Walt realized she wasn't scared. Her hiccups were gone. She was unaffected.

At least by Sarge.

Her eyes, however, mirrored his torment. Unwanted desire burned hot and primal in her core. Both of them felt it. Neither one of them wanted it.

He looked away first. He was the one in the position to do the right thing. Her instructor. Her first-line supervisor. It was his job to keep them on track. Keep it professional, no matter how hard it got.

Son of a …

He forced himself to watch Sgt. McCain begin his daily questions about the crimes that had occurred the previous night. The murders. The rapes. The car chase gone bad. With each question, recruits dropped like belligerent arrests being tazed, their tongues tied, answers incoherent.

Sarge's gaze glistened with enjoyment. The man *loved* every bit of their discomfort. He thrilled at making them ill at ease. Because the day would come when these recruits would be at a community meeting and a citizen would put them through a similar drill. Learning to deal with being put on the spot was lesson number two for the day. An uninformed cop, made for an easy target. A knowledgeable cop, could mend fences.

Yeah. Focusing on Sarge was much better. Much easier.

The drill forced the recruits to come to terms with their training extending beyond the hours of the academy. They would be living, breathing, and eating everything the academy dictated. They would learn to incorporate the news with their family television time. Their car stereos would tune in to news stations, not their favorite playlists on satellite radio. In the next six months, the job was going to transform them into new human beings. They would change into someone they wouldn't recognize today.

For some, it would be for the better, for others…

Walt stole a glance at the woman standing in front of him, expecting to see that knowledge sinking in and maybe a last gulp of freedom lost forever. What he found startled him and caused him to sway a fraction of an inch. Something he hadn't done since he went through the academy.

This time, he couldn't look away, because her gaze wasn't fixed in fear on the brick wall or Sarge like the rest of her class. No, she was still watching Walt.

And *son of a bitch*. He was stupid enough to look right back at her … and smile.

CHAPTER FOUR

Filing into the locker rooms, Kiley noticed, for the first time in her life, the guys were at a decided disadvantage. The women had a line of four. The men, however, were crowding forty-four into a room that, from all appearances, was the same size as the women's locker room.

She couldn't help being somewhat pleased by their discomfort.

"I don't think you'll have time to fix your hair, Tibbs." Her sister added a totally inappropriate finger to her comment, before pushing Kiley into the women's room. Tibbs had no time to reply before they disappeared out of sight, but the male laughter echoing in the hallway, let them know he wasn't about to back down.

It was the first time Kiley had gotten a look at the man who'd been foolish enough to laugh at her discomfort. She supposed if she'd met him in a bar, she'd describe him as good-looking. Dark hair, dark eyes, tall and built. Not as hot as Officer Raynham, but still a man to catch your eye. His personality, however, stunk. The anger he directed toward her and her sister, negated any of his physical attributes; he was ugly to the core.

She sighed. The last thing they needed was an enemy on the second day of the academy.

"Really, Lee? Geesh, the man probably hates us." She grabbed her sister's arm and tugged her in front of the mirror while the other two women went toward the compact locker area. "I'm the one who needs help with my hair, not Tibbs." Her plea sounded almost desperate even to her own ears.

"He was told to get a haircut. Maybe we should just cut ours. It'll grow back." Lee looked at her in the mirror, uncertainty wrinkling her brow.

As the older twin, Lee had made the rules, and Kiley followed. Lee wanted to play baseball; Kiley played. Lee wanted to run track; Kiley joined the team and stayed right next to her. Lee wanted to sneak out on a date … yeah, Kiley covered for her and worried the entire night until Lee finally tip-toed into the house at two a.m.

That was the one time Kiley had put her foot down. Lee may not have gotten caught by their parents at seventeen, but Kiley had refused to play mother again. She'd defined the rules for Lee that night while sitting across from her on the bed. If her sister tried it again, Kiley would be sitting in the front room, with their parents when Lee tried to sneak back into the house.

This was the second time in their life, Kiley was going to stand up to Lee. Because Kiley knew, beyond a doubt, neither one of them should touch their hair. Like Samson, when Delilah chopped off his locks, they would lose their strength. Not because it made them who they were, but because it defined who they weren't — quitters.

"No. If you don't want to help, that's fine. But I will *not* cut my hair. And neither will you." Her voice held the conviction she hadn't had before Officer Raynham's words of encouragement.

How was it possible that he'd known what she'd been thinking? How had he said the perfect thing to keep her from doing what she didn't want to do? And how was she going to stay away from a man like that?

"Of course I'll help you. Don't be ridiculous. Besides, you'd look like Shirley Temple if you cut your hair, *Curls*." Her sister tugged on Kiley's curl.

"And you'd look like a little boy if we cut yours," Kiley retorted.

Her sister changed the subject. "What did Officer Raynham say to you? Did he chew you a new asshole?"

"Really, Kay Lee?" Kiley laughed at her sister's expression. Lee hated her given name and had declared it too cute for a girl like her at the age of eight. But she was wrong. Despite being a tomboy, her sister was beyond cute. If truth be told, Lee had a graceful elegance to her beauty that was in total contrast to the way she saw herself.

Lee's hands tightened in Kiley's braid, holding her head still and forcing her to answer the question about Officer Raynham. "No, he didn't chew me out at all. He was very ... thoughtful."

"Thoughtful?" Lee snorted. "Don't tell me he already hit on you?"

"Of course not! It wasn't like that at all." There was no way she'd tell her sister about the chemistry between them. Or how he'd looked as if he'd wanted to kiss her in front of the entire academy.

"Then tell me what it *was* like?" Lee's voice tinged on anger.

Kiley shook off the fantasy involving her new boss. "Stop it. It wasn't anything like that. He just told me not to cut my hair, that Sgt. McCain was testing my strength."

"He warned you?"

"No. He reassured me that I was fine and that I wouldn't have any problems." And had somehow made himself even more delectable in her eyes … if that was possible.

Lee finished the braid and tucked the end under with her barrette. "Wow. He sounds like a good leader … or —"

"There's no *or*. He's going to be a great boss."

Lee looked uncertain, but a glance at her watch brought her back to a more comfortable conversation. "You better hurry. I've got report writing, but if I'm not mistaken, you've got to change for physical training."

Kiley groaned, and her sister laughed.

"I'd take your place if we were identical, but I'll never pass for Shirley Temple."

"And I'll never pass for a boy!" Kiley threw back at her departing sister.

***

The first day of PT was always eye-opening. Walt could tell which recruits were athletic, lifted weights, or had a runner's body. What visual inspection couldn't show was the fight inside the individual. And sometimes the one he least expected would rise to the top because of his or her dogged determination and desire.

Gibbons didn't have the desire. She didn't want to be here. She was a nurturer at heart — a caretaker. He glanced back to check on her for the twentieth time, she was falling *way* behind. She'd be out of sight once he rounded the next corner and the dilapidated neighborhood would swallow her whole with overgrown hedges blocking any possible view he'd have of her. She needed to pick up the pace, except she wouldn't. She lagged because she was running circles around recruit Allen who'd clearly done nothing to prepare for the physical side of the academy.

"Take up the lead, Rodriguez." Walt left the front of the line to the recruit fresh out of the military and pulled off to the side, jogging in place on the cracked blacktop until Gibbons and Allen caught up.

"Doing okay, Curls?"

"Yes, sir," she replied with more ease than he'd expected considering her cherry complexion.

"How about you, Allen?"

"Ye … yes … siiir." Allen's "sir" came out on an exhale that drained the last ounce of color from his face.

Eyeing Curls further, Walt realized she hadn't worked up a sweat. At this rate, she could turn purple and collapse from heat exhaustion. "You're not sweating, Curls."

"No, sir." Her voice was strong, totally unaffected.

"Did you hydrate this morning?"

"Yes, sir. I just don't sweat much, sir. Which makes me turn a little redder than most people when I run."

Allen stumbled, and they both reached out to keep him from falling on his face on the cracked sidewalk. Walt pulled up to a stop.

"Walk it off, Allen."

Allen nodded, too exhausted to even acknowledge the command with a verbal response as sweat poured from his body.

Grabbing Curls' arm, Walt pulled her to a stop when she started walking next to her squad member. Unlike Allen, she didn't huff and puff until she blew the trees down. Nor did she drip up a stream.

"Do you have an underlying medical condition I need to be concerned about?" He couldn't stop his eyes from looking for a physical defect. A defect he certainly didn't see.

At five foot two, her short legs actually appeared long and smooth. Perfect for wrapping around his waist. Her flat stomach called for his tongue to run the distance to her navel. And her hips. A groan escaped his mouth. Her hips advertised the perfect shape for him to grab as she sat on top of him.

He tried to bring his eyes up to her face, but they stopped at the rise and fall of her breasts, the rhythm threatening to undo him. And just as he thought he'd escaped the danger zones, Walt observed a sweet tendril of hair sneaking out of its new braid along her neck demanding to be tamed.

Holy mother, he was hurting.

She laughed. A cute jingle that made him want to smile.

"No, *sir*. Do *you* have one *I* should be aware of?" Her eyes traveled the length of him, pausing where he wanted them to.

Damn, he shouldn't be wanting anything.

Her left brow rose in a silent question. Daring him to handle his problem.

He ignored it.

"No, Gibbons. As your PT *instructor*" — he may have emphasized that a bit too much — "I was just wondering if your reddened complexion, your lagging behind, and your lack of sweat were signs of a medical condition."

She actually laughed at him. Again. She laughed at her instructor … when she wasn't supposed to. It was a first. And Walt realized she was a first in every possible way. She tempted. She teased. She tested every part of his self-control. And she didn't even realize she did it.

Or maybe she did.

Her voice held the control he didn't feel. "For whatever reason, I don't sweat very much. Which causes my face to turn red." Her voice dropped a fraction in an obvious attempt to spare the feelings of her classmate. "I lagged behind because Allen needed someone to encourage him to keep going. Otherwise, I'd be giving you a run for your money." Her eyes strayed for a second time.

Maybe she wasn't in control.

"What kind of run did you have—"

A shot echoed through the neighborhood, interrupting the question he shouldn't ask.

"Get down!" he yelled at a stunned Allen before shoving Gibbons over a hedge at the edge of the sidewalk. Branches scraped and caught, but Walt knew it was better than a bullet piercing her body. He landed on top of her. A position he would have loved — without gunfire as their background music. He rolled, grasping on tightly to her small frame till his back was to the gunman.

And she was protected.

Exactly where he wanted her, as more shots rang out across the street. He didn't have time to analyze the deep need gnawing at the center of his gut, ordering him to keep her safe.

It wasn't a normal reaction with a fellow officer. And it wasn't welcomed. But it was there.

A deadly silence filled the streets. No birds. No dogs. Just her breathing intermingling with his own. On the hard, grassless turf in front of a rundown house. He released her soft, supple body and denied any reaction flooding his system. He wanted to touch her and be touched. Instead, he moved away. Jumped into a squatting position to check on Allen. The other recruits. And the unknown gunman—all in one look.

She was up next to him peering through the brush, mirroring his movements. Her breathing now erratic with the adrenaline dump she didn't know how to control. He pulled his phone out of the strap on his bicep and handed it to her.

"Call 911. Tell them we have shots fired in the middle of the eighty-seven-hundred block of Kensington. The shots are possibly coming from behind 8723. Unknown suspects."

He turned and was gone.

CHAPTER FIVE

Holy crap. Holy crap. Holy crap.

Kiley watched Officer Raynham check on Allen and then signal to the rest of her squad at the end of the block to stay down and out of sight. She dialed 911 with fingers that wouldn't bend — knuckles locked into place, refusing to move. Giving up on her adrenaline-stiffened digits, she poked the numbers a second time while taking deep breaths to gain control of her out-of-control body.

"9-1-1. Call taker seventeen. What's your emergency?" The voice at the other end clearly wasn't experiencing tingling fingers that wanted to freeze.

"We have shots fired in the middle of the eighty-seven-hundred block of Kensington." Kiley repeated Officer Raynham's instructions while trying to locate the man through a small hole in the hedge.

"Did you see someone shooting a weapon?" The call taker's voice still hadn't reached the stage of being awake.

"No, but —" Kiley started.

"Is anyone injured?" she interrupted.

"Not that I know of —"

"We'll have officers en route. Do you wish to be contacted?"

She was going to hang up. Kiley could visualize her hand moving to disconnect the call on the keyboard in front of her. "Yes!"

"What is your address, Ms. Raynham?"

"My ... what?" The call taker's use of Officer Raynham's name set Kiley back, slowing down her ability to process anything. Everything.

"The address you're calling from?"

She should correct her. Tell her that her name wasn't Raynham. Instead, Kiley focused on the job and turned around to read the street address numbers boldly displayed in black on the beige porch.

"I'm at 8716 Kensington—"

"Officers are en route."

"But —"

The line went dead. Kiley stared at the phone, wondering if she should call back. She tried to locate Officer Raynham across the street as another shot echoed through the neighborhood. The sudden image of him lying on the ground bleeding to death clouded her vision.

Oh. My. God.

Blood washed through her veins and flushed through her ears. Her breaths came short and fast at the sudden thought of losing him. Her stomach turned. Made her want to vomit. Just moments ago, he'd been on top of her, removing her from the line of fire and protecting her from whomever was shooting ... now he could be dead.

She had to *do* something!

She glanced down the road and looked for her classmates. Allen was on the same side of the street as she was, hiding behind a car that was parked along the road. His breathing even more labored than it had been when he was running. The rest of her class was nowhere in sight, probably hidden next to houses down the block.

Fisting her stiffened hands, Kiley forced blood back into the offending appendages and took off in a squatted run. She reached the end of the hedge and whispered in a desperate yell, "Allen!"

The man stared off into space, his focus unknown. Again, Kiley yelled for her classmate.

This time, he looked up and caught her movements. Getting to his feet, Allen began to come to her. She quickly waved him off, then made a mad dash to his location as he moved down the length of the beat-up Cadillac.

"Get behind the tire," she hissed. The man's lack of focus was causing him to lose sight of what was important — staying alive.

Allen did as he was told, and Kiley peeked through the window of the car. A glimpse of movement on the left side of the house caught her attention. Officer Raynham jumped the tall wooden fence into the backyard of 8723 Kensington. She quickly handed the phone to Allen.

"Call 911. *Don't* let them hang up on you. Tell them Officer Raynham is at 8723 Kensington in pursuit of a suspect in regard to the shots fired in the middle of the eighty-seven-hundred block of Kensington. *Do not* let them hang up. Give them a description of everything that is going on. You got that?"

She looked at the man trying to dry his sweat-drenched hands on an equally wet pair of shorts. He was nodding his head and staring down at the phone.

"Allen!" she hissed again.

His head snapped up, and she caught his gaze.

"*Do not* let them hang up. If they do, you call them back and stay on the line. Make sure they know Officer Raynham needs help — and that he's unarmed."

Allen nodded more enthusiastically, finally grasping the importance of his role.

Kiley took a deep breath and flexed her hands once again.

"What are you going to do?" He looked as lost as she felt.

"I'm going to help Officer Raynham. Make that call." Before he could say anything else, Kiley dashed from the concealment the car had given her and ran. Heart pounding louder than her feet hitting the pavement, she watched the front of the house for any sign of danger.

Too late, it hit her that she could be watching the wrong house. Just because Officer Raynham had jumped this fence didn't mean the shooter was inside.

A new spurt of adrenaline had her heart deafening her ability to hear anything else. Her feet moving faster than they ever had in her life, she sent up a silent prayer not to get shot in the back. Her breathing hitched as she stumbled on the curb and grasped at the grass rushing toward her face. She dug in and refused to let herself fall as she grasped the ground and flung it backward in the most ungraceful frog leap or bunny hop in history.

After several crawl-hops, she righted herself in time to fall at the base of the privacy fence Officer Raynham had gone over. She tried to listen to what was happening on the other side, but all she could hear was her own breathing as blood pummeled through her veins.

This definitely ranked up there with one of the stupidest things she'd ever done.

CHAPTER SIX

Son of a bitch.

An alcoholic, from the looks of his bloodshot eyes and gray complexion, who'd decided it was okay to target shoot within the city limits — in the middle of a neighborhood, with his son playing in the backyard within feet of the target that was mounted on a steel drum along the back fence.

He might've tried to talk to the man, except the guy had proceeded to take a swig of beer, grumble, then cuss and mutter at something or someone in the back of the garage. And despite the paper target duct-taped on the can, Walt couldn't see any holes in the paper rings. Or the white rectangular outline. For that matter, there weren't any visible bullet holes in the steel barrel or the fence. Which made him damn uncertain as to what, or who the real target was.

Walt slowly made his way toward the toddler hiding behind a mountain of trash that looked like an entire range of black plastic, capped in layers of white synthetic snow. The almost-naked child crouched down with his hands in the dirt, ignorant, or uncaring of the bugs crawling all around him. His gaze was confused and leery of drunken man still waving a Glock held loosely in one hand, while amber liquid sloshed out of a beer bottle in the other before he disappeared into the recesses of a detached garage.

Out of sight, but definitely not out of mind.

Walt didn't hesitate. He ran the length of the backyard, grabbed the small boy, and headed back. The boy stiffened. And Walt made the mistake of looking down into his large blue eyes. The gut-wrenching truth hit him harder than he'd ever dreamed possible.

The boy's father hadn't caused the terror in the eyes looking up at him.

Walt, the big, sweaty, giant of a stranger created the all-consuming fear in the boy. Walt was everything a good parent would warn the child against.

For the first time, uncertainty about his decision to take the boy made him falter. Obviously, the kid had drawn the short end of the stick when it came to fathers. And Walt was betting his mom was a victim. But she had taught him what to fear: his father and strangers — like Walt.

His expression would live in Walt's mind for an eternity.

He wanted to be the man the boy could trust. To look up and know that everything was going to be all right. To know that Walt would protect him at all possible costs.

He told himself it didn't matter. The kid's immediate safety was his focus. He lifted the boy over the fence, and just as he was about to drop him to safety, the drunk yelled. The boy whimpered. And someone hit the ground on the other side of the fence with a feminine intake of breath he shouldn't recognize. Someone with enough curls to notch up his own anxiety.

"It's Gibbons," she whispered. "Hand the child over."

His heartbeat kicked into overdrive. Did she ever do what she was told? Not only had she put herself in the line of fire by running across the street, but she was standing on the other side of the fence, ready to take the weeping boy who would direct more attention her way.

And possibly draw fire from the drunk in the garage.

Son of a —

Walt stepped on a nearby bucket and looked over the edge at the angelic face on the other side of the fence.

— bitch.

Anger threatened to undo him. He'd known it was her before he caught sight of her rosy face. Part of him admired her. And wanted her. In more ways than he had a right to think about since she was his recruit.

And all that just served to piss him off even further.

"Hand him to me. Then you can hop over," she commanded as if she were in charge of the situation.

He ignored her tone. "Take him. Go back across the street and wait for my *real* backup to arrive. I think there's someone else trapped in the detached garage in the back yard. The suspect is a white male, about thirty wearing a white undershirt and jeans." Anger blasted his words in her direction. He couldn't help it. She had to know her place … or get killed.

And that was not an option.

He didn't wait for her to argue. He dropped the boy into her arms and jumped down. Then he told himself he would not kill her if he made it out of there alive.

The sultry sound of her voice comforting the boy leaked through the fence. "Shhh. It's going to be okay."

It worked. The scared-shitless toddler quieted. And as her voice traveled away from the fence, Walt's blood pressure returned to normal — right where it should be when facing an armed, crazy drunk without a bulletproof vest or a weapon on his hip.

Sirens murmured in the distance as Walt moved closer to the garage stuffed with clutter. At least Curls had listened to *part* of his instructions. The cavalry was en route.

Of course, that could be good … or it could be really bad. The boy's father could become more enraged and take it out on whomever he was yelling at in the back of the garage. Or he could remember his son and look for him.

Growing closer and closer, the sirens bounced and skipped through the neighborhood. Until they stopped. Leaning against the weathered, wooden planks of the garage, Walt tried to hear what was going on inside, but the police activity in the front of the residence overrode everything.

A drift of grey escaped the doorway of the structure. Ash floated and spiraled among the smoke toward the overhanging trees in a mad rush to leak from the enclosure. A faint cough seeped through the dilapidated boarding.

Dammit.

There *was* another person inside, a woman gagging on the smoke.

"How could you be so stupid?" The man coughed and spat as he exited the run-down building, his fist entangled in the hair of a small woman as she clung to his hand. Her face, scrunched and drawn in pain as her legs tried to keep up, but dragged in the dirt. Struggling to stand, her feet scrapped across the concrete stepping stones as he forced her forward with an urgency he hadn't shown earlier. Her jean shorts were dirty and her gray tank top pulled against the ground, exposing her bra at the neckline.

Moving into position to tackle the suspect who now had the gun in his waistband, Walt stopped when he dropped her in the dirt and asked, "Where's Jamie?" Fear radiated from every fiber of the man's body.

"I … I don't know." Her voice tortured, the woman scanned the yard. Her husband twisted. Turned. Then whipped around, desperately searching for the missing boy. His search found Walt.

Expecting him to draw his weapon, Walt hunkered down, ready to attack.

"Have you seen our son?" His eyes wild, the man looked back at the garage with horror.

"Your son is safe. We need to —"

"Take my wife to him. I need to try and save some of my tools." Without waiting for instructions, the man walked back into the burning structure.

"Wait!"

But the man was gone.

Walt ran for the frail slip of a woman, helping her to her bare feet as she cowered and tried to sink away toward the ground.

Squatting down with her, he took the moment he didn't have and tried to ease her fears. "It's okay. I'm a police officer. I'm here to help."

If anything, his declaration made it worse. Her bottom lip quivered, and her fear-washed eyes sought out her drunken husband. The deep blue bruise forming on her freckled cheek spoke volumes about what she'd endured before his arrival. Her haggard appearance and the yellowing of old bruises on her arms and legs also told the story she probably wouldn't divulge.

Anger built in his chest, gurgling to the point of a boil. He wanted to close the door on the burning garage. Trap the sick son of a bitch who'd done this to his wife and welcome him to the hell he deserved.

Instead, Walt coaxed the woman toward the back door of the house as two officers jumped the fence.

"He went back in the garage. He's angry, drunk, and he's got a gun in the front of his waistband that he was shooting a few minutes ago. I don't know what he was shooting at…" He let his voice trail off, hoping she'd give up the truth.

"There … there … was a rat in the garage," she lied.

Walt wanted to roll his eyes. Tell her to stop making excuses for the man. He did none of that. He turned to the officers and said, "He's completely unstable. Watch yourselves." The two officers pulled their weapons and positioned themselves behind cover as Walt hurried the woman into the house, and the officers began yelling for her husband to come out of the garage.

Inside the back door, she paused, "My husband …" She wanted to go back to the man who didn't deserve her, it was written all over her face.

He tried to smile, but wasn't sure he carried it off. "Don't worry about him. Let's get you out front where your boy's waiting."

Her eyes widened. Her quiver of apprehension changed into a taut line of determination and she moved through the kitchen without assistance. Slumped shoulders straightened and the curtain of hair she'd hidden behind was shoved behind her ears.

Walt stopped her at the doorway. "Is there anyone else inside?"

She shook her head and waited for him to release her. Hurrying through a clean but run-down house, she burst into the front room, where a couple toys lay in the middle of the rug. A torn couch with sagging cushions faced a large, old, projection-style television set.

She flung open the front door, her earlier fear no longer visible as she looked up and down the street riddled with police cars and uniforms running in their direction. More sirens blared in the distance; the air horn of a fire truck sounded as it cleared a nearby intersection.

Walt grabbed a young officer he recognized. "Jones. Take her down the street. The recruits have her kid."

"Yes, sir." The young officer didn't hesitate, but once she found the direction of her son, the victim took off ahead of him, leaving Jones running to catch up.

Walt turned to go back through the house.

"Raynham!" The voice of his old patrol sergeant stopped him in his tracks. She didn't wait for pleasantries. "What's going on?"

"I was running with the recruits when several shots were fired from the backyard." He nodded his head toward the victim's residence. "I sent the recruits for cover and then found a kid in the backyard. I lifted him over the fence to a recruit. Then I found a drunk white male with a gun. About that time, a fire broke out in the garage, and he pulled the woman out by her hair."

"Was that her?" Sergeant Heins pointed down the street at the woman being reunited with her son.

"Yeah. She looks like she's been beaten. The suspect went back in the garage. You've got several officers in the backyard with him." Walt began walking toward the house, expecting the sergeant to walk with him. She didn't. Her hand grasped his arm and pulled him back.

"Go take care of your recruits. I'll take care of my officers. And don't let the woman leave. I want someone to talk to her." She didn't wait for his response. She walked into the house, unsnapping her holster as she went.

Shit.

"Sure, Sarge. I'll go babysit while you have all the fun." But she was gone, leaving Walt in the middle of the walkway talking to himself. He wanted to go to the officers but knew Sgt. Heins had the situation under control. And he wasn't exactly dressed or armed to deal with a man waving a gun.

Plus … Gibbons needed him.

He looked down the street in time to see her hand the young boy over to his mother. Her hair, curls falling in every direction, still held twigs from the bushes they'd vaulted. Her arms had small scrapes where blood and dirt intermingled. And her T-shirt clung to her in a way it hadn't while she was running – emphasizing her femininity and vulnerability. Like maybe something had caused the woman who didn't perspire to actually become human and sweat like the rest of the human race. Her eyes appeared lost, like she needed him.

No.

Gibbons wasn't the only recruit who needed him. *All* the recruits needed him. They *needed* to know how to react, how to listen to orders when violence broke out, what was acceptable, and what wasn't.

And then … if he could help it, Recruit Gibbons would never be in the line of fire again.

Curls be damned.

CHAPTER SEVEN

"One month into the academy and you're failing PT? How is that possible?" Her sister looked at her as if they were strangers.

"I don't know how it's possible. I just am." Kiley blew out an exasperated breath.

"Ask Officer Raynham for help; he'll see you through it."

A bitter noise disguised as a laugh escaped her mouth. "Are you kidding me? He's the reason I'm failing!" She pushed back the blond curl threatening her sanity for about the millionth time that day and threw her head back on the antique Victorian sectional their grandmother had given her. Kiley's damned hair had the nerve to fall back in the middle of her forehead. She'd laugh if it wasn't so pathetic.

Then she hiccupped.

Ahhh!

Maybe she was losing it — screaming in her mind was *not* a sign of sanity.

She shoved her hair back, making sure gravity took care of the problem as she leaned back farther and caught her sister's expression. She hated the sympathy washing over Lee's face even more than her hair. From her upside-down vantage point, it looked a heck of a lot like pity.

Lee pulled a clip from her silky brown hair and trapped the annoying stray away from Kiley's face before draping her arms around Kiley's neck. Just like she always did — the big sister consoling the younger sibling who couldn't quite keep up.

Except Lee was only two minutes older, and just once, Kiley wanted to be the one consoling her.

Slipping out of the embrace, Kiley got up and crossed the living room. It was the exact opposite of Lee's sleek modern town-home. Kiley's apartment was country chic with white-washed wainscoting and distressed hardwood floors. That sounded better than what it really was, older-than-dirt, and looked better with her overstuffed cream sectional loaded with lacy pillows of every color. The couch took up most of the room, covering all the flaws and provided the barrier she needed from her sister.

"He can't totally hate you … he gave you a nickname," Lee argued, refusing to let the topic die.

"A nickname that is so girly it even gives Tibbs ammunition to insult me? That's not exactly a favor."

"You are girly; it fits you. It has nothing to do with whether or not you'll be a good cop." Lee wasn't going to back down.

But Kiley wasn't done making her point. "Isn't that why you dropped Kay? Because Kay Lee was too cutesy?"

"I dropped Kay when I was a kid, because we both know I'm not"— her fingers curled into quotations —"cute."

No, she was a natural beauty who didn't see herself that way. Yet she loved the color pink, even now she was rocking a bright pink tank top and white shorts. It was pointless to even argue.

The ring of Kiley's phone rescued her from the debate, but before she could grab it off the kitchen island, her sister hit speaker.

"Hello," Kiley yelled over the back of the couch.

The line crackled.

"Hello?" she repeated, then paused, waiting for the connection to clear.

Leaning over to read the caller ID on the screen, Lee picked up the phone and handed it to her. "It's Andrew."

"I can't hear you, honey," Kiley yelled.

Andrew's irritation came through loud and clear. "I said I can't make it tonight. I'm sorry I have to work late."

"But —"

Lee didn't miss a beat. "Kiley needs a night out, anyway. No boyfriends. No instructors. No men." Her sister winked, and whispered. "Just you, me, and Katie makes three."

Kiley hesitated.

"Is that Lee?" Andrew's voice sounded strained.

"Yeah." Kiley jumped on the chance to escape her worries. "Since you're working late, I'll probably go out with her and Katie."

"You will not."

"Excuse me?" Kiley couldn't believe what she'd just heard.

"Lee just wants to get you in trouble," Andrew explained. Irrationally.

Lee stuck her tongue out at the phone but kept her mouth shut as Kiley clicked the phone off speaker.

"Lee has never tried to get me in trouble." She'd been the driving force behind some of their antics throughout their childhood, but Kiley had a mind of her own. If any responsibility was to be assigned, she knew where to place the blame.

"You shouldn't be going out with a bunch of single women," Andrew argued.

"My sister and our best friend is hardly a bunch of single women."

Lee nodded in agreement.

"No, Kiley." His voice took on a quality that prickled every hair on her body.

Kiley turned away from her sister and lowered her voice. "I don't think you're in a position to tell me what to do."

"I'm telling you, if you love me, you won't go out without me."

"That's ridiculous. You go out with your friends all the time." He had to see the irrationality of his argument.

Lee walked out of the room and down the hallway. A door closed, offering Kiley the privacy she needed with her ass of a boyfriend.

"That's different," he insisted.

Kiley scoffed. "Exactly how is that different?"

"Because I'm in a high-stress job, and I need to unwind every now and then."

Anger raised her volume two notches. "And I'm not?"

Andrew said the unthinkable. "You're in a police academy that requires a GED. How hard could it be?"

A very unladylike noise escaped her mouth, followed by something that sounded very similar to *screw you*.

"Lee's looking for a hook up, isn't she? She's got someone she wants you to meet." Andrew accused.

Kiley snorted, unable to think of anything to say to his ridiculous accusation. This wasn't the man she'd fallen head over heels for. He was a stranger, who placed himself on a pedestal above her, not the other way around.

Andrew's anger spewed through the phone. "If you go, consider our relationship over."

"I think our relationship ended the day you decided you owned me." Kiley clicked off her phone, hanging up on the man she'd loved most of her adult life. She no longer recognized him and wondered which one of them had changed so dramatically. Maybe they both had.

She might have a blue-collar job that only required a GED education, but life-and-death decisions had to be made on a daily basis.

She thought of Jamie and how Officer Raynham had run in to save him and his mom. With no fear. While she'd struggled just to get her fingers to move. Andrew had been furious when she'd told him about it, and it had taken every last persuasive bone in her body to stop him from calling up the academy and chewing someone out.

Wouldn't that have been just great to hear Sgt. McCain ridicule her in front of her entire academy class the next day?

I don't want to hear from your wives, husbands, or anyone else that this city is too dangerous for police recruits to run through. This is our city; we will not back down!

Well, Sgt. McCain wouldn't be hearing from her boyfriend anytime soon. She was single, and a night out with the girls would be exactly what the doctor didn't order. A grin crept across her face, slowly building. It was either that, or let the tears filling her eyes spill down her cheeks.

She swiped them away and refused to let them fall. To do so, would be failure. Failure to stand on her own two feet, without Andrew holding her up. It was a price she couldn't pay for any man.

She walked into the bedroom, where her sister stood, going through her closet. Ignoring the pang of seeing Andrew's folded scrubs on the dresser, Kiley smiled at her sister. "You're right. A night out," she met her twin's questioning gaze, "is exactly what *we* need. I'll call Katie. Be ready in thirty minutes. Tonight, is *ladies'* night."

***

Shit.

That's what he felt like. Gibbons was failing, because of him. And he knew if he tried to help her, if he lifted one finger in her direction, she wouldn't. But he couldn't. He just couldn't help her become a police officer.

It wasn't because he cared about her or needed to keep her safe. Nor was it the fact that she'd given her personal phone number to the boy's mom, which was all kinds of wrong. No, it was the expression on her face when she'd given up the kid. The expression that said, no matter what, Gibbons would be there for the victim and her child. Any time of day ... or night. No matter what she was doing, Gibbons would drop everything for *that* woman and *that* child.

And as a cop, she'd meet ten people like *that* every day. It would tear her apart at the seams. Lead her to see too much. Feel too much. And then drink too much just to forget for a couple blessed hours.

Kiley Gibbons was the wrong personality for the job. How she'd gotten past the department shrink was a mystery Walt couldn't begin to solve. Her sister, on the other hand, knew how to compartmentalize her feelings and leave everything behind. Kay Lee would survive the hardships with a few battle scars, but she'd be stronger because of them.

Sprawled out on his leather couch, Walt flipped through the channels of worthless programming on TV when his phone vibrated on the end table. He debated answering the call. Especially when he picked it up and saw Bret's phone number lighting up the screen.

He tapped the answer key. Music and the din of a crowd blared through the phone. "What's up?" he yelled. Walt knew exactly where his partner was spending Friday night — The HotchPotch Lounge. The hot spot for the after-work crowd ready to ring in the weekend in the Power and Light District of downtown Kansas City. His partner was predictable, to say the least.

"Walt, my man!" Bret's tone spoke volumes about his level of intoxication.

"You're not driving, are you?" The last thing Walt wanted to do was go pick up his drunk partner.

"No! My brother's driving tonight!"

Walt cringed and held the phone away from his ear. He'd go deaf if this conversation lasted much longer. "Have a good time. You can tell me about it Monday."

He started to hang up, but Bret's voice pierced through his determination to get rid of him.

"The twins are here!"

Walt stopped, his finger centimeters away from the touch screen on his phone with the long red rectangular box marked *End*.

Twins. There was only one set of twins Bret was obsessed with — Kiley and Kay Lee Gibbons.

The pit of his gut deepened with apprehension. Walt rubbed his face before raising the phone back to his ear.

"You there?" Bret yelled.

"Yeah."

"I thought you hung up on me!"

He should have hung up on him.

Bret continued. "Dude, these two are hot! And they're drunk. It's going to be some guy's lucky night!"

Walt ground his teeth. "If they're drunk, they can't give consent, Bret."

"They're not *that* drunk. But they are definitely looking for a good time— hey!" Sounds in the bar were muffled as Bret covered his phone and spoke to someone before returning. "Just thought I'd let you know your future bride awaits."

Walt ignored the jab and asked, "Do they have a designated driver to take them home?" This wasn't just about Kiley, he told himself. Her sister was there too, and she would make a damn good cop someday. *If* she didn't blow it before she earned it.

"I don't think so! So are you coming or not? Cause if you're not—"

Walt interrupted him before he could finish. "Yeah, I'll be there." Swinging his leg off the back of the couch, he sat up and didn't wait for Bret to respond before hitting *End*. Whatever else Bret had to say could wait until he arrived.

***

This was exactly what she needed. Time away from the stress of the academy and the day-in and day-out interrogations of a jealous boyfriend. A man she'd stood behind through med school and three years of residency who actually questioned her loyalty. The final straw shouldn't have been a surprise.

But it had. He'd actually accused her of having a date. A date. And then he'd broken up with her. His ultimatum burned through her mind. *If you go, consider our relationship over.*

Pride had taken over, drowning out the soul-crushing pain caused by his lack of support when she needed it most. And she'd said good-bye. Because really, who was she kidding? The relationship was doomed.

Exactly three hours ago, Kiley Gibbons had become single, shocking Lee and Katie. They hadn't said a word. Just stared at her as she'd sucked down her first two shots. Her sister had joined her on the third round.

Kiley was free to do as she pleased. Free of stress. Free of a demanding boyfriend. And free from bulging biceps owned by a brooding blond academy instructor.

A shiver traced her spine as she thought of the man who had swayed her not to cut her hair. That first day, he'd been sexy, sensitive, and stunning to look at. Now he was overbearing, rude, and … well … She couldn't help the sigh that escaped her mouth.

He was still stunning.

Strong hands slid onto her hips, shocking Kiley out of her daydream. "I hope that look on your face is because of your dance partner."

The dark chocolate gaze fringed with the preppy sweep of brown hair did nothing for her. The man in front of her was good-looking and a great dancer. So far, he'd been a lot of fun. But if the grind of his junk against her stomach was any indication of what he wanted, Kiley needed to put a stop to it. Now.

She smiled and placed her hands over his, discreetly removing them from her hips while using her standard line that was no longer true. "I'm in a relationship, Terry."

God, had she just slurred her words? Maybe it was time to call it a night. She ignored the grin spreading across Terry's face and tried to extricate her hands from his grasp and explained, "If you're looking for more than someone to dance with, I think we need to go our separate ways."

And she needed to start drinking water, she was pretty sure her head said someone, and her mouth said thumone.

His grip tightened on her hands as he brought them up to his chest. The crowded dance floor jostled them toward the rear of the bar where aged Kansas City sports memorabilia decorated the walls and flashed in neon signs. "Relax. Just let your body go. I'll take care of you." His mouth was next to her ear, her hands pinned between their bodies as he pressed against her, forcing her backward.

She snorted through her stupidity. Terry wasn't a *nice* guy. The twinkle in his eyes had nothing to do with happiness, and everything to do with dominance. It gave her a quick dose of sobriety.

"Let me go, Terry," she warned.

His lips and tongue assaulted her neck. The move was meant to tease.

All it really did was test her ability not to grab his balls and squeeze until he screamed like a girl. He had about two seconds before she hurt him good.

"Let. Me. Go," she commanded, thankful that her recent lisp had disappeared with anger.

Instead of listening, Terry's hand strayed to her rear, causing her miniskirt to rise as his hand began to roam. His attention distracted, Kiley took advantage of the small window he'd left open when he released one of her hands. She grasped his shoulder and stomped on his soft leather shoe with her six-inch stiletto —driving the spike through the leather top until it reached hardwood floor below. For good measure, she shoved him with all of her strength.

Terry yelped as he stumbled back. "What the hell was that for?" His lip curled in a sneer. His eyes flashed a warning she couldn't miss as he grabbed his injured foot.

She returned the threatening glare. "Really, do you have to ask?"

She yanked down her skirt and brushed past him into the crowd. A few dancers glanced curiously in her direction, wondering if they should step in. Kiley swayed. The music pounded through the floor as the strobe lights wreaked havoc with her balance.

She shouldn't have drunk so much. It was stupid. If she'd left before the last dance, everything would have been fine. Someone pinched her rear as she pushed through the crowd toward the tables. Kiley turned to give him a piece of her mind.

Tibbs smiled, his attractive face having as much effect on her as Terry's had. His leer pissing her off and his bold assault nearly turning her anger into an explosion.

"Who do you think you are, Tibbs?"

"Just a guy out looking for a cheap piece of ass, and since you're giving it out freely..."

"Touch me again and I'll break your hand."

Tibbs laughed, and elbowed his friend she didn't recognize. "She thinks she can be a cop."

His friend smirked and took a swig of his beer before turning away to check out the crowd.

"You're a jerk." She stumbled to the side and circled away to the sound of his laughter. With one more dance floor to go before she entered the massive bar area, she decided to cut through the middle, but was stopped halfway through when he grabbed her elbow and pulled her backward on wobbly feet. Her balance gone, she slammed against his solid chest, getting lost in its mass.

Dazed, she looked up, past where his face had been. Into the angry eyes of Officer Raynham.

"Officer —" she started breathlessly.

"Walt," he corrected.

Until that moment, she'd had no idea he had a first name other than *Officer*. Walt. It fit in an old-world-warrior type of way.

"Walt."

He pushed her forward, separating their bodies as he guided her through the crowd. Disappointment tightened her chest.

Which was totally ridiculous. He was *one* of the men she'd come to the bar to forget. Shaking her head to clear the alcohol-induced emotions, she realized her mistake too late when the room swerved back and forth, spinning on its axis.

Kiley could have sworn Walt cussed her, or someone, under his breath. But she didn't have time to react as he put his arm around her shoulder, pulling her tightly against him, supporting her as if it he did it every day. He guided her through the crushing crowd, toward the door. And somehow his actions weren't offensive. In fact, if anything, they felt warm and loving. Everything she needed.

Heat radiated off his body as she melted into him. They walked as one, comfortable and right. Her footing no longer uncertain but flowing with his stride.

Catching a glimpse of him in the mirror above the bar, Kiley marveled at how handsome and dangerous he looked. His don't-fuck-with-me expression leveled people in their path and had them parting without hesitation. Men pulled women out of the way. Guys elbowed guys, bumping them just beyond the invisible route that led Kiley and Walt to the front door.

A pang of professional jealousy tore through her, constricting her chest. A crowd would never part on her behalf. She could be in full uniform with a megaphone yelling for the people to run for their lives as she rode on Godzilla's back through the center of the room … and she would never be able to command the respect he received with just one glance.

She was jealous of the control his presence had over people. And strangely enough, it added to the attraction she'd denied since he'd rescued Jamie.

She knew women found strength alluring, no matter what form it was packaged in – wealth, social status, or physical stature. But she'd never been drawn to it, at least not until she'd met Officer Raynham … Walt.

On him, it was lethal.

His eyes told the cold tale of what he'd do to any man stupid enough to mess with him. On top of all that, it was as if his very scent held the animal magnetism of danger — an aphrodisiac luring her to certain ruin.

Midway across the bar, Kiley got tired of the female patrons undressing him with their eyes and wrapped her arm around his waist, laying claim to the man she'd put in the *off-limits* category. Women continued to lick their lips at the sight of him, but he was marked. And with Kiley at his side, they knew there was nothing they could do about it.

The fact that she *wanted* him wasn't really a shock. It'd been there the whole time. To be single and in a position to act upon that desire … that somehow changed everything. There was no boyfriend waiting at home. She could caress those biceps that had spoken to her on her first day at the academy. She could bare his chest and run her tongue down the taut abs she felt through his shirt. Then she could ride him into oblivion, until they were both too exhausted to move.

And wasn't that the stupidest thing of all? Her boyfriend had just dumped her, and now her traitorous body was inescapably attracted to a man who wanted to see her fail.

Chapter Eight

He desperately tried to control the need coursing through his veins. His jaw was going to crack — split right down the middle and tear apart his entire brain. When he'd arrived, Bret had pointed toward the dance floor, and he'd had to search through two before he finally spotted Kiley in the back corner, where a preppy dude had nibbled on her neck while his hand had crept up her skirt. Fury had tunneled Walt's vision. The crowd had disappeared as he'd stalked the man bold enough to touch her. His recruit. His responsibility. His ... He'd refused to let his mind go any further.

Kiley, however, had pulverized Walt's pursuit of satisfaction the moment she'd driven her incredibly sexy black high heel into the guy's foot. Leaving Walt with no reason to pummel the piece of shit manning up for a confrontation — with a five-foot-two-inch woman who weighed a hundred pounds dripping wet. Fuming with frustration, he lost her in the crowd, her curls disappearing in the midst of much taller dancers and when he'd finally found her again, he'd startled Kiley by grabbing her with more force than he'd intended as he pulled her in tight and glared at the man following her.

As the threat had disappeared into the crowd, Walt had made the mistake of looking down into her eyes … and she'd literally melted into his body, causing him to nearly lose focus on what he'd come there to do. Especially when all he wanted to do was exactly what the asshole had been doing. Which made him, an even bigger asshole.

She needed to escape, and that's what he was here to do. Nothing more. But her damned curls were free and wild, just the way he'd dreamed they would be.

He'd put distance between them immediately and watched her sway on rubbery legs. Cussing fate under his breath, he put his arm around her and directed her to the door while her hair tormented his senses. Then her fingers teased and tempted the driving lust he fought to control as she held onto him for support.

They reached the door, and Walt nodded to the bouncers wearing knowing smiles. He couldn't blame them; if a guy walked in one minute and left with a beautiful woman on his arm the next, he'd be tempted to shake his hand. But Kiley wasn't a conquest. She wasn't going to be sharing his bed for one night.

Unfortunately.

The hot, muggy air of the downtown bar district offered little reprieve from the crowded bar and loud dance music. Walt steered Kiley toward the parking lot, savoring the feeling of her body rubbing against his own for the few moments he had left before they reached his car. The painful pleasure had his dick on full alert. But he'd be damned if he was going to allow himself the indulgence. She was drunk. And she was his recruit.

At least that's what he'd been repeating over and over in his head, like a fucking mantra of celibacy.

"My hero." She giggled as he leaned her against his candy-apple-red Dodge Challenger. Her black tank dress blended perfectly with the sleek racing stripe running the length of the car. He couldn't help but think her dress and patent leather heels were meant to be sprawled across the hood. The strap of her thin, wallet-size purse draping across her chest would definitely look nice as it bound her wrists above her head.

Ignoring the car and her dress, he reached around her tempting body to open the passenger door. A small, delicate hand caressed his neck. He told himself it didn't matter.

She's drunk. She's your recruit.

Her tongue touched his ear. *Son of a —*

He pulled away, resisting the draw of her half-closed, moss-green eyes. He wanted to believe her eyes were drunk with lust … for him. In reality, it was more likely the alcohol she'd consumed. "You're drunk. You're my recruit. This cannot happen."

Then he screwed up. He glanced down to make sure she was steady before he released her. Which was exactly the huge mistake he knew it would be. His eyes snagged on the sight of her glorious cleavage, the rise and fall of her breasts his downfall as she took in several deep breaths. Her tongue moistened sweet cherry lips, inviting him to taste them.

She's drunk. She's your recruit.

He wasn't sure how long they stood there, the car door open, the light glaring from the interior. His body rock-hard with desire.

She wanted it. Of that he was certain. The depths of her eyes darkened into a forbidden forest of attraction. It didn't matter that they were in the middle of a parking lot. He was lost in the wild woodlands of her arousal.

But she's drunk. She's your recruit.

Her fist knotted in his waistband, and before he could tell her no, she yanked him hard against her soft curves. His pulse pounded in his chest as her breasts pressed against his stomach.

She's drunk. She's your recruit.

It didn't matter. He wouldn't stop her. He couldn't. He was beyond running this show. It was all up to her. He stood ... trapped in the snare of her eyes. Reveling in the feel of her body against his own. His hands palmed the roof of his car above her in a last-ditch effort not to touch her.

A gleam of white flashed as she smiled in an all-knowing feminine look of seduction success. She'd won this battle. He could do nothing ... but surrender.

***

She recognized his capitulation a moment before he did. Recognized the desire she'd lit inside him. Strength and power *could* come from a small weakling of a woman. This was nothing like her experience in the bar where she'd wanted a good time without sex. Terry had been an attractive stranger to dance and flirt with, nothing more.

That was then. This was now. With Walt, it was so much different. He saw what *she* wanted. What she desired. And what she absolutely needed. Right now.

Her hand released the top of his jeans and traveled to the inside of his thigh. His lips parted as she ran her fingers along the hard length of his quadriceps.She rejoiced in the thought of how he would use those muscles.

"I'm not too drunk to know what I want."

"Kiley ..." Hoarse and torn, his voice defined desire as he whispered her name for the first time. It was an aphrodisiac of monumental proportion. Reduced to a plea for mercy, Walt was completely dependent ... on her. Using her free hand, she pulled at his collar, reducing his height to bring his mouth to her level.

She closed the distance between them. Brushing her lips against his, teasing the soft, firm skin as a deep, guttural moan escaped him. She ran her tongue inside his mouth, exploring the fresh mint taste mixed with a flavor of raw masculinity that could only belong to him.

Heat surged through their bodies, he was still trying to resist the chemistry between them. Muscles taut, he fought to control the inevitable. But as her hand left his thigh to caress his length, he was done.

Or rather, completely undone.

His breathing became fast and ragged. There was no last-minute resistance against the driving need between them. He would do anything and everything she wanted. She should be using restraint — taking whatever this was between them at a slower pace like the cautious good girl she'd always been. But what had that gotten her in the past?

No. This need running through her body demanded satisfaction. Now. What came of it tomorrow, didn't matter.

He pressed against her, driving his impressive size against the palm of her hand. Oh, God, she wanted to free him from the confinement of his jeans.

One of his hands left the hood of his car and tangled in her curls, turning her mouth to devour her. Taunt her. Drive her mad with the skill of his tongue. His lips left her mouth, trailed her jaw to her ear before descending down her neck. By the time his lips met her shoulder, she was beyond caring who saw them. She gasped as his mouth descended to the edge of her dress, his tongue tantalizing the sensitive flesh of her breast as her nipples grew taut with anticipation.

Muted music coming from the inside of her purse broke the spell his mouth had over her body. The lyrics identified the caller with its ringtone.

And she did the only thing she could do. She pushed away the man who brought her to the brink of insanity.

"I have to take this call."

CHAPTER NINE

Saved by the bell.

Or not. His dick demanded release. His mind knew he couldn't allow. So … yeah. He was saved by the damned bell.

Son of a —

Standing in the middle of a parking garage, that was lit up like a car sales lot, with no less than two cameras pointed at his car, he watched her take the call. The extra sets of eyes were the reason he'd parked there. Yet somehow he'd forgotten about the electronic peeping toms when her lips had met his. He hadn't even registered the voices echoing off the concrete walls one level above. Proving they weren't alone.

And she was drunk. She was his recruit.

He stepped away from the car … and her. Running his hand through his hair, he wondered who could be so important she'd stop … *that.*

But he was grateful. And frustrated.

His mind said *yes, thank you*. His body said *hell no.*

He struggled to wrestle his heart rate, and dick, back into control. She had power over him, but by the look on her face, she wasn't going to entice him further.

At least, not intentionally.

"Are you hurt?" Her concern evident, her eyes rose to meet his before she turned away to gain more privacy.

What the hell? He was a cop. If someone needed help, he was the one she should be turning toward … not away from.

He closed the distance between them, focusing on her voice, not her body.

"Where are you?" she asked.

He moved close enough for her to see help was right in front of her. Once again, she turned and gave him her back.

"I need to find my sister and my ride, but I should be there within thirty minutes. Will you be okay for that long?"

Unbelievable.

She was planning to dump him. He'd come out in the middle of the night to save her and her sister from getting in trouble … her sister. He'd forgotten all about saving her sister. Once he'd seen the asshole's hand moving up Kiley's skirt, her twin had ceased to exist.

He didn't want to think about what that said about his motives for coming out to get her tonight. He wouldn't repeat the mistake he'd made moments earlier. Her sister needed to be reined in, as well, and someone Kiley cared about needed help.

She disconnected from the call that had saved them from making a huge mistake and finally met his gaze head on.

"I need to go. I'm sorry, but I need to find my sister." She didn't get very far before he stopped her.

"What's going on?"

She started to shake her head and deny anything was wrong until he cut her off.

"I heard your conversation. Who needs help?"

She hesitated. Her eyes searched his in an obvious attempt to see if she could trust him. Reading the uncertainty in the curve of her brow, he refused to release her arm when she gently tugged.

"A friend of mine is in trouble. She needs me to give her a ride to a shelter."

That was the *last* thing he'd expected. A friend or relative in an accident, or sick, maybe. But domestic violence? Didn't she realize they were mandated reporters?

"You're saying that she's a victim of domestic violence?" It was his turn to watch her face for honesty.

She hesitated, choosing her words carefully. "I'm saying a friend of mine wants to get away from circumstances that aren't the best."

She was playing a game of words, making him question her level of intoxication.

"So if it's not domestic violence, why wouldn't she just stay with you?" He wasn't going to let her off the hook. It was a matter of doing what was right for herself and the victim.

Again, she skirted the issue. "She needs a place for long term, where she'll feel safe."

His irritation mounted. Her friend was putting her in a situation that could cost Kiley her job. In turn, Kiley was involving her sister, putting both of them at risk.

"Curls, you cannot get involved in a DV situation and not report it. You are a mandated reporter —"

"No. You're a mandated reporter. I am a civilian employee."

"That doesn't relinquish —"

She cut him off. "I'm not asking you to help. I'm going back to the bar to get my sister and my ride. We'll handle it. So your precious career can remain intact."

She attempted to stomp away, forgetting that he still held her arm until she pulled up short. Then she looked down at his hand, the one that had been tangled in her hair two minutes earlier, as if it carried the plague.

He refused to acknowledge how much that bothered him. "You cannot get your sister involved. She's going to make a very good cop one day—"

"Are you saying I won't?" she demanded.

"I'm saying I don't think your sister will like this any more than I do." It was a guess on his part, but from the expression on her face, he knew he was right. He forged on. "I'll make you a deal." She looked at him suspiciously, and he released her arm, trying to show his good faith. "I'll take you to pick up your friend, and if she doesn't have any visible injuries, I'll treat it like a courtesy ride to a shelter. But if she's injured, we *will* file a police report."

"I don't think she'll like that arrangement."

"She doesn't have to like it. You don't have to like it. It's the best option you have, or I follow you and have a uniform meet you at your final destination."

Her nostrils flared with anger as she sucked in a breath. He could imagine his expression mirrored hers. He wasn't backing down.

Neither was she. "Fine."

***

He was going to kill her. Maybe not literally, but Kiley knew her career in law enforcement was definitely in the tank.

A month ago, Officer Raynham warned her against giving out her phone number. Told her it was not the *proper* protocol for a police officer. She should have recognized at the time that she wasn't the *proper* personality for a cop. Instead, she'd ignored his directive and took calls from Brandy when the woman needed to talk. And somehow, a friendship had been born.

So how could she take any other path but to rescue Brandy and her son when they needed her most?

As a kid, her best friend had lived in a household just like Brandy's. In fact, Brandy could be her best friend's mom reincarnate — married to the same drunk bastard Kiley had hated twenty years ago. If someone … anyone had bothered to listen back then, maybe her friend's mom would have gotten out of the relationship before the violence had escalated. The safe way. With a plan installed and the law on her side to keep that monster away from a little girl named Marie.

But Marie's mom hadn't escaped. The creep had isolated her from her family and friends, and the little girl with the straight blond hair had suffered. Because there'd been no one to help her abused mom. Only when Marie had become his target for destruction and she'd secretly confessed the reason for her bruising to Kiley had the family's secret leaked.

Horrified that a father could do that to his daughter and his wife, Kiley'd told her parents. But the next day, Marie's family had been gone, and Kiley never heard from her best friend again.

Brandy and Jamie weren't going to suffer like that if Kiley could help it. The little boy who'd clung to her out of pure fright on her second day of the academy was not going to relive Marie's life.

Not if Kiley had anything to say about it.

Walt's body returned to the tense rigidity he'd displayed in the parking lot right before she'd won the battle and kissed him senseless — or at least protocol-less. Despite the alcohol in her system, she could feel the strain in his muscles all the way across the expanse of the vehicle. Both hands gripped the steering wheel as he strangled it into submission and the city blocks passed by in a blur of lights and color. To anyone else, he probably looked like he was in complete control. Relaxed.

He wasn't. He was pissed with a capital P. More pissed than he'd been when he'd seen her looking up at him to take Jamie over the fence. More angry than the day he'd caught Tibbs bullying his way in front of her on their way into the academy gym and she'd let Tibbs get away with it.

After those incidents, she'd received an earful. This time, he was silent.

"Turn right at the next intersection."

He already knew she was leading him to Kensington Avenue and flipped on his blinker with a little too much force before she said the word *right*.

"It's down here on the left—"

"I know the damned address," he growled. "What I need to know is if I need a gun before we approach the house." He turned to glare at her, and despite the lack of street lights, she felt every dagger his eyes threw.

"No. He's not here. He went to the bar, but she doesn't want to be here when he gets home in the morning." She refused to let her defensiveness leak into her tone. She wasn't stupid; she wouldn't send him in a second time to face an armed man without a way to defend himself.

"Has she been assaulted?" He turned out the lights on his car as he rounded the corner.

"She didn't say," she lied.

Of course Brandy'd been assaulted. The woman had been attacked on a daily basis since her husband had gotten out of jail for discharging a weapon in the city limits while intoxicated.

The entire process had been a joke. The only thing that had come of the whole ordeal was Brandy's further mistrust of a flawed system. Because services stopped as soon as Family Services made a house call, found Jamie clean, without a mark and the house in order with food in the fridge.

Brandy was covered from head to toe in bruises, but nobody cared to offer a way out. Except Kiley.

Walt pulled up to the curb a couple houses down from the little ranch that hid such a big secret. "Call her and make sure she's alone. Then tell her to come outside and meet us at the curb."

Kiley nodded and hit redial on her phone. Brandy picked up on the first ring.

"Kiley, are you here?" She sounded scared and frantic.

"Yeah, we're right down the block. Is he home?" Kiley prayed he wasn't.

A bitter laugh filled with sorrow echoed through the line, and some of her fear disappeared. "No one could drag him off that bar stool before three a.m. And then he'll sleep it off in his truck."

Brandy knew her husband's routine probably better than most wives. She should; she had a mark for every time she saw him.

"Can you bring Jamie out to the curb, or do you have too much stuff?"

"We'll be right out." The line went dead before Kiley had a chance to tell her new friend who was actually going to be taking them to the shelter.

"Before I pull down there, I need your word you'll stay in the car." Walt's tone returned to that of her instructor. Not her lover.

"But —"

"Unless you want me to handcuff you and drive you home, promise me you'll stay in the car."

Handcuffs might be nice if they didn't involve the attitude of being her boss … which he was.

"Fine. If Jamie starts screaming at the first sight of you, don't come crawling to me for help."

Walt slammed the car into gear and closed the distance to Brandy's house without another word. A sense of déjà vu washed over Kiley's nerves as she tried to sit back and heed his warning, while Brandy tripped on an imaginary crack in the sidewalk when she caught sight of him unfolding his body out of the car. Her eyes frantically searched the area, looking for patrol cars.

She could see Walt's posture slacken. He lost the I'm-so-pissed-at-you-I-could-strangle-you hardness and … softened. How a guy as muscle-bound as Walt could make himself appear docile was beyond her ability to process. Yet there he was, as bendable and easily led as little Jamie.

Walt, in his shrunken form, leaned in and said something to Brandy as he took her sleeping son from her arms. And Brandy ran into the house to get the rest of her things.

It was an amazingly beautiful thing to see. Until he turned around. Approaching the passenger side of the vehicle, his I'm-going-to-kick-someone's-ass posture returned as he scanned the neighborhood, looking for a threat. She ignored the fact that, in its own right, that attitude was just as beautiful … in a sexy-as-hell kind of way, and opened the door to take the small boy from his arms.

"She doesn't have a car seat," Walt whispered, as if afraid he'd wake up Jamie and make her threat come true.

"I'll hold him," she volunteered.

"You're not a car seat, Curls. He won't be safe."

"And staying here is a better option?"

"I didn't say that." Obviously he didn't like her plan, but he liked the alternative of leaving Jamie at the house even less.

Brandy ran up to the car with a small bag and a toy fire truck dangling from her shaking hands. Walt's eyes traveled to her hands and Kiley feared he would ask if Brandy was using. She wasn't taking drugs or drinking alcohol, she was just scared half to death. But he didn't know that.

Instead, he asked, "That's all you have?"

"This is all we need. I've been putting away some money for the last several weeks since…" She stopped as if knowing she couldn't say anything in front of Walt, her eyes searching Kiley's face in the glow of the interior light.

Kiley nodded and leaned forward for Brandy to get in the backseat, then caught a glimpse of Walt through the rear window as she gently passed a sleeping Jamie to his mom. A very unhappy frown had appeared on his face, as if announcing their relationship couldn't possibly work. She knew he was a man who was all about the rules. But she lived in a grey world.

"Do you know what shelter you want to go to?" he asked as if he were on a call for service in uniform transporting a woman and child to safety.

"New Hope Shelter in Independence. They're waiting for us."

Walt nodded and remained silent the entire way to the shelter, his body almost brittle, and his unhappy disposition all too clear. Brandy focused on her son's sleeping face, tears silently spilling down her cheeks. Jamie was the only person in the entire vehicle who was completely content.

Kiley was well aware it was going to hit the fan after they left the shelter. He wouldn't make the mistake of allowing her to kiss him again. He was large and in charge. And she was a measly recruit failing PT.

CHAPTER TEN

They were alone. Again. Brandy and her son were safely in the shelter, where the women hadn't been too happy to see him walking in carrying young Jamie. With Walt in tow, Brandy had broken a golden rule the shelter personnel didn't care to see ignored. It was only his badge and a phone call to the station desk sergeant that had gotten them in the front door.

And would no doubt have him answering a whole hell of a lot of questions come Monday morning.

He couldn't begin to count how many ways that was going to suck. If he started counting all the rules he'd broken in the last couple hours, he'd be writing *himself* up for conduct violations. As it was, he'd been trying to keep Kiley's involvement to a minimum so she wouldn't get into trouble.

Shit.

That was the complete opposite direction he should've taken. He should've let her walk Brandy into the shelter. Let them smell the alcohol on her breath and question her ability to drive. Force her to show her ID and talk to the desk sergeant.

It would've been the straw to break Gibbons' back. Yeah, he would've been reprimanded for his part in the whole fiasco, and there'd be a permanent mark in his jacket, but he would have survived. Kiley, on the other hand, would've been canned.

Yet once again, he'd allowed himself to fall into the role of her protector as if it were a natural part of his makeup. He would be questioned, maybe a blemish on his record, when he absolutely deserved to pay a higher price for all the sins against the job he'd committed since her lips had touched his.

The memory of her kiss made him want to do it again. Make sure it wasn't just his imagination that had him all tied up in knots.

Damn, the woman could kiss.

It was, however, not going to be repeated. He had to take her home. Walk her to her door. And make sure she understood that this would never happen again. The whole night had to be a lesson of unacceptable conduct.

"Thank you." Her voice was soft, barely audible above the purr of the engine.

"Don't." His own voice sounded menacing even to his own ears.

"Don't what?"

"Don't thank me for fucking up. 'Cause this," his hand waved back and forth between their bodies as he drove, "was the biggest fuck-up of my career. And that back there at the shelter will undoubtedly come back to haunt both of us."

"How can that haunt us? We brought a woman and her child to a safe place to live, to start a new beginning." Her voice rose as her passion escaped. "I will never regret what we did. Ever."

For a moment, he thought she was talking about their kiss. Then the light bulb turned on, and he realized her focus was on Brandy and her son Jamie. Which was right where it should be, but it still didn't stop it from tearing at his ego.

"The women working tonight were not happy about Brandy bringing a man into the shelter. They called the desk sergeant."

He felt the intake of her breath as he drove north of the river in the direction of her apartment. It was about time she started realizing there was more at stake now that Brandy and Jamie were safe. Walt's career could be on the line, and her career may not even get started. They could both be down the proverbial tank if he didn't talk his ass out of this mess come Monday morning.

Some shelter employees wouldn't care what the personal cost to Walt and Kiley would be. The director might file a complaint with the department, and the whole night would be caught on videotape for the entire IAD unit to watch. After obtaining Walt and Kiley's statements, they'd check with the bar.

Shit.

Maybe he was being too optimistic expecting a blemish. From their arm-in-arm exit of the bar, to the kiss that had almost ended up with him doing her on the hood of his car in the parking garage, to him assisting Brandy into the shelter—every set of eyes in IAD would watch the clusterfuck from hell on video, and then all of it would go on his permanent record.

He didn't have to worry about *when* he was going to TAC, because now he wouldn't be going at all. If he was lucky, he'd find himself working dog watch at East Patrol Division. But if lady luck wasn't on his side, he'd be standing next to Kiley in the unemployment line.

He pulled up into the lot of her apartment complex and parked under the covered parking, the silence between them taking a toll on their moods.

"If I'm going to pay a price for what happened tonight, I'm going to make it worth my while." Her hand snaked over to his leg, and he nearly jumped out of his seat.

"What the hell, Curls?" Fast and full of shock, he couldn't help the expletives rolling off his tongue as her fingers reached his dick.

"I want this. You want this. Let's get it out of our system so we can move forward." Her hand stroked him before he could answer, but his dick did all the talking for him. Reacted like they'd never stopped in the parking lot at the bar. Once again, he was lost in the heat of her touch.

He started to say no, when his body ignored every warning signal his brain sent and he pulled her out of the passenger seat. He trapped her head by winding his fingers through her curls, loving the soft suppleness of the silken strands as he crushed her lips with his own. Punishing both of them for their indiscretions. This was all so wrong, yet oh-so-right. She was the drug his body craved. The intoxication he couldn't escape, attached to the knowledge of doom at the end of the high he couldn't resist.

She unzipped his fly, and her slender fingers wrapped around his length no longer imprisoned by his jeans. He leaned back in his seat and allowed her hand more room to explore as his mouth descended to her neck and below. Pulling down the shoulder of her dress, he exposed her breasts and thought he died of an overdose when he captured a tight pink bud in his mouth and she moaned her pleasure.

It was everything he wanted. Everything he needed. This woman, this place. It didn't matter they were in the parking lot of her apartment complex. Nothing mattered but the here and now.

Pounding on the passenger window brought his heart to a stop.

Desperate to hide his drug of choice, Walt tossed her in the backseat over his shoulder as he tried to shield Kiley, who squeaked and rolled to a sitting position. Her dress magically returned to its rightful position covering breasts he wanted to see for the rest of his life.

He reached under his seat for his Glock, remembering he had purposely left it at home when he'd gone to the bar as he pulled up his pants to cover his own nudity. An angry female face appeared in the passenger window.

Lee. Her twin.

Son of a bitch.

He'd really screwed the pooch, and by the look on the *other* Recruit Gibbons' face, she wasn't going to let him get away with it. The woman was mad as hell, and if she didn't assault him in the next two minutes, he wasn't sure anyone would be able to convince her not to turn him in.

"*Kay Lee* Gibbons!" Kiley sounded a little more than put out in the backseat of his car, the anger in her voice matching the enraged frustration of her sister.

Could this night get any worse?

But it did. Walt saw the man walking down the steps before the two sisters did. He saw the anger on his face mixed with pain. But what he also saw was something much deeper. Concern and love. And from the deep, all-knowing pit in his gut, he knew those feelings weren't for the Gibbons on the outside of his car. They were for the one on the inside, who'd just become a drug he didn't think he could live without.

He checked his pants and adjusted himself before reaching for the polished chrome door handle.

"I think the guy coming our direction probably wants to talk to you more than he wants to talk to me. As far as anyone else is concerned, I brought you home after we took your friend to the shelter, and you fell asleep in the backseat of my car. Understood?"

Her eyes enlarged, and the guilt on her face answered the next question before he had to ask. The guy in the scrubs *was* her boyfriend, not Lee's. He pushed the door open the rest of the way, leaned the driver's seat forward, and reached in to assist her out of the backseat. Never once did he look into her eyes or even try to give her the opportunity to explain herself.

She was attached to the doctor in a big way, and she had played him for a fool. Despite the burn in his gut that wouldn't stop for a long time to come, he wasn't about to betray her indiscretion. His indiscretion. There were some things you didn't stir up. And this just happened to be one of them. Other than her hair being mussed and her dress being wrinkled, anyone could, if he wanted to, believe that she had been sleeping in his backseat and not jacking him off in the front while he sucked her incredible breasts to the music of her throaty moans.

He was such an asshole.

"Kiley." The doc with the perfect hair jogged the distance across the lot. "God, baby I was worried sick about you."

"I'm fine."

Walt stepped forward to shake the man's hand. "Walt Raynham. You must be Recruit Gibbons' boyfriend." Despite what he'd seen, he hoped the man would laugh and deny the relationship. Say he was her brother.

He didn't. He just stared at Kiley, who was staring at Walt. And he wasn't about to look at her. This little bit of a woman had played him so well he wasn't sure how to react. How could he? Because somehow it all made sense. While he was trying to push her out of the door of the police academy to save her, she did the one thing she had to do to make sure he was trapped into keeping her.

Obviously he'd seen her soft green eyes completely wrong. They were more like the deceptively pretty leaves of poison ivy. Delicate and irritatingly devious.

Good job, dickhead.

***

Why did she feel like she'd betrayed him? It was supposed to be a one-night stand. A night of freedom. A night of bliss.

Instead, it'd turned into a night from hell. He *believed* she was in a relationship. And although technically she wasn't, Andrew was still acting like they were … even though he'd been the one to call it quits.

Then there was Lee, who wasn't helping at all. Arms crossed, she scowled at Walt like he'd done something wrong. Yet he'd been the knight in shining armor at the bar. The knight in shining armor at Brandy's house. And the shelter. And once again, while facing her apparent boyfriend, he was as pure as a guy could get while protecting her at a personal cost to his own reputation.

So why was Kiley angry at him for thinking the worst of her?

Because he *did* think the worst. The solemn handshake. The emotionless explanation to Andrew about how she'd called him for help when a friend was in trouble. And then his complete avoidance of any type of eye contact with Kiley let her know his poor opinion. Of her.

How had things gotten sooo screwed up?

"Wow, babe, you've had a rough night. I'm sorry you didn't feel like you could call me for help." Andrew pulled her into an awkward hug.

And there was the guilt again. Because she wanted to be in Walt's arms. She should have called Andrew for help. He would've been there within moments to help … even if he had called off their relationship. And there would have been less risk to his career. A doctor was a mandated reporter, but he would have stayed in the shadows; he would have allowed Kiley to help Brandy and Jamie into the shelter without a single thought to the amount of trouble it would cause Kiley's career. And Officer Raynham wouldn't have been forced to be the good guy.

"You're right. I just thought —"

"You broke up with her, Andrew. Of course she wasn't going to call you. Don't be an ass."

Lee's anger was like a slap in the face—for Andrew. He released Kiley, ready to argue with her sister the way they always did. Kiley wanted to thank Lee for her attempt to protect her reputation from Walt's negative judgment. Walt … no, she needed to think of him as her boss, yet she wanted to turn to him and tell him, "See, I wasn't playing you. I am single." Then she would turn to Andrew and put him in his place for showing up unannounced and acting like the pain he'd caused had never happened. She should let them both know she'd understandably been on the rebo—

The rebound. Was she on the rebound? Was that why she'd acted so out of character and attacked a man she barely knew not once … but twice? Despite the fact that she knew he was trying to get her kicked out of the academy?

Tired of running from the truth, she turned to face the fallout from a night of bad decisions. Andrew was verbally sparring with Lee, the words lost forever to Kiley. Officer Raynham was playing knight once again, holding Lee back before she struck out at Andrew and made the night even worse. All of them were gathered in the parking lot because of Kiley.

Geesh.

How could one person cause so much turmoil? Close to having her tears spill over and completely putting herself in the pathetic category, Kiley was done talking. She didn't want to look at Walt. She didn't want to talk to Andrew. Nor did she want to listen to her sister's advice. All she wanted to do was go to bed.

Alone.

"It's been a long night. I'm going to bed. Thank you for your help, Officer Raynham. Lee, I'm fine. Andrew I'll talk to you ... tomorrow. Good night."

Kiley turned away from the three people who got under her skin more than the rest of the world combined and left them standing in the shadows from the streetlights to figure out all their anger on their own.

Sometimes it was just better to go into your cave and hibernate ... for about three to five months.

***

Rebound sex. *Jesus.* He should have known.

Granted, it was better than thinking she'd played him. But...

"I don't know what you did for Kiley, but obviously you were there when she needed someone. Thank you." The good doctor held out his hand as if Walt was supposed to shake it.

It took every ounce of his self-control not to send her Dr. GQ ex-boyfriend to the emergency room — on a stretcher. Ignoring the outstretched hand, Walt turned toward her sister. "Let me know if she has any more problems with Brandy," he said and walked away.

Leaving Kiley's Dr. Perfect to question her sister. "Brandy? Is that who they took to the shelter? When did she meet her?"

Walt didn't wait to hear Lee's response. The twin had given him an evil look as he'd nodded good-bye. She'd seen his indiscretion. Witnessed him taking advantage of her sister. He knew beyond a shadow of a doubt she would've tried to drag him from the car and throttle him if the good doctor hadn't been on his way down the stairs from Kiley's apartment where they probably lived … together. Slept … together. Shared pleasure after pleasure … together.

He started the engine to his Challenger with a roar, then peeled out of the lot, eager to leave the woman who drove him insane, and her lover, behind in the dust. His cell phone beeped.

Images of Kiley calling him from the inside of her apartment sent his heartbeat into double time. Maybe it wasn't rebound sex. Maybe her ex had given her the wake-up call she'd needed. Then, faced with the truth of her feelings, she'd gone for broke. Made the move that had been building up inside both of them for the past month.

"Raynham." His voice sounded like he'd run a marathon.

"Officer Raynham. This is TAC Dispatcher Jenkins. Radio six sixty is requesting your presence at Forty-fifth and Elmwood to translate on an operation one hundred. Are you available to respond?"

In the background, Walt could hear the familiar noises of the communications unit bustling to get everything together for a long night dedicated to talking an unstable individual, out of doing something stupid. And if they needed a Spanish translator, the TAC unit always called him first.

He didn't hesitate. He wasn't going to be able to sleep anyway. Better to work than lie in his bed wondering what it would be like to be inside the recruit with the long blond curls.

"What's the safe route in?"

Chapter Eleven

"He's gone." Allen looked like he'd just lost his best friend.

"Who's gone?" Kiley asked as she bit her lip. Anticipation of seeing Walt walk out the back door of the academy had her stomach doing sky dives. Not that she'd ever jumped out of a plane, but she imagined this was what it felt like.

The weekend had been too long. Too short. Her world was a mixed-up mess, and she wasn't sure what direction she was going. Uncertainty had driven her to hide in her cave. Watching the phone. Hoping. Listening to messages on her voice mail from Andrew and Lee.

Her sister had gotten a short voice mail in return. "I'm fine. I just need to figure some things out."

Andrew got a text. *I need time to think. We'll talk soon.* Then he'd tried to have a conversation through text messages, and she'd ignored his pleas for forgiveness.

But *he* had never called. Never texted. Didn't give a single sign that he wanted to continue what she'd started.

God, she'd been an idiot.

Her damned curl woke her from her thoughts as it drooped on her forehead, and her stomach jolted with a hiccup.

Wonderful.

"Officer Raynham. He's gone." Allen's voice drilled through her mind.

Her heart crumbled. *Oh, God.*

Visions of Walt's car being mangled in a car wreck after he'd left rubber in her parking lot swam through her head. Or what if Brandy's husband had found out? What if he'd followed them and confronted Walt … who'd been unarmed. Lee had probably been trying to tell her. It had probably been on the news, but she hadn't turned the TV on. She'd been content to wallow and stare at her phone.

And it was all her fault.

Kiley's knees buckled. Allen reached out to steady her. Her vision darkened. Her mind screamed, "*No!*" She forced the word "What?" from her lips.

Walt couldn't be dead. He couldn't be—

"Are you okay, Kiley?" Allen's voice was full of concern. But she needed to know.

"What happened?" Her voice sounded hollow … lost.

"Are you okay?" Allen repeated.

"What happened?" she demanded.

"Kiley, you really don't look that well."

"Just answer the damn question, Allen!" The silence around them filled her ears. Every recruit in her class was going to witness her meltdown. But she didn't care. She had to know what happened to the man who had turned her world upside down.

"What was the question?" Allen looked down at her hand clutching his arm, fingernails digging into his skin.

"What. Happened. To Wa — Officer Raynham?" Every word tore at her chest, the gaping wound making each word softer and more painful than the last. If anything happened to him … it was her fault.

"He got the transfer to the tactical unit he wanted … effective yesterday."

"Attehhhnnn-Hut!"

Recruits scrambled for their formations. Allen reluctantly released her and then dug her fingernails out of the skin on his forearm, his eyes watchful for any sign of her collapsing. Shaken and wobbly, she was so damned thankful for Walt's transfer she wanted to shout with joy, "*He's Alive!*" Instead, she hobbled to her spot, unsure if she had enough blood flowing through her extremities to give her the strength she needed to stand at attention.

"What's wrong?" her sister whispered in her ear as she grabbed Kiley's arm and assisted her to her spot in formation.

Kiley pushed her away. "Go. I'm fine." But her big sister stayed, in the middle of A Form, instead of being at the other end of the parking lot standing at attention, determined to take care of Kiley no matter what the cost. Angered that her stupidity was going to get Lee in trouble, she pushed her twin away a second time. "Really, I'm fine. Go."

"Recruit Gibbons! Front and center!"

"Yes, sir!" both sisters yelled, trying to take the blame for the other.

Kiley somehow beat Lee to the position directly in front of Sgt. McCain, who glared at the curl that defied being tamed as it swayed across her forehead. He stepped forward and shoved his face under the brim of Kiley's ball cap. Her focus was no longer the brick wall behind him but the coarse ink-black hairs connecting his eyebrows.

"Is there a reason you're swaying like a gawd-damned white flag, Gibbons?"

Not sure how to answer that, Kiley teetered on her heels. Sgt. McCain reached out and grabbed her bicep, squeezing it so hard she felt the pain on the opposite side of her body.

"Sir?"

"Unlock your knees, recruit. Before you fall on your sister and embarrass her as well as yourself." Sgt. McCain's words didn't reverberate through the back lot like they normally did. This order was meant for her ears alone, making the command even more deadly than any previous dress-downs he'd given.

Kiley bent her knees. Her stability returned.

"After inspection, I want to see you in my office. Is that clear, Recruit Gibbons?"

Fear returned. He *knew*. Walt must've confessed … everything. And that was why he wasn't here. That was why he'd been transferred without any notice.

Her sister interjected. "Sir, if I could—"

He didn't give Lee a chance. "I think you've covered your sister's ass enough, Gibbons." This time, his deadly words were spoken in her sister's face, and she didn't waver.

Her response was immediate and strong. "Sir. Yes, sir."

He stepped away, leaving Kiley stunned and Lee the ever-obedient soldier, staring at the brick wall waiting for further instructions.

"Return to formation."

"Yes, sir," the sisters said in unison before glancing at each other and running for their designated spots among their peers.

If she was ever going to die of a heart attack, this was going to be the day. Guilt and shame washed through Kiley when she thought of how much trouble she'd created for Walt and Lee. It was *all* her fault. She'd been the reason they'd gone to the bar. She'd been the one out of control and the reason Walt had felt the need to jump in and save her from herself. If she'd listened to him when he'd said she was his recruit and nothing could happen between them, he'd still be here. To top that … she'd been the one to get him involved in Brandy's problems. Every last bit was her fault.

Inspection carried on without so much as a hitch. The new instructor was introduced, a female with more starch in her shirt than all the rest of the instructors combined. But at least she didn't step in the first day Walt was gone and say his squad was less than ideal.

Besides, it seemed everyone else had their crap together, while she was a disaster.

"Dismissed!" Their new form leader gave the command.

Recruits went about their business. Some glanced in her direction, others ignored her—afraid whatever trouble she'd gotten herself into would rub off on them.

Which pretty much left her in the position of being a pariah.

Lee caught up with her. "It's for the best."

"I know that." Her voice sounded defensive, immediately bristling her sister's feelings. Kiley turned and smiled. "You're right. It is the best-case scenario."

"So what happened before inspection? Why did you almost pass out?"

Kiley couldn't help the color rising in her face. She lowered her voice as they pushed through the hall full of black-and-white uniforms. "I thought he was dead. I didn't know it was just a transfer."

Lee actually laughed before she leaned in and whispered, "You've got quite an ego if you think your kisses are deadly — or was it your touch that killed him? A little too much pressure during the hand technique you were teaching him? Do you think we should register your hands as lethal weapons?" She grinned and giggled as Kiley shoved her away. "The concealed carry permits are downtown." Her sister took off down the hall, leaving Kiley's face a shade close to purple.

God, she was never going to live that night down.

She took the stairwell to the upper level and approached the sergeant's office. The man was sitting behind his desk. Officer Dugan sat in one of the two chairs in front of him.

"That will be all, Officer Dugan." Sarge looked down at a file in front of his desk. Walt's old partner stood up, his eyes widened in what looked like panic when he saw her. His head moved in a slight shake while his eyes tried to convey a hidden message. Kiley stared at him, trying to understand the cryptic meaning but failing miserably. Something bad was coming. And it didn't just involve her. It involved Walt. Otherwise, Officer Dugan wouldn't be so scared.

"Have a seat, Gibbons. Dugan, close the door behind you."

"Yes, sir." Kiley swallowed down the lump of fear and did as instructed, sitting on the edge of the cloth-covered chair.

"Is there something you want to tell me about this past weekend, Gibbons?" Sgt. McCain's face was as serious as a detective at a homicide scene. And somehow that analogy didn't seem too far off base.

Was she looking at the death of her career, or Walt's? Maybe it was a double shooting and both of them would be taken down from one single bullet — in the form of the wrong word that slipped from her mouth during this interrogation.

If Sarge asked specifically about Friday night, she wouldn't be able to lie. She'd fess up to her bad behavior in a heartbeat. 'Cause she didn't have an excuse for it. And unfortunately, she didn't think she would change a thing if she had to relive the entire night. Which was really unfortunate for Walt.

"No, sir." She put the conviction of her actions behind her words.

"Did you go out with Officer Dugan this past weekend?"

"I… " Dugan? Stunned by the question, she stammered for a moment before she could answer truthfully. "I … absolutely not, sir." And that wasn't a lie.

"Let me rephrase that…" Sgt. McCain's eyes were glued to her face before they moved to the nervous tick of her shaking knee. Kiley froze the disloyal appendage and continued to look at him expectantly while secretly ready to barf her guts up.

She hiccupped instead, and Sgt. McCain's eyes narrowed.

"Did you meet up with any instructor on Saturday night?"

She paused and thought about his question. "No, sir."

It wasn't a lie. It was the absolute truth. On Saturday night, she and Andrew had been busy with their one-sided text conversation.

Friday night was a different story. On *Friday* night, she'd had her hand down the front of Walt's pants and his mouth on her breast.

But Saturday night, she was completely in the clear. Saturday night was discretion free.

"Nothing happened between you and an instructor on Saturday?"

He didn't believe her, but she felt comfortable with her statement. It was the complete truth.

Until he rephrased it to Saturday. Because technically, what happened at the shelter and at her apartment complex in Walt's car … had been on Saturday. But it hadn't been Saturday night.

She changed her approach. "Can I ask what the problem is, Sarge?"

Sgt. McCain leaned back in his chair, studying her further. Watched her next hiccup shake her body. His elbows rested on the leather armrests of his desk chair, his fingers meeting in the center of his chest, tapping together in a pyramid dance.

The dance stopped.

She stared over his shoulder, at the wall of plaques and certificates. There was no way she could look him in the face.

"The main answering system for the academy received a call this morning stating that a female recruit named Kiley had been at The HotchPotch Lounge in the Power and Light District on Saturday and ended up making out with an instructor in the parking lot." He moved his head to the left, directly in front of the black and gold unit citation plaque she'd focused on. Again, he watched her for any hint of deception.

And there was plenty there — the frequency of her hiccups increased. Her heart rate matched that of a fox trying to outwit the bigger and stronger hunter. But she'd learned how to face adversity, show fear to a bunch of two-year-olds and they'd eat you alive. She pictured Sgt. McCain's bald head as that of a young Charlie Brown and held his steady gaze.

"No, Sarge," (*Charlie*), "nothing like that happened on Saturday night." She had no problem hiding the fear that was skipping through her body from *Charlie*. Like all her toddlers who had skipped around the circular mat in her classroom, *Charlie* was not going to know the fear he could create.

"So nothing happened this past weekend between you and one of my instructors?" he asked one last time.

She hesitated, knowing the next lie was closer to a real lie than the others. "No, sir," she replied. Walt was no longer one of Sgt. McCain's instructors; if he had been, they'd both be screwed.

Her body ramrod straight in the chair directly in front of Sgt. McCain's desk, she was positive Walt had no intention of going out with her again. Otherwise, he would have called. And until that very moment, she'd held on to some kind of hope that he would. That what they'd shared hadn't been cheap. Or a one-night stand in the making.

With realization came clarity of where her true feelings lay. She knew beyond a shadow of a doubt … she belonged with Andrew. They had too much history together to throw it all away. Walt had been a mistake during one night of break-up hell and drunken debauchery. He was … rebound sex. Attraction strengthened by alcohol and her emotions of rejection.

"Go to class, Gibbons. If I hear of anything more, I will end up sending it over to IAD to investigate." His last parting blow did nothing to ease the tension ratcheting up her body.

"Thank you, sir." She took the dismissal and headed out the door, her stride long, her escape quick before Sarge asked a question she couldn't answer. She turned the corner and ran smack-dab into the middle of a brick wall. A very familiar brick wall.

"Walt." Part of her wanted to hug him, reassure herself that he was alive and well and nothing had happened to him. The other part wanted to chew him out for not calling.

Which was completely ridiculous. She'd just decided she belonged with Andrew.

His hands grasped her biceps. She froze looking up at him … searching. He set her aside like a piece of furniture blocking his path. As if he hadn't kissed her senseless. As if Friday night was just a figment of her imagination. A daydream to pass away a boring night.

He didn't even look at her. Instead, he dismissed her with a formal greeting, "Recruit Gibbons." Then he walked past, and addressed Sgt. McCain. "Sarge. There's something I need to talk to you about."

"Come on in, Raynham. Have a seat."

Walt turned and finally looked at her. Or rather, through her. Then he closed the door to her chapter in his life.

Hell. Who was she kidding? From his reaction, she didn't even rate a paragraph in the book of Walt.

CHAPTER TWELVE

Five months of paramilitary black-and-white penguin uniforms, while being scrutinized, criticized, and ostracized, left Kiley craving an entire day poolside at her apartment complex with Andrew. Instead, she'd put on her stupid costume and had driven to East Patrol Division, where her existence alone would irritate the officer unlucky enough to have a stranger in his domain for an entire shift.

She grumbled and mumbled her displeasure, talking to the radio as if the DJ would reply. "A recruit should be allowed two days off without having to deal with this crap."

She pulled into the fenced lot and parked among the seasoned officers arriving for their night shifts and drug her reluctant body out of her little blue Prius. A few officers responded to her greetings of "Hello, ma'am," and "Good afternoon, sir" with cursory nods, while others ignored her gnat-like existence with ease. She wanted to tell them it wasn't her choice to be here. In fact, this was the very last place she wanted to spend her Saturday.

She entered the sterile renovated bank building that was anything but clean, and took the funneled hallway toward the desk sergeant's area with faked excitement plastered on her face. To the outside police world, this was her opportunity of a lifetime.

In reality, it was a job to endure in order to collect a paycheck in a bad economy.

The desk sergeant sat in a glass alcove staring over the division's detention unit, which happened to be full of unhappy officers and even more disgruntled clientele. It was enough to make Kiley give a *woohoo* of excitement.

The desk sergeant met her eyes in the reflection on the window overlooking the surly arrests before she turned around. "It's all fun and games until you get to the booking, the reports, and the stinky cells."

Not knowing how she was expected to respond, Kiley went with the standard answer, "Yes, ma'am."

Which brought a smileless chuckle from the woman with the prematurely grey hair. "What's your name?"

"Kiley Gibbons, ma'am. I'm here for a scheduled ride-along with forty sector."

Kiley stood with her hands behind her back, feet shoulder-width apart. The parade rest position had become a topic of debate with her sister, who was completely at ease standing like that for hours. Kiley felt like starting the chicken dance with her elbows flapping while her vest created the look of an overstuffed mother hen's chest. Everything about it was unnatural.

The desk sergeant's eyes strayed to one of many curls threatening to bounce out of Kiley's hair clip.

"My husband must be getting soft." When Kiley didn't reply, she added, "You still have hair on your head." She turned to get the night's lineup off her desk, giving Kiley the opportunity to glance down at the gold-trimmed black name plate on her uniform. *McCain.*

Crap.

Not wanting to go on the ride-along in the first place, Kiley hadn't followed her normal routine of plastering her hair to her head. And there was no doubt she was going to pay for that come Monday. *Her* Sgt. McCain, the male one with the balding head, would make sure of it.

"You'll probably be riding with radio 341. He's been a training officer in the past. Sgt. Heins will give you your assignment. Her roll call started," she glanced at the old chrome clock on the wall, "one minute ago."

Crap. She was late.

"Thank you, ma'am." She nodded and retreated to the back of the station, where her clumsy entrance into the cramped roll-call room didn't improve her outlook for the night.

Several mouths smirked as she tripped on steps that were ridiculously placed in the middle of the room like an invisible blue line. It was almost as if the stairs had been strategically located to trip every nervous recruit daring to enter the law enforcement lair. Sgt. Heins looked up from the stack of papers strewn out in front of her on the long table lined with uniforms, her blue eyes and freckles glowing with her warm smile.

"Every single one of these sorry excuses for a human being has taken a trip down those stairs. Including myself. I'm Sgt. Heins. Take a seat next to Officer Raynham at the other end of the table. You'll be riding with him."

Officer … who? Her heart thudded to a stop. Surely she'd misunderstood. Or maybe he had a brother. A sister … a wife. Her eyes flew to the other end of the table.

Holy crap.

"Yes, ma'am." Despite the lack of a heartbeat in her chest, Kiley acknowledged the sergeant.

Her knees shook with emotion she couldn't identify. Maybe those broad shoulders occupying the second-to-last seat weren't the same ones she'd clung to as his tongue had explored her nipples four months ago.

Maybe he had a twin. It was possible. She had a twin. There were lots of twins nowadays.

The golden boy's head never lifted from the documents in his hands, but she didn't miss the sharp elbow he took from the smaller officer to his right. The two seemed familiar in a déjà vu sort of way. Partners. Like Walt and Dugan had been on her first day at the academy.

But Walt was in the TAC unit, not patrol. It couldn't possibly be him.

Please don't let it be him.

Trying to quietly control her breathing, roused by a cruel fate that threw her into roll call with an officer named Raynham, Kiley didn't think her chest could get any tighter.

She was wrong.

The moment she sat down, recognition of the body next to her hit like the butt of a shot gun in her shoulder. Only this time, it was in her gut, making her breathing jagged at best.

Get a grip, woman.

The whole thing was silly. The man probably had enough ego for the entire room with some to spare. She reminded herself that she only rated a paragraph in his life. Maybe now she'd been reduced to a sentence.

Curls had nice grip.

Oh, God.

She tried to calm her reaction and failed miserably.

Officer *Walt* Raynham. Not a cousin with the same last name. Not a brother. Not a twin. It was the one and only man with broad shoulders and an expansive chest who'd driven her to do the unthinkable. One night she wanted to take back … but couldn't.

His bulletproof vest made his brawn appear even more expansive. Then again, by the looks of his biceps, he'd wrapped his muscles with more muscle. He was larger than the last time she'd seen him, if that was possible. And his fresh scent was still tirelessly attractive.

Crap.

Sitting next to her, ignoring her existence, was the same man who'd come back after his transfer to the TAC unit and told her sergeant about her relationship with Brandy. How it had gotten started, how it had developed, and how she'd skirted the law to take her new friend to a shelter. The same man who'd almost gotten her kicked out of the academy.

Stormy blue eyes accompanied by a polite nod finally acknowledged her presence before turning back to the computer printout in his hands. And the dismissal stung. He acted like they didn't know each other, like they'd never met.

It wasn't chemistry that was making her breathing erratic now. It was inner feminine outrage.

She tried to listen to Sgt. Heins, who continued to brief the sector about the gang homicides occurring in their area. Kiley knew she should be paying attention — learning. And she most definitely should have put the memory of being in his arms in the trash a long time ago. Instead, she found herself daydreaming about his large, masculine hands running smoothly across her body. Teasing, caressing — not holding on to a boring slip of paper filled with police jargon.

Ugh. She wasn't sure who deserved her anger more. Him or her. Because things were different. She was different. And she wasn't about to let one night change her future.

***

Son of a bitch.

This was going to be a long night. Of all the weeks for his unit to work in the field for the patrol officers to get in their annual in-service training, it had to be her week at EPD. Of all the recruits to get thrown into his car, it had to be her.

Curls gone wild. Curls that would tease his body. Curls he could hold as her tempting mouth tortured him beyond his dreams. Curls, he knew from first-hand experience, were wild and luxuriously soft.

"Earth to Raynham."

Walt looked up at his boss. "Sorry, Sarge."

Shit.

No Curls on the rebound was going to get in the way of his career. He put down the pickup for homicide he'd been studying before Curls walked in and laced his fingers together on the table in front of him. His practiced image of cool confidence was about to break.

Maybe one night would drive her out of his head…

And who was he kidding? Curls wasn't just a recruit with a nickname attached. Curls was Kiley Gibbons. The woman who'd gotten under his skin. The woman he'd nearly thrown everything away for in the heat of passion four months earlier. And the woman he'd nicknamed Curls so the boys and girls in patrol couldn't give her something more painful or mean-spirited.

It was the best one he could think of, and it drove his libido crazy. Yet kept his heart out of the picture, exactly where it belonged.

Curls fit in his life; Kiley did not.

"Show Gibbons a good time, but let's be careful. Do the necessary paperwork, put the bad guys in jail, and all let's go home safe — HBO." Sgt. Heins closed the sector folder, ending roll call and signifying it was time for Walt to introduce his partner to the recruit who'd be spending the shift in their car.

His partner beat him to it. Reaching across the table, Jimmy's hand extended. "Hi, I'm Jimmy Hendricks. The big guy's partner, not the dead guitarist." She took his hand in a soft and delicate handshake.

"Kiley Gibbons. Nice to meet you, sir."

"You can drop the sir. While you're with us, it's Jimmy and Walt." Her eyes darted to Walt, who tried to shrug like it didn't matter.

Jesus. It was going to be a long night.

Jimmy continued talking, completely oblivious to the awkwardness of the moment. "We're only a step above dog shit. The *boot* over there drooling at you," he pointed to the newest member of the team, "he's dog shit."

Her follow-up smile was wide and innocent. "I guess that makes me dog doo-doo."

Walt coughed through his laughter and pushed away from the table as his partner cocked his head, wondering if he'd actually heard her correctly. Curls still didn't use bad language. It was refreshing.

He hated it.

Knowing he had to play this out, for her protection as well as his own, Walt held out his hand, and she grasped it more firmly than she had Jimmy's. "Recruit Gibbons. It's good to see you."

"I thought you went to the TAC unit." She let the statement speak for itself. Not prying but definitely hoping he would fill in the blanks.

"We are in TAC. We're filling in for patrol officers who are at in-service training this week. Jimmy's my partner." He released her hand, wishing he didn't want to hold it longer.

Her eyes communicated the knowledge that their history put them at risk. What she didn't know was that Curls had captured his heart well before *doo-doo*.

CHAPTER THIRTEEN

Going in search of a wanted fugitive would have been a welcome distraction from the silent man taking up the majority of the front seat. Instead, he took the accident in the middle of a busy intersection.

Walt had traded fast-paced excitement and adrenaline so Kiley could experience the tempers and heat of rush-hour traffic — from the front seat of the car.

What the heck was wrong with him?

People driving stupidly, cutting into spaces that didn't exist, were the calls nobody wanted, even Kiley – especially when she was stuck in the Crown Vic that smelt terrible and blew hot air through the vents. The long wait for a tow had been torturous. Jimmy yapped on and on and had taken the lead with her training, which consisted of forms and more forms. It was annoying at best in the cramped vehicle filled with more police equipment than Kiley thought possible, but at least she didn't have to come up with something to say to the silent man next to her as they finally left the scene.

"We'll stop and get something to drink. You want to make sure you stay hydrated in this weather." Obviously Walt noticed her discomfort. She wanted to tell him water wouldn't cure her — being a hundred miles away from him would. Yet he looked completely at ease with the heat … and sitting next to her. She wondered if she'd ever be that comfortable in her uniform. Because she already knew, sitting next to him, would always be a chore.

The soft, throaty voice of a dispatcher broke her train of thought. "Three forty-one."

"That's us. You better answer it." Walt pushed the mounted laptop in her direction.

"What? I don't know how —"

"Three forty-one." The dispatcher's voice held an underlining tone of *hel-lo, wake up boys.*

"Say three forty-one and give our location of Twenty-seventh and Prospect." Walt's deep voice soothed over her wired nerves that wanted to jump and fray as the dispatcher waited for a reply.

She picked up the mic and pushed the button, looking to Walt for direction. "Three forty-one…" He whispered their location again, and she repeated his words into the warm plastic receiver in her hand. "Twenty-seventh and Prospect."

If the dispatcher was surprised by a female voice on the radio, she didn't show it as she coolly gave their next call.

"Three forty-one, 10-7 on a reported disturbance. 2836 Scarritt. The caller is a three-year-old boy who states his mother is screaming."

"Click on the call on the laptop. It will automatically put us out of service at 2836 Scarritt." Walt taped the computer screen where the call was highlighted.

Kiley tried to focus on his instructions, but the address resonated fear. She knew the occupants. Prayed it was just the young boy trying out a system he'd recently learned. She clicked on the address. "Is that it?" Her fingers shook from adrenaline she shouldn't be feeling.

"That's it. Now we handle the call." He turned the police cruiser northward, not the least bit fazed by the information they'd received.

Her heart rate, however, was accelerating at an alarming pace. "They're not going to give you more information?"

"Unfortunately, no." He didn't seem disappointed or anxious.

Yet there were so many possibilities out there. "Is anyone still talking to the boy?"

"If they were, she would have told us." The traffic light turned red in front of them, and Walt eased the car to a stop.

"But we don't know if someone else is there or if she fell down. We don't have enough information." She was looking at him now, expecting him to do what, she wasn't sure.

Jimmy answered from the backseat, where he lounged with his hands behind his head, legs stretched across the vinyl bench. "That's the way most of your calls will be. If you get more information, you'll be lucky."

Walt turned onto Scarritt Avenue. Unbuckling his seat belt, he parked behind an old pickup on the one-way residential street.

"That's the house down there on the left. The one with the white shutters." He nodded toward a run-down, single-story house with grey paint peeling off. A house Kiley recognized.

She had to tell him.

But he would kill her.

Or he could get killed.

She got out of the car and followed him along the sidewalk, trying to convince herself she was overreacting. Yet knowing more information would make him better equipped to handle the situation.

One house.

Two houses.

She couldn't wait. She grabbed his forearm. "Walt."

He hesitated. Glanced at her before turning his eyes back to the house. "Now's not the time for questions, Curls." He patted her hand in reassurance and tried to remove her fingers from his arm.

She held firm. "Walt."

He stopped trying to pull away. Studied her face before turning back to watch the house. "Why do I get the impression you know something about this house?"

Letting out a breath she didn't know she'd been holding, she confessed, "That's Brandy's house. I helped her move in two weeks ago with her son, Jamie."

If he were the eye-rolling type, she figured he'd be doing it right about now, or at least looking up to the heavens for assistance. Instead, the muscles in his forearm grew taut. His fingers flexed. He looked more like he was going to pummel somebody's face in. Maybe she should be the one looking up toward the sky for help.

He chose to cuss and put her in her place.

"Shit, Gibbons. Weren't you ordered to stay away from her?" He didn't wait for an answer. He stopped his partner from heading toward the rear of the house. "Jimmy, the woman who lives here has a history of being a DV victim. Her husband is a mean drunk who I've had the pleasure of meeting. He had a gun last time, waving it around and shooting. He's 10-31."

He turned toward Kiley as he unsnapped his holster. "Get back in the car." "Jamie won't open the door for you." She looked him in the eye and knew the moment he surrendered.

His jaw clenched as his hand ran across his clean-shaven cheek. "Stay behind me at all times. Is that understood?"

"Yes, sir."

The word *sir* suddenly made all the sense in the world. It set boundaries that she hadn't set for herself. Told her the difference between them — the impossibilities of the whole situation. Not to mention, her boyfriend, Andrew, was sitting at home watching football. Alone.

They crossed the weedy front yard at a diagonal. Walt avoided the bowed, wooden steps leading to the front door and hopped onto the end of the weather-beaten porch while Jimmy positioned himself at the rear corner of the house. Walt then gave Kiley the okay to follow with a head nod.

But what had taken one quiet leap for Officer Raynham required Kailey to lift, pull, and scrape the front of her shirt against the muddied porch floor. By the time she made it next to him, her hair was slipping out of its clip in chunks, her shirt was filthy, and a stray cat hissed then skittered off the other side of the porch. She brushed off her hands and stood behind the man big enough to *be* the actual door he was knocking on.

"Police," he announced to the occupants.

A dog barked across the street. Kiley's breathing bounced off the ceiling. And the fresh scent of Officer Raynham's cologne tempted her overloaded senses. Yet nothing happened. The house remained silent.

He knocked again. Louder. His fist rattled the flimsy, wooden door stained with years of dirt. "Po-leece!" he announced, his voice full of authority.

The dog, now on full alert from the screened-in porch across the street, responded in turn. Its bark resounded through the neighborhood of similar homes in various stages of disrepair. More dogs voiced their opinions, high and low, bellowing against the intruders on the block.

Kiley began to wonder if they were home—hoped they weren't. She glanced at the dingy lace trimming the front window. It swayed.

"Someone's at the window," she whispered.

Walt looked over his shoulder just as the curtain swept closed. "Did you see him?"

She shook her head. "No, but I saw a small hand. I think it's Jamie."

"Three forty-one." Walt spoke into the mic on his shoulder, heat radiating off his body and mingling with her own.

"Three-forty-one." The dispatcher's voice popped the bubble of silence around the porch.

"Do you have the caller's name?" Walt sounded hopeful.

"Negative, three-forty-one. The call taker couldn't understand him."

The dispatcher's lack of information irritated the nerves at the back of Kiley's neck.

Walt gently tapped on the window. Then he addressed the kid inside without seeing him, "It's the police, Jamie. We're here to help your mommy. Can you let us in?"

The silence loomed like the clouds, thick and unforgiving, hanging in the air as an uncomfortable reminder of how far away they were from shedding light on the situation.

Kiley waited and watched the two officers and their silent form of communication as Walt leaned around the corner. Without uttering a word, they'd developed a plan; leaving her in the shadows of the unknown — uncertain what they should, or would do.

"Jamie. My name's Walt. I'm here to help your mom. I've got Kiley with me. You may not recognize her in uniform."

His eyes scanned her face, and she could have sworn he mumbled, "I don't know how you could miss her with those curls."

"Jamie, it's me. It's okay," Kiley said into the edge of the window.

The door lock tumbled. Sliding and screeching to a sudden stop, the handle turned, creating an opening about an inch wide.

"Three forty-one to three forty-one A, the door's open. I'm going in."

With his weapon drawn and pointed toward the floor, Walt crouched off to the side and slowly pushed the door open wide.

A bare-chested Jamie in droopy pull-ups stood in front of them. His thumb crammed in his mouth, while the index finger of his other hand twirled a lock of hair and his bare toes wiggled as if saying hello. A glass jar full of grocery store flowers stood on the entry table behind him, surrounding his head in a halo of happy colors as his golden locks reached out like curly rays of sunshine.

Despite her hatred for her own hair, Kiley had fallen in love with Jamie's waves instantaneously four months earlier. Everything about him was perfect. Even his little pop-out tummy sporting a little bubble belly button that begged to be tickled.

Jimmy came out of nowhere and eased in front of her as Walt holstered his weapon and went down on one knee, where he began talking to the boy with a gentle voice and an easy smile. Jimmy scanned the house for a threat, covering the big man while Jamie waddled toward them. Once he was within reach, Walt gently grabbed the child and quickly moved him to the porch with Kiley.

"Take him to the car till we clear the house." It wasn't just an order. It was a demand. He wanted no part of her or Jamie getting in the way. Again.

Kiley knew her place. Knew she didn't have the skills — yet. Nor did she have the equipment. A gun would be nice to have in her hand when she faced Jamie's crazy, violent dad.

Kiley squatted down low and held Jamie in a tight embrace.

"It's going to be okay," she whispered as she held his cheek in her palm. "Everything's going to be okay. Did you call 911, Jamie?"

His thumb came out of his mouth far enough for him to talk but not far enough to release the wet, pudgy digit.

"Uh-huh." His head bobbed, and he pointed to the side of the house with his free hand.

Her heart hitched. "What's over there?" she asked.

"Mommy. Thee's in the thellar." His thumb still didn't come out of his mouth, and despite the obstacle and the sheen of tears threatening to spill from his eyes, Kiley felt the urgency of his words. His mom was in the basement laundry area that could only be accessed from the exterior of the house.

"Is there anybody else here?" Kiley asked as the sounds of the two officers searching the house made Jamie flinch with each thud and each call they made to announce their presence.

He shook his head back and forth, his entire body following the movement.

Walt and Jimmy came back into the front living room. Walt's face looked like the eye of a hurricane, deadly calm surrounded by anger so intense it could tear the walls down around them. "I thought I told—"

She didn't wait for his lecture. She passed on the information they needed to rescue Brandy.

"Jamie said his mom is in the basement. There's an exterior door leading to it on the other side of the house. He thinks she's alone."

Walt gave her a curt nod, and the two headed for the cellar while Kiley, still holding Jamie tightly to her chest, headed to the opposite side of the porch to watch their descent.

"Three forty-one," Jimmy's voice broadcasted over her radio.

"Three forty-one, go ahead."

"Start an ambulance for a woman with a head injury and what appears to be a broken arm. She is unconscious but responsive."

Kiley got lost in the deep sorrow visible behind Jamie's long, curly lashes. The sheen was gone, but the golden hues wept without tears. Cried without moisture. And pled for help without a sound.

"Can you tell me what happened, Jamie?" She persuaded him onto her knee, where he suckled his thumb and stared at the door to the basement.

For a moment, she didn't think he'd answer. Then his thumb slowly slid from his mouth, and he said, "Daddy pushed her."

Kiley's heart cracked, exposing tender nerve endings that wanted to scream throughout her body. A child his age shouldn't have been subjected to something so horrible.

"Pushed her where, Jamie?" she coaxed.

"Downstairs."

"Where'd your daddy go after that?"

His shoulders raised, then lowered, his pain wiped away by an unemotional and detached reaction for his dad; as if his father meant as little to him as a stranger walking down the street.

Sirens wailed around the corner and blared down the street as the red-and-white ambulance approached the scene. Jamie tucked his head into her neck and held on tightly as he hid from the noise. Two paramedics climbed out of the vehicle and grabbed a metal gurney covered with a blue plastic mattress from the back.

A sound from inside the house brought Kiley's attention back to the basement doorway. Walt bound up the steps like an adolescent on a food run, except he didn't have the body of a teenager — his uniform held the age of authority and the rubber gloves encasing his hands were covered with blood, not catsup.

For that one single moment in time, their eyes met and Kiley felt his embrace from across the porch. Which made absolutely no sense whatsoever.

CHAPTER FOURTEEN

He was home.

In a run-down, smelly, pest-infested house, he had somehow found what he'd been looking for without even knowing he'd been in search of anything. Yet when he saw her holding the boy with curls as wild as her own, he felt as if he belonged to something bigger. Better. And knew beyond a shadow of a doubt, the universe had put them in this time, this place, with this magic for a reason.

Because together they could face anything.

He looked down at his hands. The rubber encasing his skin was covered in blood.

You're delusional, moron.

There was no magic involved in violence. A woman and a child were stuck in the middle of a hopeless situation until she took a stand against the one man who stood between her and freedom. And problem with that? They were snuggly wrapped in a system that didn't have the teeth to pull them out of the dark hell the man created.

Snapping one glove off over the other, Walt directed the ambulance crew down the steps to take care of the battered woman, who would live despite the lack of desire in her eyes. He glanced up and saw the pain on Kiley's face as she watched him remove the evidence of Brandy's injuries from his hands.

Angry with the whole damned world and feeling helpless for the first time in his life, Walt shoved the bloodied rubber gloves into an overflowing diaper pail on the porch. Breathing in and out and watching the gurney bounce down the steps to the cellar, he took an alcohol wipe from his pocket and rubbed down his hands.

He was hardly husband material.

Nor did he want to be. His life's dream had come true. He was the second newest member of Tac Team Six Sixty and there was absolutely no room for a woman in his life.

This thing, whatever it was, had to be an alter ego, a fantasy. Because nothing could replace his life as a TAC team member. *That* was a dream come true.

***

Kiley jumped at the contact. She would have fallen over if Walt hadn't included her in a warm embrace that surrounded Jamie. Her heart filled with something close to pure —

"The media's here. It's time to get Jamie in the back of the ambulance. They'll be bringing his mom up soon." Her knight in shining armor was shielding them once again.

"Of course." In what should have been an awkward dance but wasn't, they moved down the steps together, sparing Jamie the onslaught from an overly eager reporter with a story to get.

"Hey, Curls! Was the child hurt?"

Kiley stumbled as the nickname Walt had given her rolled off the reporter's lips.

What the—

"You need to step back, sir." Walt's voice held the warning she wanted to issue.

"Sure thing, as soon as my photographer gets the shot. How do you know the kid, Curls?"

Kiley felt Walt's growl. Then looked up in time for the photographer to get the shot he was seeking. The photographer she knew, and thought she'd seen the last of when he washed out of the academy shortly after Walt went to TAC. Tibbs was back behind a camera, not the badge and he was feeding the reporter with information … about her while he grinned and walked with a self-assured swagger in his cargo shorts and t-shirt. Again she was amazed how a man could be so good looking and ugly at the same time.

"Step back now," Walt ordered.

The reporter pushed. "What was the nature of the call, Officer…?" The reporter bobbed and weaved, trying to get a glance at Walt's name tag.

"We were dispatched—" Kiley started, hoping to give the man a piece of information he wanted so he would wait with the rest of the reporters across the street.

"We don't talk to any individual reporter. Wait across the street like the rest of your *professional* colleagues, and my sergeant will be over to brief you as soon as she arrives." Walt's speech wasn't just for the obnoxious little man with the perfect hair and designer suit being followed by Tibbs, it was another warning for Kiley to learn her place.

Crap.

They reached the ambulance, and Walt grabbed the door, then glared at the reporter, who finally became smart enough to back away. Kiley stepped inside the ambulance with an extra boost from Walt, and the door slammed closed, muffling the outside world.

Seeing a blanket wrapped in plastic on the side bench, Kiley tore open the package and wrapped the disposable warmth around the boy who had stolen her heart not so long ago. Despite the warmth of the evening air, Jamie had begun to shiver and welcomed the layer. A search for a clean Pull-Up, however, came up negative, so Kiley hugged Jamie tight while rocking back and forth, comforting the small bundle who'd seen too much. She wasn't sure how he'd gotten in the house, but at some point, Jamie had known to lock himself inside, away from his dad. The man Kiley had thought Brandy had escaped.

Obviously not.

The ambulance door opened wide, and Walt's face appeared. His eyes more distant than they'd been at roll call, he surveyed her and Jamie from head to foot without any hint of emotion before backing up and making room for the paramedics to load Brandy's gurney inside.

Strapped to a backboard with wide bands of gauze tape, her head was bandaged, and her left arm was immobilized with a splint across her rib cage. An IV had already been started in her good arm, and her eyes were closed under her forehead wrinkled with pain.

"Mommy?" Jamie's voice sounded smaller and weaker.

Brandy's eyes opened slowly, "Hey, baby." Her voice held as much emotion as Walt's face.

Nothing.

"Everything's going to be okay." Her eyes drifted closed. "Mommy fell down the steps, but these people will put me back together. I'm not Humpty-Dumpty."

Kiley couldn't help it. Her nerves were frayed, her heart was sick, and the rebuttal of the facts spilled out as if her life depended on it. Because Jamie's did. "Jamie told us the truth. He said his daddy pushed you. You—"

Brandy wouldn't hear it. She chose what side to lie on. The wrong side. "He's just a confused little boy. Leave him be. We haven't seen my husband since we moved in here."

Kiley knew she was lying. Everyone knew it. And there was nothing they could do about it.

"Brandy—"

"That's enough, *Officer*. We'll be fine." Her friend's voice held a warning Kiley couldn't miss. Brandy would walk away from the only person in their lives who could help them, if she persisted for prosecution. She couldn't force her to talk. Couldn't force her to take the risk.

Brandy fumbled for and then grabbed the paramedic's arm who'd been busy hooking monitors up to his patient. "Please. I'm pregnant. Can you check on my baby?"

Kiley couldn't stop the sudden intake of breath whistling across her teeth. "How far along are you?"

Brandy didn't look at anyone. She just continued to hide behind closed eyelids before confessing, "Two months."

Two months. She'd been lying for two months.

It stung. It hurt. The betrayal nearly strangled her heart.

Until Jamie reached up and touched her cheek. His eyes tender. His love evident. His pain as real as his mother's.

It was the first hint that Brandy had never really left her husband. In the entire five months since their friendship had started, Kiley had never felt deceived. But Brandy had lied. A lot.

And for at least two months, Brandy'd been lying about her survival of domestic violence. She hadn't survived. Not yet, anyway. Instead, she was secretly encircled deeper than she'd ever been — pregnant with a second child and saying her firstborn was a liar.

When the truth was written in his eyes.

Chapter Fifteen

"She insists she fell. The neighbors say they didn't hear anything, nor have they seen a man over there." He didn't tell Sgt. Heins they'd seen a white female with curly blond hair who looked like the recruit standing next to him numerous times in the past couple weeks.

He also made sure he didn't look in Kiley's direction. "We've got no witnesses other than the boy, who told the 911 operator his mom was screaming. But he told Recruit Gibbons his daddy pushed his mommy down the steps." She actually had the nerve to try and butt in. He cut her off. "Yet when we arrived, he was inside the house with the door locked. And," he added for Kiley's benefit, who was shuffling back and forth just dying to get a word in, "there's no evidence of the man ever being in the house."

"What about the flowers?" Kiley's voice sounded desperately mad. Because she was, and the truth was smacking him in the face. She had no business butting in as he briefed the sergeant. The wide white hallway of the hospital left plenty of room for her to be standing twenty feet away minding her own business. But not Kiley Gibbons. Nope. She had to stick her nose in where it didn't belong. She had no business being a cop.

Son of a bitch, would he ever be free of her?

"It just means that the relationship she said was over … wasn't." Walt stepped to the side and allowed a cute nurse into Brandy's room. He should be watching her. Getting her phone number. But he didn't. Instead, he was listening to the pain in his ass on his right.

"You *know* he did it," Kiley insisted with more anger than she should have shown in front of the sergeant. If she wasn't careful, she'd be the one answering questions.

"The detectives will try to work the case, but knowing something and proving it are two different things, Gibbons. I think that was covered in the first week of the academy." Sarcasm dripped from his voice as he tried to shut her down.

"Did the crime scene techs find anything?" Sgt. Heins ignored their squabble.

"No." Walt believed Brandy when she'd emphatically denied her husband had ever entered the house. The man didn't have to go inside to push her down the cellar steps, and with the only witness being a three-year-old whose story was full of holes, the case was going nowhere fast.

Of course, Kiley would say Jamie told her everything. But it wasn't everything, and she was a recruit with no child forensic interviewing training. Brandy had lied to her repeatedly; she'd even hidden a new pregnancy from Kiley. Which meant she'd seen her abuser on the sly without Kiley's knowledge. All that, compounded with the relationship Kiley had with the victim and her son, proved Kiley was about as unbiased as he was unattracted to the recruit who drove him nuts.

This case was going nowhere.

Again.

"Make sure you notify Division of Family Services and—" An orderly wheeled past them with Brandy looking as if she was close to knocking on death's door, her body covered from chin to toe in a white sheet. The cute nurse followed, but his eyes were stuck on Curls, watching her reaction to the scene.

Dammit.

"Why does she look familiar?" Sgt. Heins asked to no one in particular.

Walt kept his mouth shut.

"You said she's been a victim before?" Sarge wasn't going to let it drop.

This time, Kiley answered for him. "Yes. She was assaulted a few months ago when Officer Raynham was still an instructor—"

"That's the woman from the burning garage off Eighty-seventh and Kensington?"

"Yeah," was the only answer Walt dared to give as the intercom paged Dr. Barton to Radiology. He stared at Kiley, willing her to let the silence linger.

"It seems to be an awfully small world for you two to end up on this call and me to be the sergeant … again." Sgt. Heins waited for an explanation.

Walt let her draw her own conclusions. He certainly wasn't sure why or how this whole thing had occurred.

Kiley persisted. "She's a friend of mine. We can't let the system fail her again."

Walt could hear the IAD investigators knocking on his brain and had to stop himself from groaning. Curls definitely had the sergeant's full attention now.

"I see. And I'm sure you let Officer Raynham and dispatch know that you had a relationship with the victim *before* you responded to the call?"

Walt recognized the moment Kiley saw what he'd been protecting her from. Defeat was not a pretty picture, even on a beautiful woman. Sgt. Heins would take care of them, but she sure as hell didn't like being left in the dark. Which was exactly what he'd been feeling, right before he'd crossed that front yard and Kiley had told him it was Brandy's house. Too late to do the right thing and stuck with trying to straighten out the wrong thing.

"I … I…" she stuttered.

He did the only thing he could. "It was my fault. She wasn't sure if it was the right address or not." That was the excuse he'd been giving her for the past hour as he'd yelled at her in his head. "I chose to go, anyway." Which was also true. He could have ordered her to the car or pulled back and observed the scene until another car arrived. Instead, he'd gone, and she'd followed.

Sgt. Heins turned toward him, her cool eyes reflecting the pissed-off woman inside. Kiley didn't give her a chance to go off on him.

"That's what he always does. Rides in to save the day."

If she thought that, why the hell did her voice hold so much contempt in its tone?

Kiley continued. "But that's not the way it happened. I had to know she and Jamie were okay. That nothing bad had happened to them. I didn't tell him until we were a couple feet away from the door."

"That's not exactly—"

"Zip it, Raynham. She and I have you pegged."

"But—"

Sgt. Heins would have chest-bumped him if he hadn't stepped back. She turned back to Kiley. "You and I need to talk."

"Yes, ma'am."

The two women walked out the door, leaving him feeling completely helpless. He was definitely living the dream now.

***

"I quit."

"Excuse me?" Walt looked up from the report he'd been writing outside Brandy's hospital room as if he hadn't heard her correctly.

He had.

"I said, 'I quit,'" she repeated with more force behind her words.

"You can't quit … we're in the middle of a shift."

It was the stupidest reason she'd ever heard. And she laughed. It was the first joyful sound that had come out of her mouth since arriving at East Patrol. And it felt really good.

"This job isn't for me. I don't like the rules. I don't like going into a call without having more information. I don't like settling for the wrong thing because policy and procedure are telling me I have to when the right thing is staring me in the face."

"So the right thing is to just quit?" His disbelief was starting to sound angry.

"The right thing is to go into the job that I think I can make a difference in."

"And what job is that? Social worker? Avenging angel? Vigilante?"

He was definitely angry.

"I think I would be happier as a call taker."

"A call taker?" He was back to disbelief.

"Yup. I talked to Sarge and realized every call I've been on has been made harder because I couldn't get information through to the right person."

"You didn't try to get information through to me." The sarcasm was back as well.

Kiley ignored it. "I've known from day one that the academy was Lee's dream—not mine. But what I've come to realize in the past couple months is that there is a job I could be good at in the police department. Something that would fulfill me the way you get fulfilled by being everyone's knight in shining armor."

"That's not what I do." He denied what she knew to be true.

"Whatever it may be, you love being a cop. Lee lives and breathes to complete graduation and hit the streets. I look forward to my paycheck. It's not me. But a call taker... I could make a difference in that job."

"For *half* the paycheck," he fired at her as he stood up to tower over her, discarding his clipboard with a loud *thlunk* on the plastic chair.

"I've made up my mind." She stood her ground.

"So you think you can just quit and they'll automatically hire you as a call taker?" His tone was beginning to get irritating. "It doesn't work that way, Curls. You have to go through the process just like any other job in this department."

Her hands snuck up to her hips. He really could be irritating. "I've already talked to Sgt. McCain. He doesn't think it will be a problem."

He looked panicked. Almost guilty. Which was ridiculous. What had happened between them had been her doing. She had pushed for more.

"Kiley, I'm sorry. I shouldn't have—"

But she couldn't let him beat himself up, no matter how much a certain part of her wanted to let him. "This has nothing to do with you, Walt. And everything to do with what I want for my future."

The silence loomed between them. Looking up into his blue eyes, she could get lost in the clouds of passion threatening to form. Lost in the fantasy that had driven her mad just months earlier. His fingers tucked an errant curl away from her face, and she knew he wanted to kiss her.

The forbidden fruit was now edible in his eyes. But he was wrong.

"Kiley!"

A deep, familiar voice stopped Walt's hand before it traced down her cheek. Stopped the distance from shortening between their lips. Her heart pounding in her ears, Kiley wasn't sure if it was from the intensity of his gaze or the fear of being caught in a situation she had no business being in.

Again.

"Kiley, I'm so glad I found you before you left." Andrew walked up and kissed her cheek for all to see. He didn't care that they were at his place of employment or that she was in her penguin uniform. All that mattered was that she was here.

Right where she belonged.

She turned and smiled at her boyfriend, who'd been called in early for his dogwatch shift. Then she did the unimaginable.

"Andrew, you remember Officer Raynham, from the academy?" She hiccupped, and both men stared at her mouth. As if they finally understood what caused her body to squeak like a frightened mouse at the most in opportune moments.

Then their eyes met. Above her head.

The pause was full of testosterone. She wasn't sure which one exuded more. Walt, who had several inches and an undeniable amount of muscle mass over Andrew, who was built for endurance during the long haul. Lean and sinewy, his deep brown eyes spoke of kindness and understanding well beyond what she deserved. When things got tough, Andrew would pull her through with every last bit of his strength. He was tried and tested. And still remained by her side.

Walt reached out to shake hands first. "Nice to see you, again."

Andrew's hand seemed somewhat reluctant, leaving Walt's gesture of civility hanging out in the air longer than appropriate. The delay left Kiley fidgety with the uncertainty and holding her breath.

The man she loved was faced with the man she lusted. And each knew the other's role in her life. But she had to give Andrew credit. Once he shook Walt's hand, he showed no signs of animosity toward the man she'd confessed as her rebound affair. Andrew hadn't seen what transpired in her parking lot. He probably imagined more occurred than what actually had. But he'd forgiven her anyway.

Because of that, they'd grown closer than ever before. And he wasn't about to let her forget.

"Did Kiley tell you the good news?" He glanced between the two of them, and Kiley's stomach dropped to the sub-basement of hell right before he delivered his knockout punch. "We're getting married next month."

Walt dropped Andrew's hand like the proverbial hot potato and did the unthinkable. He gave her a brotherly slap on the shoulder.

"Congratulations, Gibbons. I hope you're happy in your new assignment." She didn't miss the fact that he didn't wish her marriage luck, or that he hadn't used her first name or the nickname he'd given her. Confused by the wayward thoughts clouding her mind, she allowed Andrew to turn and lead her away from the man who'd tested her like no other.

"What's this about a new assignment?" Andrew asked.

Kiley hiccupped. But this time, Andrew pretended not to notice, and Kiley began to explain her decision. Talking with her hands, distracting him from the one final glance she shot back toward Walt.

The hallway was empty. His clipboard, missing from the chair. And with the knowledge that he didn't care, she turned her full attention back to her fiancé. To her future.

Chapter Sixteen

(Two years and eight months later)

"9-1-1, call taker fifty-four."

"Help. He's got a gun," the tiny voice of a young child whispered into her ear. His plea, although barely audible, dripped with fear.

As call taker fifty-four, Kiley was used to hearing the children of Kansas City, Missouri, call for help. Every 911 call taker across the United States heard too many frightened children. Some were immune.

She wasn't. Her heart fluttered with his fear. A sickening familiarity in his voice threatened to undo her. "What's your address?"

"Please help…" the child whimpered.

Kiley leaned forward in her padded blue desk chair, her heart rate beginning to run and her attention totally focused on the voice she prayed she didn't know. Mere feet away, the laughter of co-workers faded as she willed a soft, warm tone to wrap a warm blanket across the boy's shoulders. "I've got officers ready to come to your house. I just need to know your address."

She hoped his thick layers of fear would melt enough to allow him to communicate.

"Twenty-eight ... thirty-six ... Scarritt," replied the shaky young voice.

Oh, God. No.

"Jamie?"

Please let him have the wrong address. Please let that soft little voice just sound like Jamie's.

"Aunt Kiley?" His voice shook.

Kiley nearly died.

The day she'd known would come ... had come. Despite everything.

"Please, Kiley. Please help us!"

"It's okay, Jamie. I'm here, and officers are on the way. Stay on the phone with me, okay." It wasn't a question. It was a statement—his security blanket was there for as long as he needed her.

Brandy's frantic scream pierced the phone line, stabbing Kiley's ears with its sheer volume of terror. Then it stopped. Her silence crystal clear. Kiley struggled to hear Jamie's soft, shaky whisper...

"Hello?"

"I'm here, Jamie." Her fingers flew across the keyboard, updating the computer for the dispatcher sending officers to the scene as the address of Brandy's phone finally populated on her computer screen.

"What happened, Jamie?"

"He came home ... stinky and mad. He didn't like his dinner. I tried to make him happy but—"

Again, Brandy's screams drowned out her son's response. Seconds seemed like hours as Kiley waited for it to end. As if on cue, it did. And somehow it didn't make her feel any better.

Jamie's voice hiccupped with fear. "Please hurry … he's hurting her."

Body leaning forward, hands covering the headset on her ears, Kiley tried to give him assurances. "The police are coming. Stay with me, Jamie. It's going to be okay." It was a lie, and she knew it. Everything felt wrong. "Where are you?"

His response was so soft Kiley wasn't sure if her own mind filled the silence with her biggest fear. "Hiding in the closet."

Her heart skipped a beat.

Dag-nab-it.

Jamie was trapped in a small cage. No windows, no back doors … no way out. If his dad found him…

Refusing to let hope escape, Kiley took a deep breath. Defeat was not an option. The closet wasn't the best place, but it would allow the officers a little more time to get there and get Kevin under control.

"Where's the baby, Jamie?" Kiley asked.

"Please hurry, he's hurting her," Jamie's frantic plea tugged at her soul.

"They're almost there, Jamie. Who's he hurting?"

Kiley's long, slender fingers paused above her keyboard, her fingernails tapping the keys in beat with her heart as she anxiously awaited his response.

"Mommy … and Gina," whispered Jamie.

Her heart clenched so hard she wasn't sure she could free it and allow it to beat. Again, she updated the dispatcher's screen.

"Where are they?"

"In the living room. I'm in the coat closet. I know you told me to go outside if he hit her … and call 911, but I … I waited too long."

"It's okay. You're doing great, Jamie. I'm so proud of you. Everything is going to be okay." Tears threatened as the feeling of helplessness surrounded her.

"He hit her—" he hiccupped again "—real bad, Kiley. There's lots of blood…" His voice trailed off with another hiccup.

"Are you hurt, Jamie?" Kiley asked, silently praying he wasn't.

"He … he threw me." The disbelief in his voice was genuine.

Kiley had feared this day would come. The day the addiction to drugs and alcohol reared its ugly head again. The day the domestic violence turned into child abuse. The day the precarious safety net her friend had been depending on … broke.

"I'm okay, but the baby … Mommy was holding her." *Hiccup.* "She was crying. Daddy said to shut her up. Then he hit mommy. Real hard." *Hiccup.* "I don't hear the baby anymore. I just hear my mommy…" A sob escaped, mixed in the middle of a hiccup.

The desperate cries of his mom, as she took one heck of a beating from a son of a B called *dad*, said everything Jamie couldn't. Kiley refused to become sidetracked. The more information she was able to obtain, the better chance the officers responding to the call had of getting them all out safely.

"Jamie, you said your daddy had a gun?" Brandy had sworn there were no weapons in the house, other than kitchen knives. Again, the feelings of betrayal and failure encircled Kiley's chest.

"Yeah…" His hiccups softened. No longer a full-body noise.

"Do you know what kind of gun?"

"No," he confessed.

"Is it short, like your cowboy gun?"

"He calls it an … an *AR*?"

If she were a cussing woman, four-letter words would be flowing from her mouth. Instead, she bit her lip and wondered if the assault weapon was the cause of the blood. Had Kevin shot the baby? Was that why she no longer cried?

"Has he fired the gun?" Kiley's breathe caught, waiting for the reply.

"No…"

The relief sagging in her shoulders—died.

Brandy's plea, "Please, baby—" echoed through the phone almost as loud as the gunshot that followed.

Hope drifted out the window as fate slammed it shut. Overwhelming guilt threatened to undo her.

She'd jinxed Jamie. Her good friend had betrayed her children. Brandy had lied about her husband's continued sobriety. Lied about him attending counseling. Lied about him being stronger than his addiction.

How long had they been living in fear again? Had he ever been sober? Had the abuse ever really stopped?

Kiley shook off the guilt, the anger, and the fear. She had to save Jamie and the baby … and hopefully Brandy. The vicious cycle had to end … today. And with a smidgeon of luck, and a lot of help from the officers en route to their house, Brandy would live another day to follow a new path.

"Jamie."

For the first time, nothing came over the line.

"Jamie, are you okay?" She wanted to reach through the phone, grab hold of the young boy, and yank him to safety. But all she could do was try to get a response. Any response. Her question hung in stagnant air too thick to breathe.

"Jamie, you *have* to answer me." Her voice sounded desperate.

She could barely breathe. Her heart ached, a piece tearing away with each passing moment Jamie didn't answer. Had the bullet gone through the wall? Had his dad found him on the phone? Her mind raced. Her body tensed to the point of fracturing.

"Jamie? Jamie!" Seconds passed that seemed like hours. Her fingers tapped in rapid staccato on the keyboard, yet she typed not a single word.

A faint murmur broke the silence. "I think he … he killed mommy."

"The officers are almost there. Don't come out of your hiding spot, okay?" That warm security blanket she'd tried to wrap around him with her voice slipped away. She knew it. And worst of all … he knew it. His mom no longer screamed. But the faint shrill of sirens echoed in the background.

Louder and louder. Closer and closer. She updated the call to shots fired.

A hand rested on Kiley's shoulder. Her partner, listening intently for the last several minutes, knew she didn't want to abandon the boy on the other end. Especially when a picture of that boy holding his baby sister sat on the console between them.

Would they ever get there?

A loud thumping reverberated through the phone.

Oh, God, had he found Jamie?

"Don't move, Jamie. Stay quiet." Kiley held her breath, straining her ears to hear every movement, every action, every detail she could possibly make out.

Jamie's breathing became faster and louder, the hiccups replaced by sobs of air hitching through his lips.

"Police!" ricocheted through the phone line.

"Stay where you are until they come get you, Jamie. Don't move. I've told them where you are."

Kiley stiffened as a vicious growl too vile to have come from a young boy grated her eardrum. He was close. Close to the closet. Close to Jamie.

"Get out of here or I'll kill 'em all!" bellowed the deep, cruel voice of the man she'd loved to hate. A man she'd only met once despite the years of friendship between her and his family.

Jamie whimpered, the sound resembling a lost puppy. Kiley's muscles coiled as tight as a snake wanting to encircle his body in one last agonizing hug. Closing her eyes, she disconnected emotionally. She had to—to keep him quiet—to keep him alive.

"Shhh, Jamie. The police will get you out. Just stay on the line with me. Everything will be all right." She prayed she wasn't lying. But she had to do *everything* ... say *anything* ... to keep him silent. "Jamie, I know you're there, just stay quiet, and I'll keep talking to you."

The glorious whisper of "okay" made her rejoice and curse at the same time. He was okay, but the sound may have given him away. That single word kept her faith thriving and her hope plummeting.

Quickly updating the call on the computer for the dispatchers, Kiley heard patrol officers attempt to communicate with the crazed man. She watched as her own screen flashed an update of the dispatcher's communication with the officers. They could see his dad. A large white male, six two, two hundred and sixty pounds, in his thirties, wearing a white T-shirt and jeans. He was standing in the living room—armed with an assault rifle. There was no sign of his family.

Staying on the exterior of the house and wearing bulletproof vests wouldn't protect the officers from the piercing rounds of the assault rifle. Their only protection was concealment and darkness.

Everyone was weighing the risks, especially the supervisor at the scene.

The words she'd been hoping she wouldn't see bleeped across her screen:

R330 has called an Operation 100.

Kiley's hope sank. She wasn't sure Jamie could quietly endure hiding in the closet as more officers, hostage negotiators, and a tactical unit responded to the scene.

Keeping a five-year-old quiet … and hidden … for God only knew how long … was … was something she'd never done before.

She watched the screen as neighbors were evacuated. She told a story to keep Jamie quiet as a command post was located and the Six Sixty Tactical Squad dispatched.

Faith flowed through her veins and calmed her heart. The Six Sixty Squad was like a Vince Lombardi football team. Well-disciplined with a hard edge and her twin sister running point. But the extra pitter-patter in her chest was for the man who would knock Jamie's front door to smithereens with a battering ram. Walt. The man who'd been making Kiley's heart dance since the day she'd met him.

Kiley said a silent prayer. *God, please let them get everyone out safely.*

CHAPTER SEVENTEEN

Walt looked toward his sergeant, who gave the nod of approval to answer the dispatcher on the radio, "Six Sixty Squad's en route."

Training exercises complete, the squad had been packing up their gear when the operation one hundred was called. The timing was perfect. Walt obtained the safe route in to the command post being set at Scarritt and Benton Street, at the Sacred Heart Church.

"Radio six ten on TAC air."

"Go ahead, six ten," a male dispatcher responded.

"Advise radio six-fourteen to pick up the *Peace Keeper* and respond to the command post."

"Six fourteen copied. En route."

Relief poured through him. Being the support squad sucked. All tension, no action. The members of Six Ten would be the understudies this time with radio six-fourteen sitting in the driver's seat of the armored tank better known as the *Peace Keeper*. Walt would take his battering ram and Heckler and Koch MP5 nine millimeter any day over playing bus driver for another squad.

Spotting his partner of the past year taking off a pair of worn-out old combat boots across the yard, Walt yelled, "Put those shit-kickers back on, we've got an op. Let's go!"

Lee didn't hesitate. Jumping up and slamming a foot less than half the size of Walt's back into a boot that had been through more shit than a pig, she hopped while lacing it up and running across the yard.

At first, the match-up had been tenuous. The past had left her glaring at him as if he were lower on her radar than the scum dope dealers who used kids to deliver their product. When she'd come to work on the third day with an embarrassed smile and apology, he hadn't known what to think.

Then she'd told him about Kiley's confession—about being the instigator in their indiscretions, the user in search of rebound sex.

Yeah, that'd made him feel so much better. Having a connection you thought you'd felt reduced to what you hoped it wasn't … sucked.

It did lead to a partner who complemented his skills and personality. He put up with her smaller size because her speed outdid his own. He let her drive because she had NASCAR instincts. He followed her into hell because she matched its fire with more blazing heat than even the devil could handle. And he'd ultimately given up any dream of being with the woman he desired—'cause there was no way he'd take a chance of losing his partner.

Lee Gibbons was quiet, reserved, with a small, lean frame, quick feet, and a quirky personality. Commonly mistaken as an "easy target," she never allowed anyone to make the mistake twice.

Yep, his partner was the only female in the unit. And her twin sister, who looked nothing like her, was the one woman Walt wanted—but couldn't have.

Lee began asking a tirade of questions. "Where's the command post? How many suspects? How many victims? What weapons are involved? Where's the house? What type of house?"

"A man's got his wife and kids at gun point with an assault rifle, and he's losing his sanity—fast. That's all I know at this point. The command post's at Scarritt and Benton."

Their doors slammed shut in unison — closing off the fun of training, and turned their focus toward the op. Eight unmarked police cars loaded with tactical officers left the scene of their training ground in an abandoned house and headed for the *real deal* with their lights and sirens blaring. Walt knew the hostage negotiators were also on the way. From home, the office, or the restaurant where they were having dinner with their family—each one had signed on for the thankless job of trying to talk down the latest maniac with the gun who couldn't, or wouldn't, see that there was always a point of return.

Some people just couldn't recognize any way out, other than a bloody exit to hell.

At the command post in four minutes flat, they were greeted by a uniform officer with a clipboard. Young and all business, he leaned close to the window and got an eyeful of the other drawback of having Lee as a partner.

Pink.

Pink gear bags, pink clipboards, pink computer keyboard. How she'd gotten one of those put on a department mobile data terminal remained a mystery.

Even the music was *Pink*. And although the woman had a killer voice, it wasn't the type of music Walt wanted to listen to right before an entry.

Guys often asked how he could ride in the *Pretty in Pink* cruiser. But he was serious when he said he'd follow Lee to hell and back. And he didn't let a day go by that he didn't remind her of his commitment.

Lee signed the log and glared at the young officer who choked on a weak-ass laugh.

"She's worse than a wife," Walt added.

The officer's hands flailed and juggled the clipboard Lee threw in his direction. He was lucky he didn't find himself laid flat-out on the ground. Not that Lee would deck him, but whenever she gave her *crazy-eye* look that said she'd shove a guy's balls up through his mouth if he didn't shut up, it normally resulted in the officer falling on his ass to get away.

Guys were pretty predictable when it came to protecting their balls.

As the only woman in TAC, Lee had two choices: she could be the token female … or she could be insane.

Lee liked being insane.

"Dude, you're scaring the kids."

She smiled and winked. "I'm just practicing my parenting skills, just in case I decide to take the plunge."

"Uh-huh." Walt rolled his eyes and looked back to see if the log officer had passed out from relief that his genitalia had survived—intact.

"Radio six sixty," the dispatcher's detached voice interrupted.

"Go ahead for six sixty." Sgt. Reid pulled up behind them.

"Call taker fifty-four is talking to a juvenile inside the residence. One shot has been fired. Unconfirmed if anyone hit. Suspect has blood on him, but caller confirms blood was from an earlier assault."

"Shit." Lee's face turned grim with the news.

The male dispatcher was completely detached.

The call taker wasn't.

Call taker fifty-four was Lee's sister, Kiley. Sweet with her heart on her sleeve Kiley—who was capable of rebound sex.

Lee grabbed their unit cell phone and dialed. He didn't have to ask whose number was being pounded into the phone. It was the woman she loved. The one woman who could ruin their friendship.

Lee put the call on speaker.

"Hey, Kiley, it's Lee and Walt. Ask the kid where the closet is."

"It's in the living room straight north from the door."

It was in her voice. That hidden something Kiley always left out. Which was the exact opposite of what she was known for.

"What's the suspect's name?"

"Jamie's dad's name is Kevin."

And suddenly it was all too clear. She was doing it again. Putting herself right in the middle of a call that she should relinquish. But instead, Kiley was acting the part of avenging angel, ready to take on an SOB who had guided her path since the second day of the academy.

Son of a bitch.

"Kiley..." He tried to warn her.

She ignored him and continued with a full info dump. "If you run the address, you'll find Lino K. Caputo, white male, 9/20/82, with an extensive criminal history, and a Kevin Caputo with the same date of birth, but there's only a traffic ticket under that entry. There's also a Terrenzio R. Caputo, white male born in 1986 with some juvenile indexes, but he shows some more recent addresses in Springfield. Then there's a Terrenzio Lino Caputo born in 1955 who hasn't had an entry since 2000, when he was convicted of armed robbery, assault, and armed criminal action. I believe he's in Leavenworth. I'm not sure how he got associated with this address. He's never lived there. But Lino Kevin Caputo is our man."

Walt looked at her sister. His partner. Her face had that insane look without any layer of hidden humor. And he knew she wasn't going to do a damned thing about Kiley sticking her nose where it didn't belong. Because Kiley was Kiley. Because the two of them had each other's backs. Because when it came down to the people they loved and policy — they'd break every policy in the book.

This was why a man didn't need baggage. The job came first. At least it did for those dedicating their lives to it who didn't get bogged down by their hearts.

The twins were being damned stupid.

Fuck.

And once again, he was going to do the wrong thing for all the right reasons. Because somebody had to protect them from themselves.

Walt ran the suspect's address on their pink mobile data terminal mounted between the two front seats of the police car. They watched as Lino K. Caputo's name and mug shot popped up with all the bells and whistles attached. Armed criminal action—*great*. He knew all about the crazy drunk with the gun. Assault in the first degree on a law enforcement officer—*even better*. That was new to the list—with no adjudication. And rounded off with numerous domestic violence arrests listing the expected—known to be armed and dangerous.

Oh, the joy.

"I guess it's time to take care of this guy once and for all." Lee's voice hardened in preparation for battle.

"Brandy and her kids are in there, Lee. Take him out if you have to. But make sure he leaves his family behind."

"Kiley, you have to tell your supervisor." Walt instructed deaf ears.

"Jamie's five, almost six. The baby's seven months old. I don't know where they are, but Jamie thinks his mom is dead."

Walt looked at Lee.

Fuck.

She didn't have to say it. Walt knew his partner was thinking the exact same thing. Kiley blamed herself for not getting through to Brandy, just like she hadn't been able to make a difference three years earlier when the man had pushed his pregnant wife down the steps of their basement.

Three years ago.

"Where's the two-year-old?" he asked, suddenly very aware of the fact that Brandy had been expecting her second child the last time he'd been in the middle of her domestic bliss.

His question was met with silence. He asked again.

"Where's the two-year-old that she was carrying when you were still in the academy?"

"She lost the baby that night. The seven-month-old is Brandy's third child." Once again, her lack of inflection pierced his gut.

Jesus. How had he not known that?

Granted, he'd walked away from Kiley and her fiancé immediately after she'd chosen the man she loved, and he'd never looked back. Sexual attraction shouldn't get in the way of a couple in love. No matter how gut-wrenching it was.

But for a child to die on *his* call, and for him to be so caught up in the personal loss of not getting laid by Curls, that he was oblivious to it—*Jesus.*

Brandy had failed to protect her child. And Kiley blamed herself for not ensuring justice was served against the asshole responsible. But what ate him to the core was the simple fact that he'd turned his back on all of them — and failed to protect every single one of them.

Shit.

On that one call for service, *he'd* led the system to Brandy's door — and the system had failed. Miserably.

He couldn't let it happen again, yet as much as he wanted to ensure that Jamie, his mom and sister would make it out alive, he knew there were no guarantees. The odds were stacked against them.

"I'll get them out, Kiley," Lee promised her sister over the phone.

Walt corrected, "The Six Sixty Squad will do everything in its power to get the job done." Because as a team, their chances of success were increased.

Kiley's voice came across the phone hard as a rock — Walt knew it was porous. "You guys better use that 'macho bullshit' of yours and bring them all out."

"We will," promised Lee as Walt frowned and shook his head at his partner. Lee ignored his disapproval and started asking a succession of questions of Kiley:

How many bedrooms were in the house?

Where did the back door lead?

Could she draw a diagram of the interior?

Was the suspect drunk?

How many guns did Kevin Caputo own?

And did Jamie know where his mother and sister were located?

Kiley's knowledge and her skills to obtain information from callers were invaluable. Information gained from Jamie would help the team on entry, and the hostage negotiators who were arriving at the scene could use every tidbit she received in their attempt to make a connection with his wacked-out dad.

"I'm sorry I got angry. Be careful, Lee. You too, Walt."

He hid the flinch her words caused by turning away. He was an afterthought in her life. The mistake from the past who kept rearing his ugly head. He and Kiley had their own vicious cycle going that somehow seemed entwined with Brandy and her kids.

A cycle of mistakes and screw-ups. Of intensity and confusion. And a feeling of being right where he belonged.

Everything that scared him to death with every fiber of his being.

"Just tell the boy we're coming," responded Lee to her twenty-seven-year-old twin who made his heart flip-flop more than the op.

"Love ya, Ki."

Walt hated the feelings of doom that flooded his mind. Yet somehow he knew, *'Love ya, Ki'* would be the last thing Lee said to Kiley … before Jamie's dad changed their lives forever.

Chapter Eighteen

Walt leaned against the bathroom door inside the command post bus, a modern-day Winnebago housing seven computers connected to smart boards on the walls to make everything life-size. A digital floor plan of the house decorated one wall, with obvious additions made to it by Kiley's inside knowledge of the house. Another board displayed a diagram of outside and the surrounding residences along with the positions of the current police officers keeping guard of the perimeter. Television monitors, with live footage of the scene from several different infrared cameras that had been rushed into place on tall tripods, glowed eerily from the hanging mounts inside the bus. All of it looked unnervingly similar to the images of a military target in Afghanistan or Iraq on the evening news right before it was blown up for housing the Taliban or al-Qaeda terrorists.

Divided into two rooms, one end of the bus housed the tactical squad dressed in full gear ready to go, while the other was full of commanders and negotiators attempting to talk the man out.

Yeah, like that was going to happen.

Motherfucker Kevin had made a career out of terrorizing his family. From where Walt was standing, it looked like the man wanted a retirement party with a bang.

Three negotiators huddled together planning their conspiracy as they leaned over the table. The plan was to throw a cell phone in the window since Kiley was talking to the boy on the house phone. The problem … the man might begin to wonder why they weren't using the house phone.

"Make him think the kid left the house with the phone. It will buy us some time and keep his mind busy," Lee's voice interjected.

Walt watched as negotiators and commanders turned their heads toward the unsolicited piece of advice.

Oh, shit.

There was a time and a place for the tactical guys to throw in ideas. This wasn't one of them. Too damn many chiefs plotting how the Indians were going to go to war. And despite how good the advice was, the chiefs didn't like the intrusion. But Lee just stood there … holding ground like there was no tomorrow.

Think of our careers, dude.

"Thank you, Officer Gibbons. We'll take your suggestion under advisement. Now could you get my people some coffee?" The captain's obvious dislike for Lee's input blared through his tone as he turned his back. TAC officers were not welcome with his hostage negotiation team.

"That's Officer Gibbons-*Williams*—"

Walt yanked his partner backward, shutting her up before the captain turned around.

"You'll get us taken off the entry. Do you want Six Ten Squad to go in?" he whispered in her ear.

His partner's lips pressed firmly together. Everyone in the tight-knit group turned away and huddled together while examining the tabletop computer screen. All except one short-haired blond female situated in the center of the group, who winked at Lee in a feminine conspiracy that Walt had watched play out time and time again during an op. He'd never said anything to his partner. The two had worked patrol together — had each other's backs. He respected their relationship as much as he valued his own partnership with Lee.

Besides, the blond had just squelched Lee's anger with that one blink of an eye probably more than Walt's comment. Being reduced to wait staff by *Captain Jackass* was not in his partner's personality.

Thank you, Jesus, for bringing another woman to the table.

"Coffee, tea, milk?" Walt whispered in Lee's ear as she retreated for the drinks.

"Anything you wish, *sir*." Lee's sickeningly sweet response was followed up with a feminine eyelash flutter and a sway of her hips. The accompanying shoulder bump would've knocked a lesser man on his ass.

Walt blocked the aisle as he turned his back to the negotiators and addressed his partner in the small kitchenette located in the middle of the bus. "Careful, you're pushing buttons that don't need to be pushed."

"Can they go any slower?" Lee responded in a hushed exclamation. "If we wait much longer, they'll all be dead, and where will Kiley be then?"

"Are you any different?" Walt asked his smartass partner, who actually poured coffee like she did have experience as a waitress.

"What's that supposed to mean?" Lee's voice turned to ice, making Walt wonder if he should let it drop.

"I mean," he started slowly, hoping the blow wouldn't hurt, "how are you going to take it … if we don't get those kids out?"

Memories of Jamie, his tiny little squirming body in Walt's hands while he sneaked through a trash-filled backyard, came back to slug him in the head. Would he be able to handle seeing the little boy who'd tugged at his heart and shattered it with his fear, if they found him lying dead on the floor?

Or the little boy who'd stood sucking his thumb in the doorway before he'd waddled over to Kiley? Somewhere deep within a maze of walls he'd erected around his heart, the word *family* had resonated. Could he survive if *that* kid didn't make it out alive?

"This won't be the first or the last time we see kids die senseless deaths on this job," Lee argued.

"Yeah, and a little part of you dies every time." Walt watched his partner, waiting for the acknowledgement of weakness. She refused to let it show.

A mirror image of his own denial.

"Oh, like it doesn't happen to you, too? Give me a break, Walt." She started to turn away, to keep the conversation *safe* between them as she arranged the cups on the tray for balance. Neither one of them wanted to talk about her sister. They avoided the topic of Kiley like a diabetic avoided sugar. Too much of a good thing was all bad.

But something made her turn back, risk the conversation that could be deadly to their partnership. "I'm talking about *Kiley*. You're the only person in this department who knows what she's going through. She's *living* this hell with that kid. And right now, she's closer to him than anyone else in this world. What happens to him … happens to her."

And me. Son of a—

The realization shook him deep down where he didn't allow emotions to go. Beyond the place where the love for his parents and sister were kept locked away, there was something else. Something stronger than he'd ever dreamed, someone his soul secretly coveted.

Turning away from his partner, the woman he trusted with his life, he couldn't continue to look at her. She was the one person who would see what he desired, and recognize the fear those feelings created. She would smell it on him with every breath he took.

And the last thing he wanted was for her to recognize it before he even came to terms with it himself. Glancing up at the television screen, he watched a cell phone silently crashed through the front window of the house. He froze and watched a member of Six Ten Squad make a hasty retreat on the monitor. Captain Jackass hadn't even told Walt's squad that it was a go. The man had made the decision without having the Six Sixty Squad in position to react if all hell broke loose.

Walt heard the clatter of cups and turned to see Lee stopped in front of the forward monitor, coffee spilled on the tray, dampening the napkins with the deep brown color of cop coffee.

Then he grabbed the tray before Lee hurled it in the captain's direction. He stopped his partner from voicing her opinion of the commander's stupidity."Okay. I'll play wait staff for the almighty brains. You — go call your husband." He gave her a disapproving look that told her what he thought of her ritual to tell her husband how much she loved him before every entry they made.

Yet he couldn't deny that this time, the distraction of a spouse … was a good thing. "But make it quick. I've got a feeling we're going to be storming that house very soon."

CHAPTER NINETEEN

The screams were deafening.

Kiley pictured the door flying open. Rebounding off the wall. His hiding spot discovered, the monster found Jamie with his face buried in his knees.

"Kiley, help me," he sobbed into the phone.

She saw him scream, his beautiful curls fisted in a hand large enough to crush his skull. His dad would have never done it, according to Brandy, but his dad wasn't there. He was replaced by that … that *thing*. Like the zombie apocalypse had come true on the other end of the phone, and Kiley had to witness it all through a tiny headset.

"Mommy! Mommy!" he screamed. She didn't move. She didn't help. "Mommy!" She could do nothing but listen.

Heart pounding in her chest, Kiley could have sworn it exploded as glass shattered. Time stood still. Her ears filled with noise so loud … it was almost silent. He was screaming.

Bodies and furniture slammed to the floor — the phone bounced, then rolled. The noise increased, the images refusing to take shape in her mind. Nothing made sense. Loud pops rang through the air … voices intermixed.

The thud of footsteps vibrated the phone. In the distance, voices yelled, "Clear!"

***

Within seconds, it was over. The suspect's gun secured. Jamie safe.

Lee ...

Lee shifted off the child, still shielding him from attack that wasn't coming. Jamie looked up, confused—no, terrorized. He couldn't tell who was the good guy ... and who was the bad guy. The entire scene was too much for his young mind to process as he gasped for air.

"Shhh. It's okay. You're safe," Walt coaxed as he approached the child who continued sucking in air as if he were drowning. Soothing noises did little to calm him, and it took everything in Walt's power not to join the kid when he saw his partner.

She was bleeding. Badly. The bright red flow seeping through the back of her uniform kicked his heart into overdrive. Rodriguez was trying to slow the flow with pressure, but it didn't look like enough.

Walt silently prayed as he pulled Jamie into his arms. *Don't let the kid see the blood. Don't let him see his dad.* Only then did he realize most of the blood around them wasn't the suspect's blood ... but his partner's.

Heart in his throat, he looked to Lee for any sign of reassurance, while the mad gunman lay sprawled out on the floor with two gunshot wounds to the chest and one to the head. He wasn't going to be threatening anyone anymore. The crazed look on his face had disappeared — one eye stared blankly at the ceiling. The right eye, only partially visible, dangled out of the socket. Blood and brain matter oozed in a downward trail to the floor from the wound at the bridge of his nose. He wouldn't hurt Jamie again.

"Six sixty, the house is clear."

Lee's eyes scrunched closed in pain. Someone cuffed the suspect, which seemed to be overkill at this point, as Walt sent up another silent prayer, *please let it be a flesh wound*, and called in medics. "Six sixty-two. We have an officer down. Send in EMS."

Walt towered above his partner while assessing Lee's injured back before she finally looked up. The agreement they'd made long ago passed between them. She didn't have to say a word for him to understand.

"It's not time for that. So forget about it. You're going to be fine."

They both ignored the emotion threatening to take over. Focusing on the job helped. For Lee, the job was survival.

Her teeth sunk into her bottom lip as Rodriguez applied pressure with both hands to her wound. It was serious. The blood was … everywhere. The adrenaline rush that had seen Walt through the entry tripled as consciousness became a struggle for his partner.

"Take Jamie outside, Walt. And find the baby." Her voice sounded strong. But it was a lie.

He wanted to scream at her. She shouldn't have been on this call. She knew these people — had emotional ties to these people through her sister. She shouldn't *be* the one with a bullet in her back.

Lee's brown eyes wavered as she tried to focus on another team member across the room checking the pulse of the battered young woman lying on the floor next to the couch. Walt would have never recognized her. Brandy's right cheek was swollen twice its normal size, reaching up into her eye and pushing the bottom lid closed. Her skin had washed to a gray tone with the loss of blood and made the bruising stand out even more. Her nose had dried blood caked around it, its cute, little upturn angled to the side in an unnatural curve. The gunshot wound to her abdomen went through and through, leaking blood all over the beige carpet in between the couch and coffee table.

The officers may not have been able to see blood on their first arrival, but after two more people had been shot, the room appeared to be painted in blood.

"I've got a faint pulse over here. Send in more medics!"

Brandy was alive, despite looking dead. Walt looked toward her daughter lying on the couch. Her crystal blue eyes blinked up at Sgt. Reid. She was conscious.

He turned back to his partner. "The baby's okay."

A faint smile touched Lee's lips. She could no longer focus on his face, which scared the shit out of him as Rodriguez worked his ass off to stop the bleeding. Covered with blood up to his elbows, his upper body strained to apply pressure to the wound on Lee's back.

Walt called to other members of the squad to help with the boy.

"Just get the kid out of here and let Kiley know he's okay. And could you call … Mack?" Lee's voice weakened. Her proximity to death showed in the acceptance of her tone.

"I'll call Mack, and he'll be there at the hospital waiting for you." *Jesus, how did you tell a man his wife had been shot?* "Where's the damned paramedics?" Walt demanded, holding Jamie's head tight against his shoulder to keep his young eyes from seeing more than he'd already seen. As if on cue, two paramedics, a man and a woman, cleared the front door and headed in his direction. Then they split, one went to Brandy, one came to Lee.

He moved to the side as Rodriguez started explaining Lee's injury to the personnel more equipped to deal with her injuries.

"Is Jamie all right?" Lee's voice strained to make it to Walt's ears over the conversation about her status.

"Yeah, I think so."

"Take him outside…"

"When you go out, we'll go out." No way was he leaving his partner's side.

"No. The two of you need to call Kiley … together." The last ounce of Lee's energy went into her order.

The same order his heart had been screaming for him to do. An order his mind had ignored. He belonged with his partner. Not the boy. Not making notification to family members of an injured officer. Not calling Kiley—the woman who held them all together. He belonged right here. Right now.

"Go…" Lee grunted as they moved her onto a backboard, her inhuman noises making Jamie burrow his face into Walt's neck.

More paramedics entered through the shattered door and divided up among the scattered bodies. One glance at the hand-cuffed suspect told them he was to be bagged and tagged for the M.E.'s office. Walt carried his bundle outside as team members and paramedics lifted Lee from the floor to the gurney on the count of three, his heart tangled and confused.

This was exactly what Walt didn't want. His footsteps falling heavily across the wooden floorboards on the porch, he walked away from his partner in her time of need to call another woman who needed him more.

***

"Can we call Kiley?" Jamie's whisper barely reached his deafened ears.

He stood outside the house, holding his cell phone in his hand and the boy closer to his body. Everything felt so right.

And so wrong.

He wasn't supposed to want to comfort this child. He wasn't supposed to call Kiley. Let alone want to hold her and comfort her. None of this was supposed to be in his life.

Ever.

"Yeah, Jamie. We'll call her." Only he didn't know what to say.

"Do I … do I know you?" Jamie asked, his voice wavering.

"Yeah, we met a long time ago." He smiled gently.

The kid had probably seen too many cops in his short life. Walt would be the last one he'd want to know when he got older — the one who'd failed to lock up his father the first time they'd met. Failed to save his baby sister or baby brother a few years ago. Failed to keep his mom and baby sister safe today. And he was just as responsible for pulling the trigger on Jamie's dad as Rodriguez was. The rounds may've come from Rodriguez's gun, but Walt had been the one to knock the door clean off its hinges for the team to make entry. For Lee to grab the boy and roll away and for Rodriguez to take the fatal shot on his dad. All three rounds in the suspect had been fatal. And each one had been delivered by the number two man in the door.

"Back when my dad…" Confusion scrunched the boy's face.

"Back when you met Kiley." That was all he needed to focus on. Not the violence or his dad. But Kiley. The woman who was just as responsible for getting him out alive as Six Sixty Squad was. "Let's give her a call."

Walt tried to hide the shaking of his hand as he pressed in the number. It was time. Not only did Jamie need to talk to her, but

Kiley needed to talk to him. She'd gone through just as much, if not more than what the squad had by staying on the phone with Jamie. She couldn't react to the violence she witnessed — couldn't fight back to save the innocent. And she'd probably heard Lee's attack firsthand.

Walt had to be the one to call her. He had to do it. For Kiley, for Lee, for Jamie and … for himself.

"Lee?" her voice quivered with hope.

"No, Kiley, it's Walt." There was a painful silence on the other end, and Walt struggled for the right words to say. "I just wanted you to know—"

Kiley interrupted, "Is Lee dead?"

Walt sighed. "No, but..." His voice shuddered and trailed off. Unable to voice his fears in front of Jamie, Walt turned his head away from the young boy, who was stronger than him. "She's been shot. And it's serious."

"Oh, God." He heard the self-hatred in her voice. Knew she blamed herself. But Lee was just as headstrong as Kiley. There was no way she would have recused herself from going on this call.

"*We* chose to go on the call. Lee wanted to make a difference. And she did. She saved Jamie. I've got him here. He *needs* to talk to you." He hoped his tone conveyed the message for her to hold it together. Jamie needed both of them right now, more than ever.

"Of … of course. Has anyone called Mack?"

"No. Lee asked me to call him, but I called you first."

"Thank you, Walt. Thank you so much for taking care of Jamie. I'm…" Her telltale hiccup told the story. "I'm okay."

He knew it was a lie.

Her voice steadied. "Can I talk to him?"

CHAPTER TWENTY

Walt stepped out from the shadows of the house, still holding the young boy who clung to his neck, as he paced the gurney on its relay to the ambulance. Lee struggled with ragged breaths through the oxygen mask covering her slender face. Still, she managed to hold up a balled fist in the air. Walt reached for it.

Knuckles bumping, they gave their customary conclusion to a successful op. Their voices in unison, "HBO," sounded for all to hear. His voice clearer than Lee's weak attempt muffled through plastic.

Walt's smile faded as his partner's hand dropped and slid off the side of the gurney where it hung … lifeless … swaying with movement, until a paramedic picked it up and laid it next to Lee's body. That was the last thing Walt saw before the door to the back of the ambulance slammed closed.

His chest thick with emotion, Walt turned away from the red-and-white lights coloring the houses within the neighborhood. Siren blaring, the departing ambulance took the baton in the next leg of the race to save Lee's life. Two more paramedics rushed from the house, competing against death with Jamie's mom loaded on a gurney. Another member of the tactical team assisted by carrying an IV connected to the woman's arm. She was loaded into the second ambulance as quickly as Lee had been. Unsure if he should allow the kid to see his mom in such bad shape, Walt chose to turn away and hide the gruesome view.

"Is that my mommy?"

Shit.

He wanted to lie. He didn't. "Yeah, they're taking her to the hospital. She's been hurt real bad."

The siren blared, and lights flashed as the second ambulance drove through the crowded street toward Newman Medical Center, the best trauma center in the city. The boy's mom was gone—a second set of lights and sirens cutting through the night sky.

Jamie's bottom lip quivered. Walt wanted to join him.

Son of a bitch.

A third set of paramedics exited the house with the infant strapped to a child's backboard and distracted Jamie from thoughts of never seeing his mom again. Even on the miniature board, the baby girl appeared lost in straps and braces. Walt didn't know where to turn with Jamie in his arms. Should he see her? Was it his last opportunity? Yet blood covered his sister as well. It seeped into the sheets on the gurney. And she hadn't made a sound.

Walt turned away from Jamie's family, shielding him from another terrifying scene, and didn't give him the choice. He'd seen enough. Been through … enough.

A paramedic approached Walt with arms extended. Her attempt to take Jamie met fierce resistance. He whimpered and clung to Walt's neck, grasping and squeezing. Jamie hid from the horrors of the night.

"It's okay, Jamie. She won't hurt you. They're going to take care of you." Walt attempted to soothe the child, who refused to relinquish his grip. Reminding him of the day when Jamie had been only too happy to get away from him as his dad had taken target practice in the backyard.

"Raynham." His sergeant's voice made him jump. "Sorry." He rested his hand on Walt's shoulder, consoling and reassuring without a word. "Why don't you go with him and make sure he gets settled in at the hospital?"

The suggestion held more meaning once Walt met his eyes. *Yeah, you can check on Lee while you're there.*

"Keep us posted." The pat he added on his back said that it was time to go.

Walt didn't hesitate. "Yes, sir." He didn't need any more encouragement. The Children's Hospital stood next to Newman Medical Center, where Lee would be fighting for her life. Walt stepped toward the ambulance but came up short when a microphone was shoved in his face from behind.

"Handled by officer? Isn't that a reference to a call without paperwork? Or is that code for killing a man?" Blinded by a glaring bright light, Walt couldn't see the breathless reporter questioning him. Jamie's arms squeezed around his neck, reminding him of his purpose.

With his blood pressure rising, Walt held his temper in check and responded through gritted teeth. "For us ... it's something different."

"HBO when you're holding the man's son?"

His words froze the blood threatening to boil in Walt's chest. The reporter knew the relationship between Jamie and the *neutralized* suspect—yet he brought up the death like it was nothing.

Walt turned away from the annoying piece of shit. The blinding light met his stiff back as Walt rearranged Jamie in his arms.

They would not get a view of the boy for their ratings.

Sgt. Reid and a uniform officer intervened—and saved the reporter from Walt's fist and the cameraman from eating his equipment for dinner.

In actuality, Walt knew his sergeant had probably saved him from criminal charges and losing his job, but neither seemed very important at the moment.

He stepped into the ambulance, ducking his head in the tight enclosure before the door sealed off the cruel outside world. Still holding Jamie, Walt sat down on the side bench too small to hold him comfortably and waited for the hatred to rear its ugly head in Jamie's eyes. He got none of that.

"He turned into a monster." A tear rolled down Jamie's cheek. "I haven't *really* seen my dad…" It was obvious as he bit his lip and scrunched his brow that Jamie couldn't judge the time frame. "For a while. It wasn't your fault." Again, his lip quivered uncontrollably. "He would have killed us."

Walt hugged the boy tightly, his small frame seeming so fragile while his heart displayed a strength most men didn't possess. "I'm sorry your daddy died. I'm sorry for what you and your family have gone through and continue to go through. But I'm very glad you're going to be okay."

Jamie clutched Walt's neck as tears streamed down his face, his bottom lip completely out of control as it shook and he struggled to gain his composure. Walt laid him on the gurney, determined to show as much strength as the kid in front of him.

He failed as tufts of the young boy's brown curly hair fell on the white sheet.

He should have killed the son of a bitch two years ago.

But he hadn't, and Jamie's mom would probably die because of him. His sister had unknown injuries. And Walt's partner fought for her life.

Walt found himself cataloging Jamie's injuries, each one representing his own mistakes. Scars and bruises, tears and sorrow that Jamie wouldn't have today — if Walt had been a better cop.

Bald spots riddled Jamie's head. Blood matted the hair he did have. Bruising discolored the side of his face. Swelling pulled the skin tight around his eye and mouth. The other side—marred only by tears—gave him a Phantom of the Opera appearance, making Walt wonder if the scars to his soul would mimic those suffered by the masked character.

His blood-stained T-shirt, stretched out of shape, did little to cover the massive bruising to the little boy's shoulder and arms. His elbows and knees bled freely—evidence of his flight and landing with Lee as they'd escaped his violent father's grasp.

All of it could have been avoided if Walt hadn't gotten emotionally involved and had done the job he was paid to do years ago.

***

Lee was in surgery.

It was a good thing. At least that's what she kept telling herself. Mack was somewhere in the hospital — watching the procedure like a hawk — while Kiley sat off by herself in the wall-to-wall cop-filled waiting room.

Waiting.

She didn't bother to hide her tear-stained cheeks from the department members who approached and stayed long enough to offer words of encouragement. She was alone. In a room full of people. But when he walked through the door and captured her gaze, everything changed, and she did what came natural — she ran sobbing into Walt's arms.

Then Walt did what came natural to him. After holding her tight, he walked her back to her chair and asked if he could call Andrew.

It hurt so badly, she cried some more. Shaking her head, unable to talk, she took the Kleenex he offered without saying a word.

Her husband... No. Her ex-husband would come ... if she called. Andrew would be by her side through everything. Taking care of her. And her needs. While wearing an expression of guilt that would make her want to apologize again and again.

No. Andrew was the last person she needed to see.

"Lee didn't tell you?"

The look on his face answered for him, he knew she was divorced. Knew she pathetically kept Andrew's name. Knew she had a gaping hole in her chest from her failed marriage.

She sighed and confessed her biggest failure, realizing that the moment she chose not to lean on Andrew, it finally was finally over. "We're divorced, but you already knew that." If he felt anything beyond pity, she couldn't see it in the depths of his eyes, so she leaned on the shoulder he offered without another word of her marriage.

"I just thought you might want him here with you...because of your history." When she shook her head, he continued. "So you're a single foster parent?"

Kiley laughed through the tears. "She told you about that, huh?"

"It might have been the diaper runs that made her mention it." Walt smiled down at her.

Kiley cringed. "I suppose my desperate calls in the middle of her shift might have an effect on her partner. Sorry."

Walt tousled her curls then listened to stories about her last foster kids. Politely nodding, asking questions when she stopped talking and keeping her mind occupied while wearing an expression Kiley couldn't read.

That'd been three hours ago, before the clock started to pass each second in slow-motion misery. And still they waited. He sat with her, got her coffee, and tried to get her to eat something. She refused. Not until Lee was safe. When the stories about her experiences as a foster mom ran dry, they were left rehashing the night. Over and over.

"How was Jamie? Really. I know he was hurt worse than he let me know." She needed the truth, and she hoped Walt saw it in her eyes. When he didn't hesitate to give it to her, she was glad he understood.

"You should have seen him, Kiley. I've never seen such bravery in all my life. He's got bald spots on his head. His face is bruised and battered. His arms and legs are covered with cuts. But he was more worried about his mom, his sister, Lee, and you. None of it mattered to him. He just wanted to make sure everyone else was okay."

Kiley smiled as more tears escaped.

"He apologized to *me*. Brandy has to be one hell of a woman to overcome a husband like that and give her son a sense of right and wrong in the process." He was silent for a moment. The conversation of a group nearby filled the gap as she leaned against his shoulder, their fingers entwined. "I'm sorry," he whispered in her ear. She looked up, met his gaze riddled with his own guilt, unsure why he felt the regret that darkened his lapis blue eyes.

"I should have recognized she was a good person who needed a friend years ago. I'm sorry I tried to stop your friendship."

It was weird. Almost as if … Kiley's friendship with Brandy was understandable. Because under other circumstances, she could be in Brandy's shoes. That's how slowly the domestic violence had crept into Brandy's life, and apparently how quickly it had returned. A childhood sweetheart who had been Brandy's dream, had turned into her nightmare with drugs and alcohol.

"Do you think she'll be okay?" Kiley asked.

"I don't know."

Walt explained how Jamie's father had used him like a human shield, taking away any possibility for Lee to get off a shot. Her sister had taken the only route possible to save him. She'd grabbed him, forfeited herself, and let Rodriguez take the fatal shot. But Kevin had had enough time to take a couple well-aimed shots at her sister before Rodriguez could get the job done.

Lee … oh, God, Lee.

New tears fell freely as images of her sister's sacrifice screamed through her head. At least one of those rounds had entered Lee's back while she'd rolled away from Kevin and protected Jamie.

Walt gave all the details, holding nothing back. She hated it, yet loved him for sharing. Without the knowledge, she'd be utterly lost. They both knew he wasn't supposed to talk about the shooting before giving his statement to detectives, but Kiley was thankful he recognized her need for details. And broke the rules.

Struggling to maintain his own composure, Walt held her like he'd never touched her before, and she melted into his side, completely at home. His body warmed her heart. His closeness tugged at her sanity. And his eyes made her lose reality.

With so much pain and anguish came a mixture of pleasure and guilt. Lee was fighting for life while her sister enjoyed the comfort of her partner's arms. Yet she couldn't let him go.

"Kiley?"

She looked up and saw her pain reflected in Katie's green eyes. A year older, everyone believed Katie was her twin, not Lee. It never bothered Kiley, until now as she watched the face of their childhood best friend crumble.

What if Lee died? What if she no longer had her twin by her side — her true best friend in the whole world? What if Katie made two and Brandy never got the chance to make four?

She stood up and hugged Katie with all the love she had and made soft noises of comfort as Katie sobbed. At five foot seven inches, Katie's heels made her tower over Kiley, her long blond hair, full of smooth waves, slipped over Kiley's shoulder. Katie always made Kiley feel short and awkward with her elegant suits and designer stilettos. Even now, with her suit wrinkled and mascara smudging under her eyes, she caught the attention of every uniform in the place. Including the elusive Rodriguez.

Katie pulled back and wiped her eyes with a tissue Kiley hadn't seen crumpled in her hand. "How is she?"

Kiley never got a chance to answer. Mack walked into the waiting room with a female surgeon, both looking tired and strained. Her brother-in-law's normally perfect hair strayed in all different directions as if he had wrung it out with his hands. His face didn't hold that boyish grin her sister loved so much. He looked like his wonderful life had just taken a turn into the dark depths of hell.

A hush went over the room—all eyes tunneled to the one woman with wrinkled scrubs as she stood in front of them like a god. A god who held Lee's life in her hands.

Kiley looked for any signs of hope in her eyes. In Mack's.

There was none. But the doctor gave her speech like she had so many times before, while Mack looked down at his feet.

"Your sister's injuries were extensive. The bullet went in her back, tearing apart her spleen and appendix. We removed both. The liver was lacerated along with the muscles in the hip, but we were able to repair the damage. The hipbone was miraculously spared, and the bullet exited the thigh without causing further damage."

As a sigh of relief went around the room, Kiley and Katie shared a watery smile and squeezed each other's hand. But the doctor stopped their minor victory celebration and squashed the optimism. "Blood loss has been, and continues to be, the major issue. The next twenty-four hours will be critical for Kay Lee. We've done everything we can. Now ... we can only wait."

Lee's future was out of this woman's capable hands.

Kiley couldn't help it. From somewhere deep inside her, more tears sprang forward, and she broke, no longer able to hold any of her emotions in check. Walt was there, and despite the woman clutching her hand, Kiley turned toward Walt's chest, just as Jamie had done hours before. She wanted him to block out everyone — the chief, the commanders, the officers. Everyone who didn't really know Lee. Who didn't believe she would never give up the fight.

Even Mack, who'd been on a whirlwind romance with Lee for less than a year before they'd married, had given up on her sister. It was written in his eyes—science didn't lie. She never looked at Katie, she just released her hand and went where she knew the fight would never be over. 'Cause if she looked at Katie and saw the same reaction Mack gave, Kiley's world would come apart at the seams.

Frustration and anger seized her. She wanted to rant and rave. But in the midst of dozens of officers, she and Walt were alone in their hope — and their grief. Without support, Lee could very well lose her battle.

But Kiley knew, within two people, hope still lived, despite the odds.

CHAPTER TWENTY-ONE

All bad things happen in threes. At least that's what the cops were whispering.

Leaning back in the stiffly cushioned hospital recliner that made for a lousy bed, Kiley rubbed her neck and stretched her arms as monitors beeped and hummed around her sister. The starkly white walls and medical equipment colored in blue and a hue of beige had started to close in on her in the early-morning hours. Until Mack had brought her to an area of the hospital she would have never seen without his access. A place of solace and reprise for her tired body. A small empty locker room for female staff members. With a shower. Mack had given her a pair of scrubs and some toiletries and told her to clean herself up.

"Lee won't want to wake up and see you looking like that." He'd smiled and ruffled her curls. "Text me when you're done, and I'll come get you."

Now it was his turn to take a refreshing warm shower and Katie was off in search of food, cause despite her rail thin figure, the woman ate like a horse, especially when she was nervous. And Walt had joined her. Kiley couldn't help but think they'd make a good couple, but neither one seemed interested past the joint concern for Lee, and making Kiley more comfortable.

Yet as much as everyone's concern helped, it didn't make up for the impersonal sterility of her sister's room — the typical intensive care unit with solid side walls and floor-to-ceiling glass separating it from the nurse's area. The tubes flowing toward Lee looked like a jumbled ball of yarn that had been in the possession of a cat for about a day and a half and through the night, the nursing staff had amazed her with a personal caring touch and their magical knowledge of what tube went where.

But all she wanted was for Lee to be in her own bed of white down and pink pillows with her husband waiting on her hand and foot.

She closed her eyes and let out a breath. The surgery had gone well, she told herself. Lee had made it past the first twelve hours, and Kiley refused to believe anything worse would happen.

The cycle of three had been met. Jamie's dad had died. Unfortunately, Kiley couldn't view that as a bad thing. Brandy was hanging on by a thread. And Lee was going to pull through after sustaining a gunshot wound to the back.

The commonality — all three had been *shot*. Only one would die. Because Kiley wasn't going to allow it to happen any other way.

Walt walked into the room and handed her a bag with a breakfast wrap and a large tea. A slow, easy smile spreading across his face that looked as tired and worn-out as Kiley felt. Yet despite his lack of sleep, he looked incredibly good.

Too good.

Keeping her voice to a whisper she asked, "Where's Katie?"

"She offered to help set up a table of food for everyone in the waiting room."

Kiley smiled. Of course she did. Katie was at her best when she was running the show.

"How's she doing?" Walt's low tone caressed her.

Kiley squirmed in her makeshift bed as she closed the footrest. "She's doing really well. She woke up for a minute, but I'm not sure she was coherent."

"Did she say anything?"

"It didn't really make any sense." Now she'd really stepped in it. How did she tell Walt that Lee was mumbling about him doing his job while she lay in a hospital bed with critical injuries? She knew Lee didn't mean anything by it. Walt was the best partner she'd ever had, and Lee loved him like the brother they'd never had. But…

"What'd she say, Kiley?" His voice had taken on the manner of instructor/recruit, bristling every nerve in her body.

Fine. She didn't have the strength to protect him from the ramblings of her drugged-up sister. "She said"—Kiley's voice projected louder than it should have—"'Step up, Walt.'"

The tiny fall at the corner of his mouth said it all. And Kiley regretted opening her mouth.

"It doesn't mean—"

"It means everything." His eyes shot to Lee's monitors, watching the steady rhythm of her heart.

"She's heavily medicated—"

"We have an understanding." He confessed. His voice jagged and rough.

"The doctor—wait. What understanding?"

He turned away like maybe *he* regretted opening his mouth. Kiley looked at her sister. Looked at the monitors. Their beeping filled the silence with a foreboding Kiley knew she'd have to face.

She swallowed her fear and set down the food in the chair as she got up to stand behind Walt, as he looked out the window with a view of a catwalk leading to a parking garage across the street. She raised her hand to his arm and he flinched at her touch before turning around.

"Sometimes partners have an agreement with each other. In case…"

What was left unsaid … said it all.

Oh, God.

The whole time she'd thought Lee had been reliving the shooting and giving her partner instructions about what to do during the assault … Lee had actually been planning for whatever happened when she was no longer around. Lee wanted Walt to "step up" and take care of whatever he was supposed to when her sister died.

Kiley's knees quivered just as Walt's arms embraced her against his solid chest.

Alarms rang in a room down the hall. "Code blue. Code blue. Room five fourteen," sounded in the hallway.

A sob escaped Kiley.

She knew that room. It was Brandy's room. The room she'd been going back and forth between in the wee hours of the night. Brandy had regained consciousness and asked to speak to her social worker, who just happened to be next door at the Children's Hospital with the kids at the time. When the social worker had arrived, Kiley had stayed with her sister.

Now she wasn't sure if she'd ever see her friend again. How could she be alive and talking one minute and on death's door the next?

This could not be happening. Fear of losing everyone she loved crushed at Kiley's chest. Tears spilled down her cheeks, dampening Walt's shirt.

Just as she sensed him tightening his hold, Kiley pushed him away. She stalked her sister, refusing to accept their decision without a knock-down-drag-out fight. "Don't you dare give up like that." Her voice shook with fear and anger. "You're not allowed to make pacts with anyone…" she finished the sentence with a whisper in her twin's ear, "…but me."

Movement near the glass wall to the ICU nurse's station brought Kiley's gaze away from her sister. Desperation assaulted her as Brandy's caseworker breached the doorway.

"I don't care what kind of agreement you made." Her voice cracked. She continued her rant to her twin. "You don't have the right to leave me out, and you don't have the right to leave me behind."

For the first time in their relationship, Kiley hadn't noticed Walt move closer. Maybe it was because she was as mad at him as she was at her sister. The two of them had *no* right. It had been Kiley and Lee against the world since the day their parents had died. The four Musketeers reduced to two. One alone was … nothing.

And no one had the right to break the bond of *all for one and one for all.*

No one.

Not Donna, the woman walking in the door with bad news written all over her face. Not her sister's absent husband, who'd gone to shower. And most certainly not the man who worked with Lee night and day and had the ability to make Kiley act like a stranger in her own skin.

***

Bad news was coming. It didn't take a PhD in psychology to read the social worker's face. Two people were dead.

"I'm sorry, Kiley..." The social worker stood at the door, the corners of her mouth drawn tight, her eyes bright with unshed tears. The wrinkle of her brow tipped him off. There was more than just Brandy's death weighing on her shoulders.

"But ... she was just talking," Kiley insisted.

"Her doctor advised her in front of the detective and me that she was not going to live; the damage to her body was too severe. The detective asked her if she wanted to make a dying declaration. She did."

He watched as Kiley took in all the information. She'd shut him out a moment ago, but she needed someone to make it through this clusterfuck.

He moved closer.

Tears spilling down her cheeks, she turned and glared in his direction before addressing the social worker. "What did she say?"

The social worker's fingers clenched the clipboard in her arm as she delivered the message that was uncomfortable ... at best. "She said she brought you into their lives several years ago because she knew the day would come when Kevin would kill her. She said her children need a mother, and she wanted you to take custody of Jamie and Gina."

Kiley's chest expanded. Her brows lifted into peaks of visible pain. She hadn't known Brandy's fears mirrored her own. Apparently that was the one topic they'd never gotten around to discussing. Walt wanted to wrap his arms around her. Comfort her the way she needed. Instead, he stood by and helplessly watched.

The caseworker continued. "She said she wanted you and your husband to adopt her kids."

"Of course I'll take the kids, Donna. But I..." She stopped and stared at the social worker who was dressed well beyond her years in elastic-waist pants and a polyester jacket. "I'm no longer married."

From the expression on her face, the social worker wasn't aware of the change in Kiley's marital status. No doubt she wondered where that left the validity of Brandy's statement.

Walt wanted to tell her the truth. Kiley was just too selfless to talk about her problems. She wouldn't burden Brandy with the pain of her divorce. She'd bear it alone. Apparently Brandy never asked about Kiley's husband—her ex-husband of almost eight months.

Hell, even though he'd known about it, Kiley hadn't mentioned it to him either...not until today. In fact, Kiley still had the man's name on her department name tag and wore her damn wedding ring, for Christ's sake. How was he supposed to act around that?

Not that he'd counted the eight months since her divorce was finalized, but he knew it was over. That was the one thing Lee had shared with him often. *"Kiley really needs to get out and date. It's been two months since her divorce was final."* Or *"Kiley's sitting at home again. After eight months, you'd think she'd be hitting on every horny cop who stopped by to talk to her."* That particular comment had earned her the silent treatment for an entire shift.

"Walt..." It was Lee's turn to shake things up. Again.

Walt moved forward as Kiley stood at the foot of her sister's bed, smiling because her sister was awake, but hurt because her sister wanted *him*. He also saw how torn she was by her loyalty and love for her friend's children that demanded she convince Donna she was still the right choice for a home for Brandy's kids.

"I'm here, Lee." Walt responded loudly enough to include Kiley in the conversation.

Lee's eyes remained closed, but her voice held strength. "Step ... up."

"You know I would if you needed me to, but you don't. You're going to be fine." He tried to reassure the only woman who truly shared his life.

Electronic alarms blared next to him on the monitor. Numbers flashed in neon shades of green and blue across the dark screen. Walt watched in shock as Lee's heart rate nose-dived, and nurses rushed toward the room.

The social worker stepped back in the hall, looking like she was going to break if she had to witness another person's death. Walt wanted to yell at her to hold her ground but focused on Kiley as she ran for the opposite side of the bed.

"Don't you dare leave me!" she pleaded, her voice desperate as she held on to her sister's hand. "I love you, Lee."

A nurse gently pushed Kiley away as she laid her sister's hand down on the bed. Walt did the only thing he could. He was there. Next to Kiley to grasp her empty hand before she could feel the void.

A doctor Walt didn't recognize appeared at the bed. "Clear the room," he ordered like a sergeant at a crime scene.

Walt pulled a reluctant Kiley from the room and approached the social worker without hesitation. He would respect his partner's request.

"I'm Kiley's fiancé. We'd be honored to have the kids."

CHAPTER
TWENTY-TWO

Kiley wasn't sure where to go.

She'd listened to Walt and Donna make arrangements to drop off the kids. At her house. People were coming and going out of her sister's room, and the horrifying thing was that most of them were the same people who'd rushed into Brandy's room.

How long had it been? Ten minutes? Twenty minutes? Could it have been thirty minutes since Brandy died?

And now her sister was on the edge …

Mack appeared out of nowhere full of anxious questions Kiley couldn't answer and then turned toward his wife's room. The room he shouldn't be in. But it was the room no one was going to keep him out of, and relief washed over her. He would make sure Lee was okay. Any other outcome was … unthinkable.

A nurse who looked like she was still in high school, began shooing them toward the waiting room. Kiley let Walt's large arm wrap around her and guide her away, but her head craned in the opposite direction, seeking a glimmer of hope in the mass of doctors and nurses surrounding her sister.

The only good sign she saw was the lack of someone in scrubs straddling Lee's body while performing CPR like they did in the movies. Voices were loud. Medical terms were confusing, but no one yelled "clear" and sent electric shock waves into Lee's heart. She was alive.

The monitor hanging from the ceiling with its darkened background screen was the last thing Kiley saw. A wavy blue line—Lee's heartbeat—staggered like the thin blue line police officers walk. Pulsing with conflict, it's irregular up and down pattern was consistent with its struggle to stay on the beaten path.

There will not be three deaths.

Donna pushed open the doors to the waiting room, where officers still stood vigil, waiting to hear about Lee. What the officers got was a completely different tidbit of news.

"I'm glad to hear that you and Kiley are engaged. It will make the adoption process that much easier. However, the placement will be considered temporary until it goes through the courts. Kiley is one of our regulars, but the entire adoption process will take time. Other family will be located and contacted. A background will have to be run on you, Mr....?"

Walt filled in Donna's question without hesitation. "Walt Raynham." He handed Kiley a tissue that he magically materialized out of thin air. Kiley wiped away the tears staining her face, uncertain what the heck was happening.

Donna's smile didn't quite reach pleasant with the strain of the situation bearing down on all of them. She shook Walt's hand before turning to Kiley. "What I really need to know is if Kiley's up to it?"

Kiley'd never had the social worker's sympathetic eyes directed at her. The new perspective — the receiving end — wasn't a position Kiley had ever expected, or wanted to occupy. When they'd worked together in the past, it'd been in regard to discussions about Brandy, Jamie, and Gina, their progress and any safety concerns. But this...

"I'm not going through anything compared to what the kids have experienced. We'll be good for each other." And they would.

Walt squeezed her shoulder, bringing her back to reality. It wasn't just her and the kids. He was in the picture as well. Part of her wanted to kiss him with everything she had, for stepping up and ensuring she got the kids.

The other part wanted to kick him to the curb, she was not a debt made to a dying partner. His partner was very much alive, and she wasn't going anywhere. And the *last* thing Kiley needed was a man who didn't *want* to be married to her living under the same roof with her and the kids.

One ex-husband was enough, thank you.

"Where are the kids?" she asked with a lowered voice. The tiled waiting room with its black vinyl seating, that made it look more like an airport terminal than a hospital, was full of men and women in uniform. They were anxious to hear about her sister, but were getting a full episode of drama in the life of Kiley Gibbons instead.

"They're still at Children's Hospital. The doctors agreed to keep them for observation last night, but they'll probably be released this evening. Will you be able to manage it?"

"Yes." Her voice sounded stronger than she felt.

Plans started forming in her head—plans that kept her sanity intact and her feet in place when all she wanted to do was run back through the doors to her sister's bedside, while bowling over anyone and everyone who stood in her way.

She'd have to call her emergency babysitter.

The kids' belongings would have to be gathered from their house—their old house.

She had rooms ready—for her next set of foster kids, but with a few additions they'd be perfect for Jamie and Gina.

Minus the mom who loved them with everything she had.

Kiley's eyes began to form more tears. She willed them away.

Her basement, in the middle of being transformed into a family room/play room for her foster kids, would have to be completed.

But mostly she needed to talk to Walt. To set ground rules. Boundaries. The kids didn't need a temporary dad. If he was going to do this, he needed to know it was *forever*. Not the marriage. Neither one of them wanted that. But the role of parent—he could never turn his back on Jamie or Gina.

Ever.

It looked like divorce number two was already in the works before she even said the words "I do."

***

He was not going to over-think his decision. Lee had asked him to *step up*. He'd stepped up. End of story.

Yet somehow it felt like the beginning of a new chapter. His life was on a roller coaster that he wouldn't be able to control. Two children and a wife were going to roll, twist, and dictate his future from now on.

Something foreign began to build in his throat. Sweat beaded on his forehead. If he had to put a name to it, he might label it as panic on someone else. For him, the type of anxiety rising through his body was not conceivable or acceptable. He forced it down to the depths of his own personal hell that it had risen out of and focused on the commitment he'd made.

Members of his unit were staring at his arm wrapped around Kiley even though he'd held her tight throughout Lee's surgery and several times after that. He could tell they didn't see the real meaning behind it—to keep her knees from buckling. No, his squad had expressions that threatened to unnerve him—like they'd known he'd been having a secret affair with Kiley all along. Like they knew she was his destiny or something.

Like … hell.

It was stupid. And if they didn't knock off the smirks, back smacks, and eyebrow wagging, he was going to punch the ever-living shit out of each and every one of them.

Which was exactly what Lee would have done. Not Walt. He was the partner with the cool head. Lee was the passionate fuse. She hadn't been up until the day she said 'I do.' Then every call seemed to trigger some kind of connection for her. She related to this, she related to that. And now he was doing the same thing. Apparently when it came to getting married and having children, his personality would change just like Lee's had. Proving every last theory he'd ever had about TAC and marriage—they didn't mix.

Rodriguez was the only one who looked at him with a suspicious eye. He understood. A wife and kids had no place in their lives. And Katie…she looked scared as hell. Standing next to Rodriguez, she was the one other person Lee had included in the pact. Walt would step up and take care of Kiley, with Katie's help.

He leaned over and kissed Kiley's head, making sure everyone knew the affection was real.

He'd tried to warn Lee away from the good doctor, Mack. Sure, her husband was a great guy, but a doctor and a female cop? What chance did that marriage have of surviving? Especially if, by some miracle, Lee did survive. How could Mack let her go back to the life she loved that had almost taken her from him?

Walt knew what it felt like to lose someone to the job. Knew the pain and despair and hatred that would come. As a traffic officer, his dad had worked countless wrecks on city streets, country lanes ... freeways. He'd called Highway 169 his station because he'd spent more time working accidents there than anywhere else. It was also where he'd worked his last accident. Where he'd died.

The traffic unit was the one job in the department Walt's mom had made him swear he wouldn't work. That wasn't a hard commitment to make. Freeways scared the hell out of him.

The other promise his mom had made him vow was to kiss his wife and kids good-bye and say, "I love you," every day. No matter what. Again, he'd made the promise without a second thought. It was a simple promise to make. 'Cause he wasn't getting married. Ever. And kids—they just weren't in his future.

Until five minutes ago, when everything had changed.

The frosted glass door opening to the hallway opened. A preppy guy dressed in designer clothes reeking of money walked into the waiting room as if he owned the place. His level of comfort and the cameraman, who also looked like someone Walt should know on a first name basis, pushed their way past an unsuspecting young uniform stationed at the entrance. Luckily, Rodriguez caught the movement out of the corner of his eye, reacted, and moved in to cut the intruder off before Walt had to extricate himself to handle the problem. Rodriguez had seen enough reporters, trying to sneak where they didn't belong, to handle the brazen pup trying to make a name for himself.

Yet something was different. Hairs on the back of Walt's neck rose to a heightened awareness. A few more cops joined Rodriguez to move the *problem* outside peacefully.

Because the guy was definitely a problem. To the female eye, Walt had no doubt his face was pleasant, but he appeared disturbingly familiar with his hair swishing across his forehead in a salon-style haircut while his boyish grin didn't even come close to reaching his eyes. It was the feigned innocence so many women fell for, like that of Kiley's ex-husband—sincere, caring, a trustworthy, stand-up guy.

A total asshole to the core.

He'd wanted to high five her when she told him not to call Andrew. But this wasn't her ex, and despite the fact that he didn't belong there, he seemed somehow connected to Kiley in a way that didn't make Walt feel any better. Especially when the asshole's eyes narrowed in on her. Like he knew her—and despised her.

Walt's arm instinctively tightened around her shoulder.

A swoosh of air released behind them and the door to ICU opened, followed by, "Kiley."

She turned toward the voice of her sister's husband. Extricating herself from his grasp and leaving his attention divided between the man who *could* be delivering bad news, to the guy at the door who *was* bad news.

"Mack, is she…?" Her voice once again tried to lie about a strength she wasn't feeling, but her inability to finish the question said it all. For everyone.

The doctor in blue scrubs, the man who Walt had barbequed with and helped build a fence around his backyard so he and Lee could adopt a dog, moved closer.Trouble, on the other side of the room in clothes that cost more than Walt's salary could afford, resisted being extricated from the waiting room.

"She's stabilized … for now. But she's not out of the woods." Mack paused, and Walt wanted to look into his eyes, search for what he wasn't saying. Unfortunately, the asshole resisting his removal across the room wouldn't allow him to do anything but stand at high alert by Kiley's side.

Then Mack's voice grew louder. As if it would make a difference in the disturbance in the room. "Up until now, I've made the error of allowing too many people in her room. That's going to change." His voice strong and territorial, he eyed the cops as if they were the barrier standing between Lee and recovery. "From now on, family will be the only people allowed in." He was in charge of what occurred behind those doors — not the nurses, or the decorated uniforms filling his waiting room.

"I understand, Mack. It'll just be me and you." Kiley's voice was filled with regret she shouldn't be feeling.

"And me," Walt interjected. "I'm Lee's partner. She's my sister in every way except blood." He could see Mack ready to deny him access. "And I'm going to be her brother-in-law very soon."

He'd said it. It was out there for everyone to hear. Everyone to acknowledge. Of course, everyone was busy going into protection mode, but that just made it worse. Fear of Kiley refusing him tightened his gut. By the look on her face as he glanced in her direction, it was on the tip of her tongue.

He wouldn't let her. He smiled and stepped forward to put his arm around his fiancée, whether she wanted him or not.

"You're not—"

He stepped all over her denial. "Next week we're getting married. And you know Lee would want me in her hospital room by your side."

When he finally made eye contact with Mack, he saw the raw pain and denial of the possibility of losing his wife, who looked nothing like the woman Walt was going to marry.

"That's fine. But *only* the two of you will be allowed to visit." Mack turned and disappeared with a disapproving glance in the direction of the scuffle at the entrance of the room. No doubt he'd take care of that problem, too, if the officers didn't handle it soon.

A bright light illuminated the room, and Walt caught a look at the man behind the camera.

Tibbs. Son of a bitch.

He was back. Bold, rude, and beyond caring for anyone but himself. The asshole had lost his partner and now had someone new with him to stir the pot. The reporter was probably cooking up more trash and Tibbs was going to make sure he got the right ingredients to go with it. There was no doubt Tibbs was the camera man who'd shoved the bright light in his face after the shooting.

"I want to talk to the officer responsible for my brother's death." Trouble's voice rose over the heads of the officers blocking his view. The camera scanned the room like a search light roaming the crowd, looking for the guilty party.

Everyone reacted. Some closed the distance to join Rodriguez at the door who looked like he was ready to take the camera away from his ex-classmate and tear him limb by limb. The short, unassuming female deputy chief who'd been in the waiting room throughout the night with her own entourage of loyal followers, knew exactly what to do. She pointed behind her and a wall of uniforms and plain-clothed officers formed a blockade. There was no way Trouble was getting near Kiley.

The DC moved her way to the front of the line, pulled Rodriguez backward and passed him off to her aide, who knew exactly what to whisper in the reluctant officer's ear to make him cooperate. Rodriguez retreated to the rear of the line with Walt and Kiley, his jaw tight, his body ready for battle. Katie moved next to him, grabbing his arm with long graceful fingers. It would have been interesting, if so much shit wasn't going on.

Little did Trouble know, he'd actually had the full attention of the officer responsible for taking out his piece-of-shit brother. Now, the distance between him and Rodriguez may as well have been a city block. Silent officers stood ready to defend Lee, her sister, and Rodriguez from a man who didn't belong in the family.

Walt remembered the computer check of the address Kiley had run the previous day. There were three males that responded to the address. Kevin Caputo and a father and a son with the same name. He searched through memories jumbled with blood, statements, and too much emotion.

Ter … the name was different. Italian maybe.

Ter—and it hit him. "Terrenzio Caputo." His date of birth remained fuzzy, but nineteen eighty six circled Walt's thoughts. "He's one of the names that came back to the address when Kiley ran it through the ALERT system yesterday."

"Terry…" Walt heard the fear entwined her voice as Kiley uttered the name. And it took every bit of his restraint not to go beat the shit out of the ass-wipe who put it there.

CHAPTER TWENTY-THREE

The monster had a brother.

And Walt was putting himself between her and Terry, blocking her view of the one man who could continue the destruction Kevin started.

How could she forget the computer search she'd done when Jamie had called 911? Yet she'd forgotten all about him. Because she'd known the victims on the call. She'd known the suspect, Brandy's husband, Kevin. She'd never heard a word about Kevin's family. Nor would she have guessed his family had any link to the address she'd found for Brandy and Jamie as a first step toward freedom. But freedom from the violence had never really existed. Brandy may have had a short reprieve, but she'd had never been free.

With the computer check back in the forefront of her thoughts, Kiley wondered how Terrenzio Caputo had used Brandy's address. Had he been involved in an accident and used his brother's address? A ticket? Or was it a violent arrest that hadn't shown up on her computer search?

The familiar flip of his hair and the glint in his eyes bordering on hatred made everything worse.

Seeing him again brought back the memories of the best and most embarrassing night of her life. The night she'd gotten drunk at The HotchPotch Lounge. The night she'd turned away from Terry's advances and practically attacked the man now protecting her with his body. It was the first and only time she'd met Terry—Terrenzio Caputo.

He was the brother who would threaten Kiley's adoption plans. More importantly, he was the man who threatened the safety of Jamie and Gina. Because there was no doubt in her mind he was a threat to the children. The unleashed anger she'd experienced in the bar, the domination he'd wanted to subject her to, and the pure malevolent intentions he'd hidden under his boyish grin were enough evidence to lock him up and throw away the key. At least in her book.

Until this very moment, everything she'd experienced in the bar had been buried under the sparks, the elation, and the regret over her reaction to Walt in the parking garage. She'd obsessed over memories of pulling him against her and wrapping her leg around him. She'd fixated on stroking him and the hot trail of kisses he'd left on her body. The entire night had been lost to the passion between them...

Terry was nothing. A hitch in the night better left forgotten. Until now. Her knight in shining armor was protecting her from the one man she would have to face—no matter what.

"I need to talk to him," she told Walt's back.

"No. You don't. Not now."

His order bristled her nerves. "Yes, I do. He's going to make a scene and cause a problem with my plans to adopt the kids if I don't."

Even from the profile view she had of his face, she saw Walt's uncertainty mixed with frustration. Without turning his back on the man he obviously thought was a threat to her safety, he asked over his shoulder, "Have I met him before? He looks familiar."

She was pretty sure the two hadn't met in the bar … unless Walt had seen Terry steer her to the back of the second dance floor in the bar. It somehow made sense that he'd come to her rescue then, like he had every other time she'd needed him. And as much as she didn't want to remind him of that night, she knew he needed to know the truth.

"He was at The HotchPotch Lounge the night you gave me a ride home when I'd had too much to drink," she whispered.

Walt brought his voice down to her level. "He's the guy who was trying to force you into a dark corner? Did you know who he was then?"

And there was her confirmation. Walt had been more of a knight in shining armor that night than she'd realized. It probably hadn't been her words of warning that had kept Terry from following her through the bar. It had been Walt's presence.

"Yeah, he's the same guy. But no, I didn't know he was Kevin's brother until this very moment. I need to talk to him." She put every bit of her desperation into the look she gave Walt.

"Actually, Kiley," Donna stepped up, joining their conversation late. "I think I should be the one to talk to him."

"Don't you think—"

"Is that Curls, the *Guardian Angel* who saved my nephew? Is she the woman he was talking to when the officer shot my brother?" Terry's voice rose above the sea of heads that refused to part for him.

A brief flash of light sliced across her face as Walt grabbed her arm.

"I think you need to go see your sister and then get your house ready for the kids." Donna hadn't finished saying "kids" before Walt ushered Kiley toward the ICU door.

Nor did he give her time to respond. Instead, he advised the social worker, with a direct certainty and ease, "We'll be home within the hour."

Like he belonged in Kiley's home. Like he went there every day and laid his head down on the pillow next to her.

He didn't. He wouldn't.

"What was he talking about, *Guardian Angel*?" she asked once they got through the double doors.

His hesitation said more than his words. "It's nothing to worry about."

Again he tried to push her forward. Kiley side-stepped him. Met his blue eyes and let him see everything she was feeling—frustrated, pissed, scared, and every other angry adjective she couldn't think of. "Which means *it is* something I need to worry about."

The sigh he released was full of frustration. "It's the same old shit, Kiley. The spin on the facts that makes a story … a story."

"So what's the spin this time?"

His fingers brushed through his wavy blond hair. "The media is calling you the Guardian Angel."

"Why would they call me that?"

"The department released the statement that a call taker was on the phone with Jamie during the entire incident, keeping him calm and gathering information for us to make entry. One reporter called you an angel. Another discovered your nickname. And then someone started calling you the Guardian Angel when the department wouldn't release your real name."

He grabbed for her arm, ready to lead her into Lee's room, his abrupt manner telling her more than his words. She pulled back—his warm fingers slipping across the cool skin of her bicep sent tingling sensations through her body.

Ignoring it, she asked, "What else are they saying?"

Again, his fingers went to his hair. She wanted to cut him some slack. Proposing to his partner's sister hadn't been on his agenda when the day had started. He was feeling as closed-in as she was … if not more. But she couldn't let it go.

"Walt. I need to know."

"Okay, okay. But Mack is not to get word of it. Not yet."

This time when he grabbed her arm to pull her close to the bank of glass walls, she let him. And once again, she ignored what his touch did to her.

"They're questioning Lee's actions," he said as he watched Mack standing next to Lee's bed, one room down.

"What do you mean her 'actions'?" This could not be happening.

"They're questioning why she didn't take the shot." His blue eyes turned dull with an emotion she couldn't read.

Incredulous, she had to clarify exactly where the criticism was directed. "They're questioning why Lee didn't shoot Kevin?"

Again, he looked like he'd rather be anywhere but standing in the hall talking to her. "It's the typical bullshit, Kiley. If there's no story to tell, someone's going to make one up. Whether it's a reporter, someone in the neighborhood, or someone on the department—somebody is going to fling some shit."

"But—"

"It happens every time an officer is involved in something. Let it go. We've got more important things to think about."

Because he was right, Kiley didn't object to his hand in the small of her back guiding her into Lee's room, or how he seemed to be mapping out the afternoon in his mind. He had a role to play. The role of knight racing the helpless princess off toward the castle on his mighty steed as danger pursued them through the forest. As much as she loved him for it … she hated it.

Hated everything about his rescue. Because it meant he was doing it for the same reason he'd become a cop. The same reason he'd gone to TAC. Because of some promise he'd made to someone and his need to protect the needy.

Not because he really cared for her.

When, exactly, that had started to matter to her, she wasn't sure, and she didn't have time to figure it out as he whisked her into Lee's room, where monitors drummed a steady beat. Her sister lay unconscious with Mack gently holding her hand as he bent down to whisper in Lee's ear and kiss her cheek.

A nurse replaced one of the many bags of fluids and began checking valves and monitors. All of which mattered to Lee's health. None of which made any sense to Kiley.

Standing behind her with his hands on her waist, Walt guided her forward. Still protecting as they inched their way forward. Mack looked up, his face strained from lack of sleep and … fear. Fear he masked as soon as he met her gaze.

"She's got the best doctors Kansas City can offer."

Kiley was pretty sure he said it to convince himself as well. "What happened, Mack?" She needed to know it wouldn't happen again when she left.

His composure threatened to slip. "I … I…" His voice escaped him as he tried to answer. He shrugged, tears brimming in his eyes. Kiley felt her own tears spill over. Mack loved her sister more than she'd realized. The night before, when he'd been all business and medical terminology, she'd wanted to lash out at him for being an uncaring husband. But she'd been wrong.

Walt came to Mack's rescue. She should have expected it. "Lee knows what's at stake, Kiley. She knows you have to leave to take care of the kids. And it's okay with her. Mack is by her side. That's what's important."

Mack *was* by her side. Right where he belonged. Right where Lee would want him. An unwelcome feeling of jealousy stirred in the pit of her stomach for the first time in her life. Jealousy of her sister—her best friend. Despite lying in a hospital bed connected to all kinds of machines and on the brink of death, Lee had everything a woman could ask for—a husband and sister who loved her and a partner who would sacrifice his future for her.

How could one woman be so completely blessed?

Mack's watchful eyes went back and forth between Lee's face and the monitors. Then he spared a moment to say over his shoulder, "I'll call you if there's the least bit of a change."

Ashamed of the brief bout of envy, Kiley escaped Walt's grasp and headed to the opposite side of the bed. She leaned over to kiss the pale skin of her twin's cheek. "I love you," she whispered. "And I need your help raising two kids. 'Cause that deal you made with your partner won't work." She brushed the hair from her sister's forehead and threatened her the way only a sister could. "The kids need you. Mack needs you. And I need you to release Walt from whatever crazy pact you made with him. Don't even think about leaving us … or I'll tell everyone at your service that you wanted to be a nun when you grew up."

With one last kiss, a tear fell on her sister's cheek. Kiley wiped away the offending moisture, then walked out of the room with the man her sister had chosen for her. Her future husband.

CHAPTER TWENTY-FOUR

She still looked damn good in his Challenger. Even with ugly green scrubs, she still sent his heart into overdrive. Like the last time she'd been in his car, and he'd nearly fucked her in the driver's seat.

Okay, maybe it'd been the other way around. She'd been the one driving the wild passion between them that went from zero to six thousand in a matter of seconds. If he let his memory get the best of him, he could taste her, feel her nipple harden with the flick of his tongue, and crave her body the way he had that night when she'd wrapped her hand around him and had driven him to the brink of insanity with lust.

And what a dickhead he was for even thinking that way.

She was asleep in his passenger seat. Exhausted. Hurting and scared. Yet her beauty did things to him. Her golden hair, curling around her face in ringlets other women paid hundreds of dollars to achieve, had made him want to lock his hands in her hair from the very first moment he'd seen her at the academy. He wanted to bury his dick deep inside her as she screamed with need and he drove her crazy with his mouth and hands. Everything about her demanded his attention. Even her mouth, slightly open in her slumber, was an invitation to explore what could have been between them.

He was totally screwed.

He wanted her so badly his dick throbbed the moment he sat down in the car, making his BDUs more uncomfortable than he'd thought possible. Memories of their one night in the front seat soared through his mind as if it were only yesterday that her breasts had been exposed and she'd been jerking him off.

Son of a…

He turned off the ignition in the driveway to her Victorian-style row-condo. Thankful they'd arrived and he'd be able to put some distance between them, he just wasn't sure he'd be able to hide the hard-on he was wearing when she woke up.

"Kiley. We're here."

She didn't move. Exhaustion had her out like she'd been drinking all night instead of worrying whether her sister lived or died.

"Kiley." His voice a little louder, she still remained immobile. He reached across the car and put his hand on her shoulder, shaking her gently. The heat under the thin cotton cloth nearly seared his palm. "Kiley!" he said more loudly than he'd planned. She stirred and mumbled and snuggled deeper into the passenger seat.

"Shit." Getting out of the car, he made his way to the passenger side and opened the door. He tried not to think about what he had to do. Thinking only led to problems. Problems he didn't need. Slipping one arm around her back, the other in the crook of her knees, he lifted her out of the car, hoping she'd wake and he could set her down immediately. Instead, she snuggled into his neck, her warm breath tickling his senses, her arms wrapped around his neck … and he knew he was doomed. It didn't matter what he did or what anyone else thought, he wanted this woman in the worst kind of way. Then again, maybe it was the best kind of way. She *was* going to be his wife.

Turning toward the house, he did something he'd never thought he'd do to his car. He kicked the passenger door closed and made his way up to the front door.

How the hell was he going to get the front door open?

"Can you tell me where your key is?" he asked.

"In the hanging pot."

If he hadn't been holding her tight, he would've kicked her butt for being so damned obvious—because *no* thief would ever think to look for her key in a plant.

Positioning his arm under her ass to support her weight with one hand while searching through the leafy fern, he easily found the plastic case and tried not to think about the ways he wanted to explore her body. He pulled the key out of the container and unlocked the front door while focusing on the fear of her being attacked in her sleep instead of the location of his fingers. A larger woman would have been difficult to maneuver. Kiley fit in his arms as if she belonged there.

He glanced around her condo knowing she was the exact opposite of her twin in everything, yet amazed at how different they were. Whereas Lee decorated in everything modern and pink, Kiley's condo looked like a blast from the past. Early 1900s past.

The dining room to his left sported a long farmhouse table built for a lot more than Kiley's one little body and opened to a small kitchen with whitewashed cabinets extending to the ceiling. Sporadic cabinet pieces were painted in an antiqued brick red, accentuated the room and giving it a homey feeling. Straight ahead, he saw the living room with a very large Victorian sectional covered in pillows that called his name. He turned and looked up the stairway to his right. It had to lead to her bedroom.

Setting the key down on the sideboard table, he noticed a pair of little bitty women's shoes he would've thought belonged to a child if he hadn't been carrying the owner of the delicate sandals sitting next to a closet. Kicking off his tennis shoes, he was thankful he'd showered and changed when he'd given his statement to the detectives at HQ. Otherwise, he'd still have on his boots. God only knew how many crime scene contaminants those things carried.

He locked her front door and carried Kiley up the stairs, taking them two at a time. Glancing inside the first two bedrooms, he immediately knew by the modern kids' décor that she was more prepared for Jamie and Gina than he'd realized. The last door at the back of the condo led to a perfectly made king-sized bed loaded with more pillows.

Pillows were ... useful.

His brain, or maybe it was his dick, immediately wanted to think about the positions he could make love to her using those pillows. A shutter surged through his body as he laid her down in the midst of the soft down mattress on her huge four postered bed.

Gawd, the thing he could do with those posts.

He reached around to pull her hands from his neck, only to find them locked. Trapping him where he wanted to be.

He closed his eyes. Too afraid to dream. To hope.

Breathing in her fresh scent, he released it along with his crazy, mixed-up expectations that her hands were telling him more. He gently pried at her hands. They tightened at the base of his skull, signaling the end of her slumber.

Her breath fanned his cheeks. Nose to nose, he opened his eyes to find the answer he needed. Green eyes, fresh as the morning grass, met his—capturing him in a mirror of desire. Every act he wanted to do with her. To her. Backward. Forward. On the bed. On the floor. In the shower. Hell, he didn't care where they did it. As long as they did it and didn't stop doing it.

It was all there in her eyes.

"Kiley…" Need grated across his vocal chords, roughening his voice and telling her everything his lost words couldn't.

"Please, Walt. I need you. Now," she whispered, answering all his hidden prayers.

That was all it took.

Her body told him how much she wanted him, but *needing* him was the answer he was looking for. It was the answer that hardened his body. The years of wanting this woman beneath him and not being able to have her were in the past. He crushed her mouth with his own. Taking … feeling her full lips the way he'd dreamed of since the last time they'd kissed.

She tasted of peppermint candy — her trick to lose her hiccups. But that wasn't all he tasted as he deepened the kiss. Exploring her mouth, he tasted what made Kiley so damned appealing. Her soft, giving nature. Her loving and loyal soul. All packaged in the sexiest damned woman he'd ever met.

Needing him as badly as he needed her, she pulled his body down on top of her and he groaned with the full-body contact he'd been denied for so long. Firm breasts rubbed against his chest while her heart thumped in rhythm with his own, in a sprint to make up for lost time. His hands raced up her sides, under the hospital scrubs. His fingers skimmed across soft, taut skin goose-pimpling under his touch. Across her stomach and ribs, he reached the breasts he longed for and flicked the front clasp of her bra open with little effort. She moaned into their kiss as he palmed her and kneaded the flesh that drove him to the brink of insanity.

Pulling away from her lips, he yanked her shirt over her head and brought his mouth where it belonged—teasing her feminine curves. Testing the tight bud, surrounded by a pale triangular tan line from her bikini, he flicked her sweetness with his tongue. Savored her taste as he reached for her other breast and teased her nipple between his thumb and index finger. She arched into his mouth, making him want to devour her even further.

Small hands raked through his hair, holding him tight as he suckled one breast and then the other while his hands pulled at the elastic waistband of her pants. Walt couldn't help thinking whoever gave her these scrubs deserved a thank-you as the pants slid down her hips and he found her going commando—no panties.

Thank you, God.

Within seconds, he had her naked and reveled at her beauty. Her soft curls haloed her head, yet her eyes and body spoke of her passionate nature that conflicted with the innocence of her face. Her tongue darted out to moisten her lips, giving away her excitement and apprehension all rolled into one.

"Are you…" He couldn't bear to finish the question. If she said she wasn't sure, couldn't go through with it…

"Don't stop."

Relief rushed through him. She was sexy. Beautiful. Smart. Loving. Caring. And tough. Everything a guy could ever want. This woman could undo him faster than any woman he'd ever met. And she didn't want him to stop.

He brought his tongue to her knees, intent on savoring every last inch of her. His mouth gliding across skin so smooth, silk sheets couldn't compete. Easing his way to her apex, her excitement nearly drove him over the edge as her hips lifted, reaching for relief from the tension that had obviously plagued them for too long. Controlling his desire, he couldn't help but nip her inner thigh as he made his way down the other leg before retracing his path to the finish line, where everything began and ended. Kiley whimpered in frustration as he flicked his tongue across her, bringing a smile to his face.

He refused to hurry. As much as he wanted to drive into her, he wanted her to enjoy their first time — he wanted the memory to last a lifetime. Because recent history had shown that life might end an hour from now or sixty years in the future. Regardless, every moment was to be treasured like there was no tomorrow.

Not to be denied, Kiley urged him on with her fingers tangled deep in his hair. He slowed his pace. Teased her. Taunted her. Brought her to the brink, then refused to let her tumble over the edge.

"Walt, please…" she begged.

But he didn't stop. His hands explored. His mouth savored. He wasn't about to let the first time pass without enjoying every last detail of her curves. Again, he caressed her smooth skin with his tongue trailing the crevices she opened to him. Her breathing more erratic, she pulled him home and screamed her release.

As much as he wanted her, her pleasure was enough for him. If she went limp with exhaustion, he told himself he would be satisfied.

He knew it was a lie. But he also knew he could stop. For her. This incredible woman who gave so much, to so many. He was lucky to be the one to give her something in return.

"Do not even think about stopping there."

She pulled him up the length of her body, and he celebrated, blood raging to areas that were ready to party. Throbbing, his dick raced for home as she yanked at his pants.

Biting her lip, he couldn't help but laugh at her determination to get him as naked as she was. His hands explored the path he'd already traveled, his tongue forging its way to her mouth, where she captured him in a deep, demanding kiss.

This was where he belonged.

***

The shock on his face as she flipped him onto his back with one swift hip thrust was priceless. She'd shown the master of defense tactics a move he'd never experienced. Despite his size and brawn, she was now in a position of dominance as her hands held his above his head, and she looked down at an incredible sexy man who was wearing way too many clothes.

There was no doubt he could take control of the situation if he wanted. But he didn't. She kissed him again. The same way he'd kissed her. Fierce and controlling. Tasting every inch of him. She released his hands to pull his shirt over his head to get a look at the most incredible set of pecs and abs a woman could imagine. Skin molded over perfectly formed muscles, layered with even more muscle. His shoulders rounded and dipped, like armor draping over biceps big enough to be her thighs. But her thighs looked nothing like the sculpted granite of his arms as he brought them up behind his head in a relaxed position of submission … and a little bit of arrogance daring her to tease him. But from the fire in his eyes, she'd bet it was his way of controlling his hands. Of stopping himself from stripping off his pants and taking her the way his body wanted him to. And she loved him all the more for his patience.

Slowly she unbuttoned his BDUs, the length of him pressing against each button of his military-styled pants, straining to be released. A muscle in his jaw twitched as he lifted his body and allowed her to pull his pants over slim hips. She knew the torture he felt. Knew the gnawing sensation eating away at him and demanding to be released as he helped her remove the barrier between them.

And she encouraged it the same way he had. With a torturous trail of kisses and nips down his neck, across flat nipples hardened with desire, down taut stomach muscles pointing toward his manhood in a glorious V. Her tongue sailed over waves of muscles on his stomach, each swell tunneling her focus.

As her tongue flicked his tip, he pulsated with desire. Air passed over his lips in a hiss as he gasped with need.

Again, she flicked his tip. Circled his head. Drew her tongue down the length of him, feeling the blood surge through his vein as his dick reached for her mouth with fervor. She captured the length of him. Drew him in, taking what she could of his glorious length. His moan reached her ears. His hands curled in her hair.

The in-control Walt was completely lost. He pulled her up his body, kissed her, and thrust his tongue in her mouth to dance with her own, while the rest of his body sought to take them to new summits.

She pulled away. Grabbed for the condoms in her nightstand and hastily tore open a package. Sitting on his thighs, she slipped the protection on him before resuming her position over him, his hardened dick teasing her clit. She rose to her full height on her knees. Let his tip tease her opening. Watching his hips rise, demanding entrance, she met his eyes full of passion before sheathing him in her warmth that brought them to their final destination. Home.

Grinding her hips into his, she lost herself in the storm. His hands caressed her, no longer allowing her to run the show. He drove her body to heights she'd never dreamed. Yet with each explosion came a new tension. The surge rose within her in a flurry of sensation as he met her rhythm and raged past, taking her with him. Their release came with so much passion, fireworks would have been lost in the background of the moment.

Kiley collapsed on his chest, surprised at how much she savored his sweat-ridden body against her own. His arms wrapped around her, their breathing erratic in unison.

"Ho-lee crap," she sighed.

He chuckled underneath her, his deep timbre welcome to her ears. "Yeah. You could say that again."

His lips pressed against the top of her head, bringing a smile to her face, before reality struck her heart.

Her friend was dead. Her sister was fighting for life. And she'd found happiness in the arms of a man she shouldn't.

As if sensing her change in mood, he pressed his lips to her head once more.

"Don't," he ordered.

Then he lifted her chin. Brought her eyes in line with his own to stare deep into her depths.

"This would have happened no matter what. We both know that. Brandy knew it. Lee knew it. That's why she made me promise to be there for you. If anything happened."

"Nothing's going to happen." Her voice tightened with emotion. A tear dribbled down her check to land on his fingers.

"Something *has* happened." He was going to make her face reality. Even in the aftermath of what had just happened between them, Walt wasn't about to lie or mask the truth. "None of us will ever be the same. Especially Lee and Jamie. Gina has been traumatized, but she won't be able to process much of it. Lee will. Jamie … Jamie is going to go through hell."

"What about you?" Her voice quivered, and she wondered if he felt what she did after the most incredible sex of her life.

"Yesterday and what happened here today"—his hand waved, indicating the bed in which they lay—"has changed my life forever."

She wanted to ask if today had made him see the future as she saw it. Together, with the kids, helping them through the loss, the anger, and the pain that too much violence had brought to their lives.

But she didn't, because she knew he was deeply affected and that was enough. It had to be.

CHAPTER
TWENTY-FIVE

Chimes, melodic and soothing, like a small-town steeple, sounded through the house.

"Crap!"

Kiley jumped from the crook of his arm where she'd fallen asleep. He tried to pull her back, but she was out of the bed before he was fully awake. Leaning on his elbows, he squinted through the bright sunlight shining through the crack of her floor to ceiling curtains.

The sight in front of him was something he'd never forget.

Kiley … naked, was more beautiful than he'd ever imagined.

She grabbed the scrubs he'd striped from her body and began frantically covering her rounded ass with green cotton before he could ask, "What is that?"

"The kids are here." Her face was full of fear. And a lot of grief that she masked as she pulled the top over her head.

Walt wasn't sure what he felt. Obviously, the after effects of mind-blowing sex were good. No. They were beyond great.

Watching Kiley wiggle into her clothes wasn't a bad thing, either. Although, he'd rather watch her wiggle out of them, but "the kids are here"? That made his stomach lurch in a direction he wasn't really proud of.

"Hurry!" She tossed his shirt, hitting him in the face as he sat up. "They can't see us like this."

"Why? Didn't you see your parents in the morning?"

"It's the middle of the day!" She picked up his pants, threw the sheet from his body and began and pulling his BDU's up his legs before he could even put his feet on the floor.

The higher she pulled, the more aware he became. And as he waved at her with all his glory, she finally took notice of what she couldn't possibly miss. Her cheeks reddened in a refreshing blush.

"I think I better finish that, or I won't be able to greet them." He smiled as he leaned forward and kissed her hard. She quickly turned away, but he grabbed her arm before she ran for the stairs. "As much as I like your current look…" He entwined a few curls in his fingers, and a self-conscious hand flew to her hair.

The mortified look passing across her face couldn't have been more endearing. Her expression of, "Oh, my God," before she pulled away and ran the opposite direction to her bathroom actually made him laugh. Yet he held it back, too uncomfortable with the happiness wanting to spread through his chest when the day was full of so much grief.

If he had it his way, her hair would look like that all day, every day. It was wild and sexy and brought images of every position they had yet to try and places they had yet to christen.

He pulled up his pants, then yanked his T-shirt over his head. Running his hands through his hair, he met her at the door, where she linked her fingers in his and led him to the stairs. He didn't want to think about what or who they were running toward. He was used to charging into dangerous situations.

So why was his heart racing at top speed?

They reached the door as the chimes sang through the house for a second time. Kiley flung open the door without looking through her peephole. A blast of summer heat and a whole lot more hit him in the face.

Jamie charged the open door as Donna grabbed for him. All she got was a handful of air as Jamie launched himself into Kiley's waiting arms. Instinctively, Walt's hand rested at the small of her back, bracing her against the onslaught that would have knocked her on her ass from the force of the collision. A weary smile on her face, Donna returned her attention to the crying baby girl enfolded in her arms.

The baby was the exact opposite of what she'd been during the worst day of her short life. The terror that had gripped her emotions yesterday had been thawed — raw. Walt froze.

How had he missed that racket through the door?

He wanted to love them unconditionally … but Jamie was talking so fast not a single word penetrated the ice barrier around Walt's skull. And the screams coming from the baby had to be audible the next block over. But the real kicker was the smell in the air. It was worse than the detention unit on its foulest day and it was coming in his direction — in the form of hell in a blanket.

He tried to smile. Tried to be comfortable holding a smelly Gina screaming at the top of her lungs as her warm diaper squished under his hands and she tested the acoustics of Kiley's hallway. He tried not to show the doubts, the fear, or his desire to give her back and walk out the door.

For the first time in as long as he could remember, he lacked confidence. Lacked knowledge. Lacked everything it took to fill the role he was playing. He was not a parent. Not a guardian or even a babysitter. He had no idea where to begin. Desperate for guidance, he looked to Kiley for direction. For the hope that *this* was *not* what the future held.

She held Jamie tightly. Swaying back and forth. The two of them staring in his direction. Waiting for him to step up to the plate and handle the situation.

He'd told Lee that he'd step up — be there for Kiley, no matter what. But what if he couldn't do this? What if mind-blowing sex wasn't enough to make him into the man she needed? Or who these kids deserved?

Kiley nodded in Jamie's direction, his head resting on her shoulder, her hand caressing his curls that blended with hers. Walt copied her actions with Gina, ignoring the stench that reached for his taste buds. He held her head against his shoulder, caressed the peach fuzz on her scalp somewhat awkwardly. Her crying slowed but didn't stop. Kiley nodded her chin and looked at his hips as she swayed.

Memories swarmed him. His dad singing him to sleep at the age of nine when his mom had been out of town for a month with her parents. His dad's deep baritone that belonged in a jazz bar vibrating through his burly chest.

He remembered the laughter when he'd tried on his dad's police uniform. The pant legs about three feet too long, the shoulders drooping to his wrists while he stood tall and proud and saluted the man he loved.

He'd be standing by Walt's side right now, if he were still alive. To change diapers. Sing songs, fill these kids with joy and laughter, or just be there and hold them when they needed it most.

But what Walt remembered most was his dad's words. "Anyone can put on a uniform and ride in to save the day. It's how a man treats his family that defines who he really is. Love, honor, and respect the ones you care about. And don't ever let your pride get in the way."

The odors disappeared. The sounds softened. The only thing Walt felt in his arms was the fragile body of a little girl in need of a dad.

***

He was singing. The voice that had whispered in her ear and hummed against her body through the morning hours was soothing Gina out of a fit of tears. His tone was a little off-key, but it was so filled with love it brought tears to her eyes. The fear that had threatened to overwhelm him and send him running for the hills was gone. Replaced by the confidant man she knew him to be.

"Dad never sang to Gina," Jamie whispered against her shoulder. "We made up a song together before she was born about roaches. I was afraid of them, so Dad came up with the song for me and Mom to kill them when he was at work." He shrugged like it didn't mean anything—instead of everything. "I think it might have been 'The Ants Go Marching,' but he changed the words."

Walt stopped singing, Jamie's pain reflected in his eyes. By helping Gina, Walt had brought out a painful memory for Jamie. Yet it was a good memory. One that needed to be cultivated … strengthened.

Pulling Jamie away from her shoulder, she brought his face up to hers and kissed his tear-dampened cheek, the salt creating moisture in her own eyes. "Then we'll have to make sure that Gina learns the song. She needs to learn about who your parents really were. What do you say we start making a video log of all the *good times?*"

'Cause all the bad times were going to be hashed out in the counseling Jamie was going to need, for years to come. Life was too complex to put Kevin in the role of just a bad guy. Jamie loved him. Brandy had loved him. And from what she'd said, Brandy'd fallen in love with a good guy who'd used bad judgment and allowed drugs and alcohol to bring out an awful side of himself no one could love.

She hugged Jamie and asked, "Would you like to show Walt your totally awesome room? Then I'll give him a break and change Gina. Nobody should have to do *that* kind of diaper on his very first time."

"Nope," Jamie confirmed. "Gina can peel the paint off the walls with those diapers." A faint smile crossed his face as Kiley set him down to scurry across the wooden floors. "Come on, Walt, if Kiley's volunteering, you need to let her change that nasty thing."

Kiley stepped forward and took the quieted Gina from Walt's arms, then winked at him as Jamie dragged a guilty-looking Walt toward the stairs. "The next one will be yours, cowboy. So don't think you're riding off into the sunset."

Walt didn't have a chance to respond as he attentively turned to listen to the lecture Jamie was giving while tugging on his arm. "Walt, there's one thing you need to understand in life. A baby girl can stink up a house just as badly as a grown man."

Man and boy left the room, hand in hand, but Kiley wasn't sure who was leading the other.

CHAPTER
TWENTY-SIX

Was it really only nine o'clock?

Kiley peeked into the room at the end of the hall after leaving Gina asleep, snuggly in her crib in the smaller bedroom. The light was out in Jamie's room, but the night on his nightstand still shone and the stars on the ceiling glowed as Walt read *Zoo in the Sky: A Book of Animal Constellations.* She smiled and left upon catching Walt's eye as he laid on the twin bed, most of his muscular body hanging off the edge. He roared like a lion for Jamie.

Sitting down in her bedroom on the four poster bed where she and Walt had made love for the first time, she didn't think she would ever view her lavender bedroom the same again. Andrew had never slept in the house, never shared the bed she sat on. The only man who had stepped foot inside her bedroom since she moved in, was Walt. She smiled, then picked up her phone from the night stand and dialed Mack's number.

"How is she?" She asked as soon as he picked up.

"She's still critical, but she's stable." His voice tired and strained, Kiley wasn't sure if he was telling the whole story.

"Has she regained consciousness?" She crossed her fingers.

"No."

She let her shoulders slump. "That's bad isn't it?"

"It's not the best case scenario."

A tear threatened to slip down her face. Nothing was the best case scenario. Best case would be Brandy here with her kids. Mack and Lee playing with them in her finished family room. And Walt…

"It's really not that bad, Kiley. I'd call you if I felt she was going to…"

He couldn't say it. Mack had lost his ability to talk about Lee like a patient, and Kiley couldn't blame him. She wasn't sure how he'd been able to do it to begin with.

"I know she's going to make it. Can you put me on speaker?" Kiley prayed he would.

"Sure." The sounds of the monitors became louder. "Okay, she's listening, Kiley."

"Lee, you have the best husband in the world. He loves you. I love you. Come home." Mid-way through her voice wavered. "I love you too, Mack. Take care of her for me and let me know the moment she wakes up."

Mack cleared his throat before responding. "I will. Goodnight, Kiley."

After the hopeful but cautious news from her brother-in-law, Kiley stepped into the shower and allowed it to work magic on her tired body. Her emotions were in conflict. Like the steam trapped in the glass enclosure that circled around the top of the shower, she swirled this way and that. The social worker's bombshell that the kids *did* have an uncle and that the courts would consider him as a candidate for adoption despite Brandy's wishes, left her raw and angry. Sad and defeated.

It didn't make it any easier to think that she wouldn't be spending the night at her sister's side. Fear of not being there when Lee needed her most threatened to drop her shoulders for good.

Mack was there, and if truth be told, Lee would probably rather have him next to her, than her twin sister fretting at her side.

It still didn't make the pain lessen.

A change in the steam brought her eyes up to the doorway that now stood open. Walt leaned against the doorframe.

"Is this my bedtime story? 'Cause I'd really like to write the ending myself." He smiled as he stripped off his snug police logo'd T-shirt and smooth, rippling muscles greeted her. She couldn't help the physical reaction he caused; the effect he'd always had on her body. Her nipples peaked, and the tingling traveled through her torso all the way to her toes as he slowly undid his pants in the striptease of a lifetime. His taut, washboard abs V'd with his defined lower abdominal muscles, pointing in the direction her tongue wanted to roam. He eased his BDUs over his manhood. Stepping out of his casual police uniform, Walt strode to the shower as if he owned the place. Owned her.

The realization should have frightened her. It didn't. This man had owned a piece of her since the first day she'd laid eyes on him. Destiny had brought him to her. Sure, he was following some agreement with her sister. But all along, she'd known these moments were inevitable.

She stepped back into the spray, allowing him to enter the shower and close the door. His eyes devoured her before they met hers, electricity sending tiny shock waves through her body. His large, strong hands rose to cradle her jaw, and everything she swore she wouldn't feel for this man threatened to explode from within her. How could she be so completely in love with him after only wanting to use his body for so many years? How could one man's touch ignite such a primitive, demanding need that she forgot everything else in the world but him? That ever-present need engulfed her body and made it no longer her own.

She reveled in the depth of her feelings as he captured her tongue in a dance that heated her body to the core. Part of her wanted to brand him and claim him, the same way he had seized her. Yet she held back. Knowing he would never give his heart to anyone but the job.

"Tell me your story," she whispered against his lips.

Leaning against the shower wall, her knees shook with want, his hands ensnaring her body. Fingers caressed her neck, her shoulders, as she clung to him. Finally, he seized her nipple between his thumb and forefinger, torturing the nub, and eliciting a moan from deep within her.

"There once was a woman in need of a man."

God, how she needed him.

"With a spirit as free as her curls gone wild." His mouth captured her breast and drove her beyond her wildest craving. "Only one man could tame her need."

His fingers slid down her stomach to explore her center. Where his fingers moved, her body demanded more.

"Please..." she cried, writhing under the teasing experience of his hands.

She felt the smile on his lips before he descended to his knees and began his exploration with his tongue. He nudged her legs farther apart, his tongue and fingers working in unison. Unable to hold herself, Kiley clung to his shoulders, her hips arching into him of their own accord.

Beyond comprehension, she heard his deep voice telling the story of her desires. His mouth encapsulated her in ecstasy as the world split apart in an explosion of color behind her heavy-lidded eyes. Spent with rapture, she wanted more. Much more.

She wanted him.

***

As she shattered around him, Walt wanted nothing more than to please her again. To watch her lose control at his touch. At that moment, she was his. In a way no other woman had ever belonged to him. It wasn't about control, or the sex. It was something that touched him deeper, in a place he hadn't acknowledged existed before today.

Rising to his feet, he lifted her into his arms and got lost in the forest of her eyes—exploring through the untouched areas, where no one else had reached. A place of peace and tranquility he'd never experienced before.

"Please…" she begged, her sweet lips caressing his own.

Her full breasts teasing his chest, he couldn't hold back any longer. He slid home — where he was tightly embraced in her warmth.

The groan that escaped him sounded fierce and demanding. Yet he held back, never wanting it to end. He stopped and enjoyed her tightness before pulling out. She whimpered her displeasure with his absence. Until he began pleasuring her with his tip. Slipping in and out. Driving them both to the brink of insanity, he rubbed and teased.

"Walt, I need … all of you," she panted.

Her nails driving into his shoulders brought him to the edge. He braced her against the wall, water slicing down their bodies. She was as gorgeous with her hair slicked back and wet as she was surrounded by curls. Her round breasts teased and taunted with their movement, looking unearthly with their glistening sheen. She threw her head back, arching into him, demanding that he drive deeper as she squirmed against him.

Unable to control himself any longer, he filled her completely. Her moist warmth pulsated against him as she once again came undone, her tightness gripping him, urging him on. Over and over, in a never-ending feeling of abandoned reality.

Time stood still, the pressure building and building, the sensations sending him home with unbearable ecstasy. The noise coming from her lips spoke of her own desire as he followed the roaring beat of his heart toward gratification.

And he wondered what he'd ever done to deserve such pleasure.

"It wasn't the man who stole the woman," he told her in between gasps for air. "It was the woman who broke the man."

And he did break.

At that moment, his world exploded into thousands of little pieces. Detonating with such force, each dream or goal he'd ever had no longer mattered. As his limbs trembled in the aftermath, he relished the snug fit inside her, yet at the same time he feared what had just happened. He'd reached her very core and found everything he could ever want.

And wasn't that a bitch.

CHAPTER
TWENTY-SEVEN

Kiley slid down the length of Walt's body, enjoying every second of contact. In the last few hours, she'd had the best sex of her life. Not only did they fit to perfection, his touch did things to her no man had ever accomplished. The fact that her heart played a role in what transpired between them was irrelevant.

It had to be.

Their future would start with a quick ceremony, followed by the adoption proceedings, and then end with an even faster divorce and a child custody agreement. It wouldn't go beyond that. Because in his heart, Walt was married to the job.

She pushed Walt down on the gray tiled bench and grabbed the soap. Lathering up the washcloth she'd hung over the door, she washed her body as he watched with definite interest. She circled her breasts, stroked between her legs before finishing with a smile. Re-lathering, she closed the distance between them and began to scrub his body with care. Savoring each muscle, each contour, each scar he'd endured throughout his lifetime. She wanted to ask about the knee surgery and the small scar on his hip. Was it from an appendectomy?

Instead, she kept silent, tracing the blemishes on his beautiful skin with the reverence of someone in love as he leaned his head back and enjoyed her touch.

Her phone vibrated on the counter, and all the tension of the day returned. Kiley dropped the washcloth and ran from the shower, wrapping a towel around her dripping form as she went to retrieve the phone before it woke the kids. Fear of bad news made her check the caller ID, which read *blocked*.

"Hello?" she breathed. The water turned off behind her.

"Hi, Curls." The masculine voice sounded familiar yet foreign at the same time.

"Hi?" she responded, hoping he'd say more. Praying it wasn't a doctor calling for a distraught brother-in-law.

"You don't remember who I am, do you?"

The humor in his voice told her she should know … but didn't. She breathed a sigh of relief, knowing a doctor wouldn't see any humor in bad news. Distracted by the man walking up behind her, Kiley confessed, "I'm sorry. I know I should—"

"Yes. You really should." He responded more cavalierly than she thought anyone could.

She shivered as Walt's arms wrapped around her waist from behind. He sought her eyes in the mirror.

"Who is this, and what do you want?" she asked in her call taker voice; the one she used when she knew she was talking to someone who had more to hide than to give.

Walt's hooded eyes widened. His hands stopped caressing. His head moved closer to the receiver. A laugh from the other end of the phone followed.

"For starters, you could give me what you just gave that brute, but—"

She didn't hear anything else. The phone yanked from her grasp. Walt walked away from her, her phone cradled to his ear. He grabbed a towel to wrap around his waist. Puddles of water littered the floor between them, each screaming the hazards they faced. One false move … and it was over.

"I don't know who you think you are, asshole—" He stopped as if to listen, his body shaking — in anger.

Never would she have imagined Walt, the man who Lee had described as unshakeable, reacting so intensely. As if the rage within him might erupt into another creature. Had she allowed the wrong man into the lives of Brandy's kids?

Big, brown youthful eyes stared at her in the mirror. Jamie's head was barely visible in her darkened bedroom, but he was there, hiding and Walt had no idea what his emotions were doing to the little boy. Kiley cleared her throat and tightened the towel wrapped around her body before turning toward Jamie with a smile. She knew it wasn't her best, and she hoped it didn't look like a half-hearted attempt at reassurance, the way Brandy had tried after Kevin beat her. Yet Kiley couldn't deny … her fear of their uncle getting the kids and her uncertainty of Walt's rage shook her view of the future.

Without looking in Walt's direction, she eased her way toward Jamie, trying to appear unfazed. Comfortable. Everything she wasn't.

"Hey, Jamie. Were you having trouble sleeping?"

"I … I…" His eyes darted toward Walt. His bottom lip quivered.

Grabbing her robe from the hook on the door, she quickly wrapped herself up more securely and stepped into the darkened room with Jamie. She bent down and took his body into her arms, his little hands snaking around her neck, his face hid in the crook under her chin.

Her eyes quickly filled with tears.

He'd been through so much. Lost so much. Was scarred so deeply. She wanted to take away all the pain, bear the burden on her own shoulders.

"It's okay, baby. We have each other. Nothing can take that away." She prayed she wasn't lying.

Part of her prayers were answered. Walt was there. Bare-chested with just his BDUs covering him from the waist down, he enveloped Jamie between them, holding them both in his arms. Hugging and comforting, despite the initial jolt his touch created in Jamie.

Looking for his eyes in the dim light, she could see the intensity, softened by shame. Walt felt responsible for Jamie's current mood, yet he wasn't. Kevin was the only one who could take the blame.

"She's right, kiddo. We'll always be there for you." The pure conviction in his voice made her want to believe his words, know the system would work — they would work.

"Do you want to talk about it, Jamie?" Walt asked the question she'd been wanting to ask since the kids had arrived.

Jamie's small hands tightened around her neck. His feet wrapped around her like a boa constrictor. His head shook in response.

No. He wasn't ready.

Again, she reassured, "It's okay, Jamie. We'll go at any pace you want." She ran her hand through his curls, loving the feel between her fingertips.

His head lifted slightly. Brows drawn, Jamie whispered, "I couldn't find the phone."

Stunned by his comment, she asked, "Who did you want to call?"

His eyes moved downward, toward Walt's feet. Jamie's teeth drew in his bottom lip. She waited for his answer. None came.

"Jamie?" she coaxed.

"I … I got…" Again, his eyes darted toward Walt.

It was Walt who finished his sentence. "You were afraid I'd hurt Kiley."

***

Son of a bitch.

People had shown him fear plenty of times. Even Jamie had been afraid of him years ago when he'd lifted him up over the fence to Kiley. But no one had ever thought he'd hurt someone he cared about. Making it worse was the look in Kiley's eyes. She understood Jamie's fear — had seen something in him that made her question who he was. What drove him. Like anger could motivate him to violence. Against her. Against Jamie.

To deny he was *that* guy would only add credence to their fears. How could he possibly prove to them he would never raise a hand in anger? He protected. Like his dad had protected. That's what wired him. His anger came when someone threatened *their* safety, not his pride. His ego didn't give a damn if it was challenged. Ever.

It had been his heart screaming in fear that sent him over the edge when the caller had made the sexually charged comment to Kiley.

He'd wanted to reach through the phone and tear the son of a bitch's throat out. Instead, he'd been reduced to dialing star five seven when the caller hung up. Tomorrow he would trace the call.

Right now, with Kiley and Jamie in his arms, there was only one thing he could do. Must do.

He dropped his arms from the hug that left the boy shivering. "If I frighten you, I'll sleep downstairs on the couch. I won't leave you; I'll be here to protect you, but I don't want to scare you."

Jamie's head burrowed against Kiley's neck. He sniffled. Raised his head and wiped his nose with the back of his hand before looking up into Kiley's eyes.

Walt couldn't tell what happened between the two. He waited. Prayed Jamie and Kiley wouldn't believe the worst of him. They were two thirds of a future he hadn't known he wanted yesterday. A future full of uncertainty and doubts based on a commitment to his partner. He couldn't fail.

Jamie turned. "It's okay. Kiley trusts you. She didn't trust my dad." His eyes dropped. "She never trusted him."

"I'm sorry, Jamie. This isn't going to be easy. All we can do is our best. Your mom would want that." Expecting him to flinch, Walt slowly lifted a palm to caress the back of Jamie's head. His hand encountered curls as soft as Kiley's that didn't jump or move away from his touch.

His voice barely audible, Jamie whispered, "I miss my mom."

"I know. I miss my dad," Walt confessed.

"What happened to your dad?"

"He was a police officer. He was killed by a drunk driver while working an accident scene."

"Were you my age?"

"No, I was eighteen. I got a few more years than what you got with your mom, and I'm sorry you didn't get more time with her. But I know she loved you and wanted the best for you."

"Does it go away? Am I going to lose her?"

"She'll always be a part of you."

"But will I forget her?" Jamie asked.

He couldn't lie. The kid was only five years old. Of course he'd forget some things. Walt couldn't remember his dad's favorite color. Wasn't sure he'd ever known. "You'll forget some things. The unimportant things. But the big part of her — her love for you and your sister — that will always be there."

Snuggling against Kiley, Jamie closed his eyes. Kiley began to hum a tune that brought a small lift to the corners of his mouth as she stood with Walt's aid and walked over to her bed to lay the small boy in the middle.

"I need to get my PJs on, and I'll be right back, okay?" she asked.

Jamie's head nodded as his eyes closed against the pillow. Walt planted his feet. Afraid to move. Afraid to scare either one of them. Or worse, both. But most of all, he was afraid he cared too damned much and wasn't capable of doing right by Kiley and the kids as he watched Kiley disappear into the closet to change.

He was a tactical officer. That's all he knew. All he wanted to know — up until his partner showed him another side to life. Somehow Lee had known, before he had, what he was missing. But he wasn't sure he could make the two worlds come together … as one. The combination went against every belief he'd ever held. And what if he gave up his first love, the job he'd dreamed about since he was Jamie's age, to a temporary family who would be gone within a few months? Or worse, a family he left behind without a father. The anguish he felt at his father's death returned. Images of his mom's pain flooded his mind.

No. After the adoption was finalized … he would walk away.

Warm, soft lips kissed his cheek. Lost in doubt, he hadn't heard a thing as he'd stood guard over the little boy who was wise beyond his years. Kiley's hand slid down his arm, and he wanted to pull her close. Strip her firm body of the yoga pants and T-shirt she wore. Instead, he stood and watched her sink down on the bed next to Jamie, still humming the tune that soothed the boy to sleep.

Someday Jamie would be their son, or at least he would legally. Then what should he do? Leave? Say, "It was nice knowing ya, kid, have a great life"?

He didn't know this boy. And there certainly wasn't a father-son bond between them. But could there be? Did he want one? The arrangement might be temporary right now, but he could make it permanent. If he could convince Kiley they were good together. Convince himself Kiley and the kids were better off with him, no matter how much time he had, than they would be without him.

Of course, all of that sounded self-serving. Walt turned to go downstairs and make his bed on the couch.

"Don't go." His voice thick with sleep, Jamie reached out, stealing a heart Walt had thought couldn't be stolen a few seconds earlier. "Can you bring Gina in here? I don't want to lose her."

Walt looked at the bed occupied with Jamie and Kiley. It was going to be a snug fit once he added his bulk to the mattress. "I don't think it's wise for the baby to be in bed with all of us. Could I just wheel her crib into the room?"

"H … h… Okay." Jamie's voice hitched with a yawn.

Walt retreated to the baby's room and silently unlocked the wheels as he watched angelic lashes flutter like wings against her cheeks. Slowly he pushed the crib over the threshold of Kiley's bedroom, careful not to wake the little girl who was to be his daughter.

He thought of Brandy and hoped she'd approve. That somehow his labeling her children as his own didn't hurt her soul but, rather, set it free.

In the narrow beam of light shining from the bathroom like a beacon directing him to his side of the bed, he pushed the crib into the room and positioned it within reach of the vacant spot he'd occupy — for the rest of his life. He gently tugged the blanket up to the baby's shoulder then turned around to catch Kiley watching him with an expression he couldn't read. He tried to give her a reassuring look before turning toward the bathroom to turn out the light.

"Jamie likes the light on."

Nodding, he silently turned around and lowered himself onto the bed, knowing he'd probably be more comfortable on the couch. The sounds of Jamie and Gina's breathing intermingled in a musical symphony of child fatigue. Cradling the back of his head with his hands and his body laid out prone on Kiley's bed that seemed too damn small, he realized he was more afraid than he'd ever been in his life. This was not a win-win situation. If he got the woman with the kids, he couldn't keep the job. And if he kept the job, there was no way Kiley would stick around. An impossible situation that couldn't work out in the end.

"Good night, Walt." Jamie's soft voice broke the silence.

"Good night, Jamie," Walt answered.

CHAPTER
TWENTY-EIGHT

He was gone.

The sun hadn't even shown its face on the horizon, and the space Walt had occupied on her bed was cold. Only she and Jamie remained lying with her comforter stretched over the top of them with Gina's crib pulled up close and her little baby snores filling the silence.

Slipping out of the bed, Kiley tucked the bedding closer around Jamie and then sneaked downstairs. The scent of coffee filled the air, and she hoped it was a sign that Walt hadn't left but had just started the day off early. After the emotional rollercoaster of the previous day, she couldn't blame anyone for needing time to think.

"Walt?" The hope that he remained somewhere hidden in the shadows disappeared in the peace and quiet.

Flipping the switch on the kitchen wall, she spotted a single slip of paper laying on the counter next to the flashing light on her answering machine. It said so much, yet so little.

Kiley,
Went in to work and then to my place to pick
up some of my stuff. Be back later.
Walt

Relief flowed through the doubt. He was coming back ... even if work came first.

Pushing the message button on her phone, she pulled down a mug and poured a cup of coffee, breathing in the deep aroma that he'd left for her to enjoy. A smile formed on her lips. He was coming back.

The mechanical female voice broke the silence. "You have two new messages."

"Hi, Kiley. It's your sister." Lee's hoarse, weak greeting brought tears to her eyes. "I'm fine. Mack's here ... stay with the kids. They need you. Love you." Lee's voice gave way to her husband's. "She wouldn't shut up until I let her call you. She's doing great, but I'm insisting she rest. I'll call later and update you."

The line went dead. Replaying the message three times almost made her giddy. Every word, every nuance in Lee's voice said she was up for the fight. Through the blurry tears spilling down her cheeks, she finally listened to the second message and wiped her tear with her t-shirt.

Sounds she didn't recognize filled her ears. No words were uttered, but something was happening. She leaned in to hear better. A breath hitched. Liquid slurped. A male voice moaned, "Cuuuurrls...." before the line went dead.

Oh. My. God. She wanted to wash her phone. Wash her ear and her mind from the disgusting sounds of the man on the other end. He knew her ... but she didn't know him.

She dialed Walt, only to get his voice mail. Disappointed and desperate to erase the memory from her mind, she began to leave a message, "Hi, Walt..." Her phone beeped with an incoming call. Quickly, she switched over. "I was just leaving you a message..."

"Really?" replied the female voice on the other end.

Kiley glanced down at the display. Donna. Crap.

"Sorry, Donna. I was leaving a message for Walt, and when the phone rang, I assumed it was him."

"He isn't with you?" Her voice held uncertainty.

She replied, "He's at work."

"I was hoping to talk to both of you before the kids woke up." Donna hesitated. "I have some bad news."

Kiley's stomach somersaulted, but she refused to hide. "What is it?"

"Have you seen the news?"

"No. I didn't want Jamie to hear or see anything." She didn't want to see or hear the news stories either, they'd all been through enough.

"There's a story about the shooting."

"What aren't you telling me?" Kiley wanted to hide her head and deny things could get worse. Lee was awake and talking, things had to get better.

"It's beyond stupid, but there's one reporter who's running with the story that your sister and the hostage negotiators made no attempt to talk Kevin out peacefully. He's saying they never planned on taking Kevin alive. Now it's getting the attention of everyone else ... including my boss."

Setting her cup down on the counter, Kiley walked through her old world living room that she'd made kid friendly after Jamie had told her she needed to childproof her house. She looked out the sliding glass door and stared at the play set in the backyard, the rising sun illuminating the set she'd picked out with Jamie; the baby swing for Gina swaying in the breeze. Everything, in her condo had Jamie and Gina's mark. "Why would your boss care if the story is so ridiculous?" she asked.

"Because we've had a few placements that wouldn't have been made if a proper background investigation had been done. And since you, your sister and Walt were all part of what happened at the house..." Donna didn't have to say anymore. If the story blew up, the adoption was in jeopardy.

Kiley closed her eyes and leaned her head against the glass. Brandy wouldn't want her kids to be placed with Kevin's brother, and Kiley wasn't quite sure she could say goodbye to them.

"I've been scrambling to get Walt's background investigation complete." Donna's tone sounded apologetic, when it shouldn't.

She knew Donna would do her best, but the sway of the empty baby swing felt ominous. The previous night Walt had lost his cool, not because of her or the kids. He'd never directed it toward them. The caller had been the cause. Yet was there something in his past that could cost her everything?

"What about the kids' uncle?" she asked.

"I'm working on his background investigation as well, so far it's very clean and he's not happy about the recent reports." Donna responded.

Kiley ran the voice through her mind, wondering if Terry was the man who'd left the message on her machine. Or could he be the one who'd called last night? "I think you should know that I've met Terry Caputo before."

"You have?" Donna was as shocked as Kiley had been.

"Yes. But I didn't know he was Kevin's brother. It was in a bar, years ago when I was in the academy. It was the first time..." The first time she'd kissed Walt. Yet if she admitted the secret she'd kept for years, she'd cause a mark on his career ... a mark he didn't deserve. "It was the first time Brandy ever asked for help. Walt and I moved her and Jamie to a shelter that night."

"You've known Walt that long?" A hint of hope was layered in her voice.

"Yes, but we weren't involved until recently." Very recently — like yesterday, to be exact. Could it be less than twenty-four hours since they'd made love for the first time?

"What brought you together?"

"My sister." At least that much was truthful. "She made us see that we were good together. Belonged together." She laughed. It really was funny how much truth was behind that statement. "And, well, if you look at the women he dated, I couldn't be more opposite if I tried. The same goes for my ex. He was nothing like Walt." It was time to bring Donna back to the important issue … the kids' uncle and her chances of getting custody. "I actually considered going out with Terry when I first met him. That would have been a huge mistake."

"Why's that?"

"Because he's smoother than Kevin. He doesn't have the substance addiction … that I know of, but … I don't know … he was … pushy."

"That describes at least half the cops I know. Including your sister."

Donna was right, of course. Cops liked to be in control. But good cops had a strong sense of right and wrong that Terry didn't. He just wanted to dominate. Which was a trait neither one of them were looking for in a father figure for the kids. She couldn't let it drop. "I didn't know he existed until yesterday. And I don't think you did, either."

"No. I didn't. But I'll conduct a thorough background investigation on both men."

Kiley didn't miss how Donna included Walt in her suspicion. "I understand. I'll have Walt call you as soon as he gets home and give you anything else you need for his background investigation."

"That's fine. I'll need to interview him, then the two of you together and then finally interview the two of you with Jamie. You'll be at the service tomorrow?"

Nothing could keep her away. Brandy's kids needed to say good-bye. She needed to say good-bye — to her friend whom she'd failed. Her friend who needed Kiley to step up and be stronger than she'd ever been before.

"Yeah. We'll be there."

A masculine voice in the background signaled the arrival of a client in Donna's office. "I've got someone here to speak to me about your case. I'll see you this afternoon."

Before hanging up, Kiley heard the affection in the social workers voice as she greeted her visitor. "Kenny Tibbs, you have grown up into a fine looking young man."

The line went dead, leaving a tight ball in Kiley's gut as Gina's babble carried down the stairwell, tickling Kiley's heart and hardening her resolve.

Terry would not get custody of Brandy's kids. She would not lose this battle … no matter what the cost.

***

The morning radio show played a hip-hop song from a recent action flick that Walt had yet to see. Surrounded by empty desks and stacks of gear that dated back before Walt joined the department, the room looked more like a storeroom than a TAC office for a team with state of the art equipment. As Walt completed the paperwork he didn't want to do, the female DJ's laughter caught his attention. "Did you see his chest? That officer would give Thor a run for his money."

"According to the last woman he was with, his hammer isn't too shabby, either."

"Hey, Raynham! They're talking about you on the radio," Rodriguez called out from across the squad room, where he sat cleaning his pistol.

Walt stiffened.

"She's not the only one saying he can swing that mallet with a driving force. There've been three or four women coming forward talking about his abilities in the bedroom." The male DJ's laughter grated on his nerves. "The question remains, how many women will line up to talk to the media and is that necessarily a bad thing?"

The female snorted. "Well, not if you're a guy. But what about the call taker? Curls, the Guardian Angel? Does she want to go where everybody and their sister have been before? And what type of guardian will she make if she hooks up with a guy who shoots first and asks questions later?"

"Son of a bitch!" His chair slammed to the floor as Walt rose to his feet, anger rolling off him in heated waves. "I'm going to ring somebody's neck." He strode over to the unit phone and called the department operator, too pissed to look up the number on the computer.

"Officer Walt Raynham. I need a Kansas City, Missouri, phone number for Q 107." A muscular arm reached around him and hung up the receiver.

"That's not the way to handle this." He turned to find Rodriguez staring at him. His face expressionless. His pistol in parts on the table.

"What the hell am I supposed to do? Stand here and let them bash Kiley's reputation into the ground?"

"You need to contact Sarge. The department has more at stake than just you and Kiley."

It was like a nail in his coffin, sealing off any chance of his career in TAC surviving. What Rodriguez suggested was common sense. The chain that made the department link together as a strong, unbreakable force would act decisively to shut down the rumors with its own media release. Any other time, he would have contacted their sergeant and passed on the problem for the brass to handle. Yet it seemed with Kiley... his brain didn't function at all. Instead, his emotions ruled.

And that could be a death sentence to him or someone else on the team.

He looked down at the form in his hand. The form he wanted to crumple and throw in the trash. The form he never thought he'd complete. The form that decided his future.

"You're right. I'll call Sarge."

Rodriguez released the receiver and walked away, leaving the dial tone ringing in Walt's ear ... and his Request for Transfer burning a hole in his hand.

CHAPTER
TWENTY-NINE

Jamie remained quiet throughout the service. Sitting in white garden folding chairs, his feet dangling over the edge, he leaned against her chest as she wrapped her arm around him. She wished he'd allowed her to hold him. Jamie, however, wanted to remain strong and she had no choice but to honor his request. She couldn't see his tears as his head bent from view, she could only feel the warm drops on her hand and hear his muffled sniffles compete with the sounds of the bird's singing as he clutched a single white Easter lily in his tiny hands.

Baby Gina slept through most of it. Resting against Walt's chest, her pink cheeks dimpled as she dreamed … and Kiley was sure the images playing through the little girl's mind were of her mother, kissing and loving on her baby girl.

The crowd was sparse, Terry was nowhere to be found.

Thank God.

A few women from the shelter. A neighbor. Some members of the TAC team who'd tried to save Brandy. And Donna, who said she needed to talk to all of them. The conversation had added a whole new dimension to her loss of direction.

Sitting under the small white tent with red carpet covering the grass, most of the adult faces were carved in granite as drizzle pinged the canvas above. The priest finished the service before moving over and talking softly to Jamie. His gentle palms rested briefly on the small heads of Brandy's kids as he said a prayer for the orphaned children. Then he turned and offered his condolences to Kiley and Walt, blessing them on the difficult journey ahead.

Throughout the ceremony, Kiley sensed Donna's guarded approval of Walt's behavior and felt a modicum of relief but knew the battle for custody was just beginning.

With everyone else walking toward their cars parked along the winding asphalt path through the cemetery, Kiley and Jamie approached his mother's casket for the last time. Armed with his flower, which drooped slightly from his caresses throughout the service, Jamie's lip quivered as she lifted him to place his gift across the smooth white surface of Brandy's final resting place. His voice remained silent — until he said good-bye to his mom. Then it waivered ever so slightly as he displayed a strength and courage that would have made Brandy proud.

"I love you, Mommy," he whispered.

Tears, which had threatened throughout the ceremony, spilled down Kiley's cheeks. Jamie shouldn't be a statistic of domestic violence. Gina should grow up knowing her mother's love firsthand. They both should have parents who loved them unconditionally. Walt's arm wrapped around her shoulder, and together, they walked through the rain holding two precious children who deserved more than Walt and Kiley could possibly give.

She felt Walt's body stiffen, then saw a man wearing a navy rain slicker with a local news station's logo on the chest walking in their direction. Instinct took over for both of them. Their strides lengthened. Their pace increased. This was not the place or the time for an interview.

Kiley caught a glimpse of Rodriguez angling across the lawn, cutting the reporter off before he reached them. Their verbal exchange drawing other officers in as Rodriguez blocked the reporter's route with each step the man tried to take. The quiet of the cemetery disappeared in the exchange.

But the reporter wouldn't stop, wouldn't let go of the opportunity he'd seized. "What do you have to say about the baby you gave up, Officer Raynham?"

Kiley tripped over the reporter's words of a forfeited child. Only the grip on her elbow, by the man who'd chosen to step in and fill the role of father for Brandy's kids, kept her and Jamie from landing in the wet grass. She glanced up and saw the truth on Walt's face — lines on his forehead formed, the length of his jaw clenched, as his eyes looked everywhere but her direction.

He *had* walked away. Once ... if not more than that. How many times had Walt cast kids aside who needed him? Would he do it again? Would he abandon Jamie and Gina — complicate their lives even further with layers upon layers of emotional scarring?

They reached the limo as the driver opened the door, holding an umbrella over their heads for them to enter the plush dry interior. Jamie climbed in his booster seat as Walt handed the now-very-awake Gina over to Kiley. She expected him to join them, but his voice interrupted her wiping of the rain droplets from the baby's face.

"I'll meet you at the house."

"Walt, we need—"

"To talk. I know. I won't be long."

The door closed with a deafening thud, leaving further discussion impossible. And doubts about the future sprouting roots that gripped her heart and squeezed. Kiley did the only thing she knew to do — she fastened Gina's seat and then turned to Jamie, "Let me help you with that, buddy. That buckle is tricky."

Life was tricky. And only patience would get her through the next hour … or two … or three, before she was able to find out what Walt had done in the past, that might determine how he would act in the future.

CHAPTER THIRTY

Having opted against a reception after the funeral, felt wrong. When they'd made the decision it seemed the best way to handle it. Lee and Mack wouldn't be there, the shelter women had to go back to work and there really wasn't anyone else Jamie could relate to other than Donna. The focus should be on him. But now that they were piling out of the limo, without Walt, and the elderly driver was helping her carry the car seats to the front door, it seemed like they should have more people around them. Even if they were strangers to the kids now, they'd be friends later.

If she got custody of the kids.

She smiled at the man with the skinny frame and suit that made his drooping shoulders look nonexistent. "Thank you. If you could just put it down on the step, I can get it from there."

"Are you sure? It's no trouble." He blew out a breath from the exertion of removing and then carrying the seat from the limo.

"I'm sure. Thank you."

He nodded and set the car seat down with a thud that seemed to embarrass him. "I'm sorry for your loss. Take care of your mom, young man."

She stiffened, then reached out and put her hand on Jamie's shoulder.

"I'm not…"

"Thank you, sir." Jamie interrupted and took the hand the old man offered. A male bonding moment happened between the two, something like a gentleman's agreement, which seemed fitting standing on the wooden front porch of her blue Victorian townhome. Then the old man nodded in her direction and left without another word.

Jamie picked up the diaper bag and tried to add his booster seat to the load.

She laughed and ruffled his curls. "One thing at a time, super hero."

"I can carry both."

"I have no doubt that you can, but I need help finding the key in that bag."

Jamie set the bag on the porch and began rummaging through the contents as she juggled Gina from one side to the next. "I'm sorry about the comment about your mom, Jamie. You know I'll never try and take her place."

Jamie busied himself with his search, talking to the diapers instead of her. "I know. Mom always said my hair made me look like you. She loved your hair, so it doesn't hurt."

A hiccup gave away his true feelings and Kiley felt her eyes begin to fill with unwanted tears. Jamie pulled the keys out with a jingle, held them high in the air and they exchanged a solemn grin. Turning before the emotion spilled over again, Kiley unlocked the front door and held it open for Jamie to pass through with the diaper bag … and one car seat.

She grabbed the second car seat and pulled it through the front door, then stopped and looked around. Something felt wrong. Like someone had been in the house.

The front door had been locked and everything appeared to be in its place. But she sensed a change. Knew in her gut that something was very, very wrong. It crept along her spine, warning every nerve in her body.

She reached out and stopped Jamie from going farther into the room. Pushing him behind her, back toward the door. Toward safety.

"What's...?"

She shook her head. Pleading in her mind that he knew when to stop, as she purposely kept her voice soft. "We need to go."

She wanted to send him out the door ... to stay and fight whoever threatened her home, the kids. But the child in her arms and the boy at her side changed her focus. She suddenly felt more vulnerable than she'd ever felt in her entire life.

Jamie's stare held the depths of his physical and emotional exhaustion. And as hard as she tried to hide her fear ... he recognized it. Understood it. Because he'd seen it on his mother's face a thousand times. His eyes widened as he gulped down the lump she'd put in his throat. They backed out of the house, and she silently clicked the door closed as Gina chose that moment to squawk.

Turning around, she grabbed Jamie's hand and ran down the short driveway and across the street. She hurried the frightened boy at her side, and the baby screamed in protest to the jostling. Kiley's heartbeat competed with the sounds of Gina's shrieks in her ears as they trampled through brightly colored lilies in the neighbor's flowerbed to a door identical to her own. Casting furtive glances over her shoulder, Kiley frantically pounded on the crimson red door ... of an empty townhome.

"Do you have your phone?" Jamie's breathless voice brought reason to the forefront of her mind.

Releasing his hand, she guided him to the corner of the porch, where they could duck behind the bushes and be hidden from view. Hands shaking, she cursed the adrenaline she couldn't use and dug into her pocket as she and Jamie shushed his sister with soothing noises.

One button and two rings later, Walt answered, "Raynham."

"Someone's in the house. Are you close?"

She heard the engine of his police Charger engage. A siren blared. "I'm a couple miles away. Where are you and the kids?" His voice held the deadly calm she'd heard the first day he'd met Jamie. He was all business. Ready to ride in and save the day; his shield of armor firmly in place.

"We're across the street."

"Are you hurt?"

Gawd, was there judgment in his voice?

He probably thought she was a wimp. She felt like a spineless weakling running from the fight that had come into her home. She should be fighting to protect the kids, not cowering behind a bush."No. We're…" She didn't want to say it. Had to say it. "We're hiding behind the bushes surrounding the front porch across the street."

"Good." She heard him radio dispatch. Knew he was calling in the cavalry to back him up. "Can you see the house?"

"Yeah, but I haven't seen anyone." Even to her own ears, it sounded stupid. Paranoid.

"Was the door kicked?" His siren became audible in the distance.

"No. I didn't see anything… I … I could just tell. Someone had been in the house."

"Nothing was taken?"

She was beginning to feel foolish on two fronts. One, she

was hiding behind her neighbor's hedge. Two, from a bogeyman who probably didn't exist.

"Is that his siren?" Jamie's voice popped into the middle of her conversation with Walt.

She smiled and nodded her head. "Yeah, it's okay, Jamie. That's Walt. He's almost here."

As she spoke, she could hear his siren turn into the neighborhood just before he silenced it.

"I don't know if anything was taken. We didn't make it past the entry," she advised as she repositioned the baby in her arms.

"I'm here." The phone went dead, and she saw his car pull around the corner. His seat belt was off and his door was open before the car even stopped. When he emerged from the side of his patrol car, his gun was drawn. He crouched in his form fitting black suit and sunglasses, looking like a member of the Secret Service as he ran across the lawns to her home. Their home.

Watching him as he spoke into his radio made her feel trapped — frozen with no place to go. She couldn't help him. He glanced in her direction, checking the concealment she knew she had, before he made entry into the house.

"Police!" His voice echoed through the streets.

She wanted to scream at him. Stop him before he disappeared from sight completely. He was breaking policy. Going in alone when he didn't have to. They were safe. To hell with the contents of her house. Why couldn't the man wait?

She pictured all the sights she'd heard when her sister had been shot. Only this time … it was Walt taking the bullet. His lifeblood spilling on the floor with no team member to eliminate the threat. No one to stop the valuable ruby fluid from draining out of his body. The amount of worry weighing on her shoulders was as foreign as the responsibility for the kids' safety.

When had she signed up for all of this?

Jamie tugged at her sleeve as she cooed at Gina. With his hand cupped to her ear, he whispered, "Shouldn't he be done by now?"

Yes. He should. The townhome wasn't that big. But he'd be thorough. Even if he didn't find anyone, he'd look for the point of entry and exit, to see if the burglar was still a threat … or catchable.

And that's what worried her. If the back door was open, if a window had been broken on the backside of the house … Walt would follow the lead, chase the suspect, or worse … end up fighting for his life.

"He's making sure everything is secure. He'll come get us in a moment." She saw the worry in his eyes and silently cursed his biological father. Jamie shouldn't be able to recognize the risk — not at his age. But he did. Thanks to all of the violence he'd witnessed and survived.

Wrapping her arm around him, she felt the shivers running through his body. Gina quieted. With a tear-streaked face, she looked deep into her big brother's eyes and reached for his cheek, comforting her brother without even knowing she did so.

A patrol car pulled up behind Walt's unmarked vehicle. The two cars were identical, except for the KCPD logo emblazoned on the car belonging to the patrol officers who pulled themselves out of their seats a little too slowly. The uniforms weren't in a hurry, as Walt had been. Their manner was relaxed as they glanced around the neighborhood.

In fact, their entire approach angered her with its silence. No sirens had sounded in the distance. Even their guns stayed holstered as they walked across the lawn, infuriating her further. She had to wonder if they'd felt any urgency at all to assist the man she … loved.

She loved him. Loved Walt Raynham with an intensity she'd never felt for her ex. The man who'd been knocking on her heart for years had broken down her barricades, despite her need to keep him out. And now that he was in, he was occupying every nook and cranny. It was wonderful. Horrible. She wasn't sure if she'd ever be able to evict him.

Recognizing the change in Kiley's and Jamie's focus, Gina's silence turned into a howl of hunger. It'd been a long morning for all of them. The baby had slept through most of it. But her bottle was in the diaper bag sitting on the floor in the entry of their home, and they were hiding behind a row of thorny holly bushes at a distance that seemed like a world away.

"They're looking over here," Jamie said above his sister's crying.

Physical concealment ceased to be important. Emotional concealment, however…

"It's okay. We'll wait for Walt to give us the all-clear sign."

A moment later, Walt met the officers at the front door. His own gun holstered, he had the diaper bag in his hand and said something to the officers before heading in their direction.

Kiley smiled at Jamie as she stood up and pulled him to his feet. "Everything's fine."

Walt had the bottle in hand, holding it out to an anxious Gina as they met at the end of the driveway. Then he picked up Jamie and hugged him hard. Jamie returned the affection easily. Needing this man who'd broken down so many of their barriers in such a short time.

Walt slung an arm around Kiley's shoulder, and she gazed at him with questions in her eyes.

"Everything's fine," he assured. His lips pressed against her forehead as they made their way back home.

Despite his confidence, Kiley knew everything was less than fine.

CHAPTER THIRTY-ONE

Kiley's phone call had reinforced his hopes and his fears. Hopes that she depended on him. Fears that he couldn't imagine a future without them. He belonged here. With Kiley and the kids. Sitting on her dainty vanity chair watching her in the mirror as she took off her makeup, while Jamie slept in *their* bed and Gina snored in the crib next to him. They made him more content than he could remember being. They gave him a stronger, deeper fulfillment than the job had ever given him.

He was home.

Kicking dope house doors and facing life like there was no tomorrow, was over. Life was full of tomorrows. It had to be.

He understood Kiley's fear. Knew the vulnerability she'd felt while holding the kids and confronting the thought of someone being in the house. The thought of not being there for them when some crazy person could have been in their home … nearly killed him. She wasn't going crazy, even though he knew she was wondering if she was. The entire night, she couldn't get comfortable. She kept checking each window, each door for a sign. For some way, somehow, someone had gotten inside. Yet everything was there, and nothing was out of place. The house had been locked tight.

He'd followed her lead. Checked everything over and over. 'Cause he'd want her to help him do the same thing. But by doing that, they were avoiding the topic they needed to discuss. Because having his secret out for not only Kiley to know, about but his co-workers as well ... hurt. The gnawing shame dug at his gut more it ever had before. He kept looking for judgment. Condemnation. Disgust. He got none of it.

And he knew he needed to suck it up. Face the past and talk about the future. Their future. They needed to make plans for counseling for Jamie, hell, for all of them. Together, as a family, they could do anything, but a little guidance with their feelings wouldn't hurt. And he had to get his past out in the open. Before it became an elephant in the room between them.

With the kids in bed, there was nothing like the present. He expelled the breath threatening to strangle him and tried to say something ... anything. But couldn't. Wavering with indecisiveness, he wondered if he should just go with the desire her braless tank top and short pajama bottoms unleashed in him. Her taut butt and perky breasts could make him forget about talking. Especially if her long, smooth legs were wrapped around him as he buried himself deep within her and her breasts bounced in his face.

The antique cherry vanity chair creaked beneath him, causing him to focus on something other than sex. Maybe it couldn't support his weight with the burden he was carrying. He looked down at the legs. Her laughter brought his eyes up to her face.

"It will hold you." She smiled, and he thought he was in heaven. She hadn't had many reasons to smile lately. He wanted to change that.

Instead, he did the opposite. He wiped it from her face. "I need to tell you about the child I gave up for adoption."

She cleared her throat and wiped a cotton ball across her eyelid, no longer meeting his gaze. "It's really none of my business—"

"It's totally your business. I was eighteen. My girlfriend was seventeen. We were young and dumb, and when my dad died, I thought sex would be the thing to fill the hole he'd left behind."

She stopped rubbing her eyes and turned toward him with a clean, fresh look that made him love her even more. Leaning against the counter, she gave him her full attention.

"My girlfriend wanted to make me feel something other than pain. It happened. And we weren't ready for the consequences. She wanted to give the baby up. She was only a junior … I couldn't raise a child by myself, and my mom… My mom was a wreck. We did what we thought was best." He ran his hand through his hair and looked at his feet, unsure what her reaction would be. Knowing they'd done the right thing, but feeling the pain all over again. The pain he'd felt every day since his son had been born. "I still think it was the best thing for the baby, even though I think about him every day."

She was down in front of him, kneeling at his feet and grasping his hands in hers. If it'd been the opposite way around, his hands would have engulfed hers. As it was, her hands didn't even cover one set of his knuckles. Her eyes shone with the tears he felt. Tears he'd cried years ago that had dried up — yet still stung.

"I know what it's like to feel the loss," she whispered. "I can't have kids. I lost the one child I…" Her tears were for her own child now. She cleared her throat. "You gave your child a chance of having a whole family, and you gave a couple the ability to have a child they couldn't have had without you. Now *we* have two kids depending on us to do what is right … because they *need* us … but I think we might need them more."

He reached down and pulled her up on his lap. As much as he wanted to have sex with her, he wanted to hold her more. Savor the gift they'd been given and let her know their relationship would be more than sex.

Sex would have a huge role. Incredible role. But their relationship was going to reach levels he'd never dreamed of attaining — a lifetime.

Her arms snaked around his neck as her legs wrapped around his waist. Desire began attacking his resolve not to push her on the floor and drive deep within the incredible woman sitting on his dick who had begun teasing him with a sensual, rocking caress of her hips. The place between her legs he wanted to devour rubbed his length, making him harder than he was trying to be.

"Kiley—"

Her finger covered his mouth, shushing him like a mother to a child. But the look reflected in the deep marine sea glass of her soul was full of an adult love. And right now she wanted him as much as he wanted her.

Then he told her the words he'd only told his high school sweetheart. The words that had lost meaning for a young couple in the pain of a lost child. Words that grew into something much larger, stronger, and tender for the incredible woman ready to rock his world.

"I love you, Kiley."

Her hands cupped his cheeks while his own made their way up her silken skin at the bottom of her cotton tank top. A smile spread across her face. A gloriously, bright, happy smile that he wanted to make sure she wore every day for the rest of their lives.

"I have loved you since the first day I saw you at the academy." Her lips descended toward his, stopping when the soft pink flesh grazed his. "Carry me into the closet, Walt Raynham, and I'll show you how deep our love runs."

He felt his own smile widen beyond the joy expanding in his chest. They looked in at the sleeping children in the other room, and then he closed the door before carrying her into the closet. Life would have its challenges, but with Kiley by his side, they could conquer them all.

CHAPTER THIRTY-TWO

The closet had proved to be a brilliant spot to make love. The air conditioning vent had blown down their backs as they heated up the space against the wall, on the floor, and in the middle of the room. She was pretty sure the closet was her new favorite room in the house, and she couldn't help but smile at the very different image looking back at her in the mirror. At the moment, she was using the closet in a traditional sense, getting ready for her meeting with Donna.

Slipping on heels to match her navy blue business suit, she took one final glance before exiting her love shack and entering the bedroom, where Walt lay with arms cradling his head and Jamie curled up against him. His broad chest was bare, and his hair had a been-loved-all-night quality that looked good on him.

His eyes tracked her as she crossed the room and kissed his forehead.

"I'm going to meet Donna. I'll be back as quickly as I can. Will you be okay?"

His finger traced her lips, reminding her of what she'd done to his body and how he'd come undone with need. She'd enjoyed watching Walt lose the cool facade of a man in charge last night, but this morning, it made her happy to see the self-assured man who could take on any task … including the care of two small children.

"I got this." He nodded toward the kids.

"And so much more," she whispered against his smiling lips before kissing him tenderly, knowing they could handle anything. Together.

***

The morning started out with all the promise one woman could ask for. Kiley's mood was beyond wonderful as she walked across the parking lot for the Division of Family Services. Because she and Walt were good together. Really good together.

In more ways than one.

A smile slipped across her face as she thought of all the things he'd done with his tongue. And all the things she'd reciprocated. Despite her initial doubts about the job, the string of women, and then a child he'd given up, Walt would make the perfect partner to raise Jamie and Gina. Nothing could stop them; she was sure of it.

Her shoulders held her confidence as she pressed the button and was greeted by a man over the intercom.

"I'm here to see Donna Townsend." The door clicked with an elongated buzzing noise, allowing Kiley to enter the social workers' office that was deserted of the normal weekday staff. Her heels clicked past the security desk, where she had expected to find the male voice behind the speaker. It was vacant.

Not particularly alarmed since weekends were only utilized for emergency call-outs and for caseworkers to catch up on their overflowing schedules, Kiley made her way down the vacant hallway. She had no doubt Donna would stand by her decision to place the kids in her care. Gossip from Tibbs and that reporter hadn't changed Donna's demeanor at the funeral, and the kids didn't know Terry. The state would give Terry supervised visitation, but in the end, Jamie and Gina would go where Brandy had requested. She was absolutely sure of it.

Until the smell hit her.

Punched her in the nose and stopped her foot from crossing the threshold to the social worker's office. Her face froze as a feeling of something very wrong washed over her … again.

It was … fresh. Magnetic — drawing her in for a closer look she didn't want to take with its heavy, nauseating, metallic scent. She'd never smelt it before, at least not in this quantity. But she knew without a doubt, the heavy scent clinging to the air spoke of blood, and death by unnatural causes.

She reached in the black canvas bag slung over her shoulder for the can of pepper spray she always carried. Her cell phone magically appeared in her other hand, making her wonder if time had warped, because she certainly didn't remember removing it from her suit pocket.

She scanned the room, seeing her friend slumped over her desk. Knowing it meant the blood was leaking from her body. And knowing she had to make sure she was alone before she could help her.

She closed Donna's door. Locked it behind her as she tried to remember the voice from the intercom. Someone else was here. Possibly someone who could help. More likely the person who had done this.

She searched the room as quickly as possible. The closet. The bathroom. Every nook and cranny. Nothing.

Knowing she was safe—for the moment—she rushed toward her friend and stashed the can of pepper spray back in her purse.

"Donna. It's me … Kiley," she told the back of Donna's red frizzy head of hair, her hand wavering over the top of the woman's shoulder.

When she didn't wake, Kiley shook her. Hoping she'd jump back from a deep sleep that had her drifting into another world.

Her body listed to the side. Her shoulders fell over the arm and threatened to knock her out of the chair. Kiley grabbed her, dropping her phone in the process to bear the brunt of Donna's weight … her dead weight.

Despite the warmth of her body, Kiley knew she was dead. The heat didn't radiate. It sank away from her skin, drifting toward the core of Donna's body, where it would eventually shrink in upon itself, like a black hole.

A black hole of death.

Refusing to acknowledge the truth, Kiley leaned her friend back in her chair, ready to lay her on the floor and perform CPR if it would save her. But the view she got, told her Donna was beyond saving. Her eyes were vacant. Her skin slackened. And the blood covering her chest was beginning to dry, the bright red fluid browning with its loss of vibrancy.

"Oh, God."

The knot in her throat forced her breathing to become shallow. Her eyes welled with sorrow — for the woman who had been more of a co-worker, than a friend. But still so good and selfless with her desire to help others. Donna was a woman dedicated to helping children … and was *dead at the hands of another.*

Without her, Jamie and Gina would be…

Dead at the hands of another.

She checked for a pulse, still not wanting to believe the signs slapping her in the face.

Dead at the hands of another.

There were plenty of cases that could lead to the death of a caseworker, but Kiley knew deep in her gut that it was her custody case behind Donna's death. It had been the reason she was working this morning. Diligently putting together the background investigations of two men. One who had been with her, and another who…

Was that Terry's voice she'd heard on the intercom? Had he been the one to buzz her in? And if so, how had he known how to do it? How had he gotten inside to murder Donna?

Was he still here?

Her mind racing with the possibilities, Kiley looked at the door. Wondered if the killer stood waiting behind the flimsy wooden defense.

Reaching down, she picked up her cell phone and saw a pair of brown leather loafers kicked off to the side. Donna's feet were shoeless. Trouser socks covered her small feet that appeared puffy.

She'd been comfortable when she'd died.

Not the state of a woman meeting someone she wasn't familiar with. But someone she'd known. Maybe it wasn't Terry. Or maybe Kiley was looking for evidence that didn't exist, just so she could make her custody battle go away.

She dialed 911, not wanting to think about anything but getting justice for the woman who deserved more than this.

"9-1-1. Call taker thirteen. What's your emergency?"

Cindy. The supervisor on the day shift.

"Cindy. It's Kiley Gibbons." Her voice shook. Taking a deep breath and concentrating on her words, Kiley slowed down the beat of her heart that threatened to take off. "I'm at the DFS downtown. One of the social workers has been killed. Donna Townsend."

She heard Cindy typing in the background and filled her in with the details she needed without having to be questioned.

"This is the second call we've received there this morning. The first one was at nine hundred hours. A nine-one-one hang-up."

"Did the officers contact anyone?"

"No. The building was secure."

"Someone let me in. I assumed it was a security guard or another social worker. Now, I'm not sure."

"The officers are almost there. Stay on the line with me."

Kiley suddenly realized how Jamie must have felt trapped in the closet with a crazy man outside. His mom injured, possibly dead — like Donna — and him being completely helpless to do anything but wait for someone else to arrive to save the day. Waiting and wondering if he was next to die.

Hunted.

But she wasn't a child. She was an adult who had some self-defense training. Unfortunately, by the looks of the two bullet holes in Donna's chest ... she was outgunned.

No. Waiting for the uniforms to arrive was the right thing to do. If they had to kick the door to get in ... let them.

CHAPTER THIRTY-THREE

"Stay with the kids. It shouldn't be too much longer."

Unless, of course, they decided she was a suspect in Donna's murder. But Walt didn't need to know that could be a possibility, at least not yet. He'd probably know if they planned on charging her before she did anyway. He worked with these detectives — kicked the doors on search warrants the detectives obtained on cases just like Donna's.

"I'll find someone to babysit. Then I'll be right there." His voice held all the love and worry she could ask for. And all the wrong things she needed to hear.

"*No.*" The detectives circling their rickety powwow table turned and looked at her with a collective question. It wasn't the whole squad, only three detectives pushing paperwork while the others were at the scene, with the body, and talking to the crime scene techs gathering evidence.

They'd already taken her statement and politely asked her to stick around for a few more minutes. But enough was enough.

The kids needed her. The only thing she was guilty of was wanting to adopt two children whose mother had chosen Kiley to raise them. Brandy had chosen *her*.

"I'm sorry. I didn't mean to yell." She turned away from the curious stares. The run-down office filled with paneled cubicles dating back before the 1970's had painted desks covered with chicken scratchings that looked worse than gang graffiti. The vinyl padded chair she occupied had been taped several times to hide the tears in its original gray covering and made her skirt stick to the surface. This was the last place she wanted to be, but it would be even worse if it was all for nothing.

She tried to convey everything she felt in a few short words for Walt. "I need to know the kids are safe and that Donna will receive justice. I'm done here. I'll be on my way home in five."

She hung up before he could respond. Afraid he'd offer to come get her. Afraid the adoption would become the focus of the investigation. She didn't want a ride. She needed the kids to be safe. Protected from any sights, smells, or conversations that would expose them to any more violence. Their lives needed to be filled with kisses and hugs, creating things, sports, games, and adventures without violence.

Besides, she'd asked one of the detectives to drive her car back to headquarters, knowing they'd want to search it. They did and they had, all routine, of course.

They were just doing their jobs.

Now, it was time for Kiley to do hers. She was going home to the most important job in the world.

***

"Is it true the shell casings at the scene of Donna Townsend's murder were identical to those used by the police department?" The reporter shoving the microphone in her face shouldn't know anything about the crime scene, or that she would leave through the employee exit through a gated parking garage.

But he was one of two who had plagued her life since Jamie had called 9-1-1. The other was Tibbs, who'd been jacking with her, since her second day on the department. She pulled her hair in front of her face and turned away. She had no doubt these two were the ones who crossed the crime scene tape after her sister's shooting. The reporter had also been the same one who stuck his nose where it didn't belong and broke the news about Walt's child, at the funeral. His timing still ticked her off. He and his sidekick, Tibbs, always seemed a step ahead of the rest of the pack — probably voted least likely to have ethical practices in journalism school. Their young, wholesome faces and clean-cut appearance were just a ruse.

And now it seemed they knew more about Donna's case than Kiley did. *Awesome.*

She pulled her purse in closer and began to jog across the street. He kept pace with her, attacking the story with a zeal she hated, while Tibbs grinned and raced in front of her to get a better view.

"Didn't you go through the police academy, Ms. Gibbons?" When she didn't answer, he resorted to using her nickname. "Curls, do you still own your forty caliber Glock?"

The reporter's words literally tripped her. Not the sprawling-across-the-pavement kind of trip, but close. Except now she saw things a little too clearly.

She spotted her car, and was thankful she'd removed her keys from her purse before exiting the building. Once in her car, she slammed the door and glared at the camera an inch from her window filming every movement she made. Turning the ignition, she jammed the vehicle in reverse, uncaring if she caught Tibbs toes as she pulled out of the spot and away from the lot. Once around the corner and out of sight, she rolled down the windows and let the summer heat escape the interior. Then she reached for her cell and called Walt.

He answered on the first ring.

"I need a really big favor."

He didn't hesitate. "Anything."

"I need you to go to the nightstand in my bedroom. There's a safe inside. I need you to make sure my Glock is there."

He was silent as he went through the house, then she heard the door clicking on her nightstand.

"It's locked." His voice was calm. Like hers.

"There's a key on the back of the headboard. I need to know that my gun is inside." She barely heard the jingle of the chain through the phone over the silent prayers she said in her head. *Please let it be there.*

His voice almost sounded as sick as she felt. "It's empty."

"Oh, God. That's what he took."

"What who took?"

"The person who broke into my house. I knew someone had been in there. I should have checked my gun — but the safe was there — it was locked. No one has a ke…" No one had the key anymore. But Brandy had had her own key to the safe. Just in case.

Walt didn't miss a beat. "Who else had a key?"

"Brandy had a copy of the key. And a copy of my house key. You have to get out of there. You and the kids are in danger."

"So you think someone has Brandy's key. They broke into the house yesterday, stole your gun, and killed Donna with your gun today?"

"In a nutshell … yes."

"That's crazy. Why would anyone—"

"I know it's crazy. But I need you to get the kids out of the house. I need you guys to be safe."

"No one's getting in here with the kids. I'll protect them."

"I know you'll protect them. I have no doubt you would kill any S.O.B. who tried to harm a hair on their heads. But I don't want them to even be able to detect a hint of danger. I don't want them to live their lives not feeling safe in their home."

"I understand. I'll take them to my place. But I need you—"

She couldn't listen. She had to find out if Brandy's key was missing. "I'm going to Brandy's."

"Kiley. You need to go back inside the PD and tell them what you know. Tell them your gun was stolen, and they can send a lab team over to process your safe."

"No."

"No?" His voice was beginning to sound angry, and this time it was definitely directed at her.

"If I go back in there and try to say my gun was stolen, they're going to hold me." She started the car. "Then they're going to send officers with social workers to come get the kids." She turned down Benton Boulevard. "Getting them back will be next to impossible, because Donna isn't our caseworker anymore and the new one will just see us as more conflict than the kids need in their lives. I'm not going to lose them. I need you to report the gun stolen and talk to the detectives."

"Kiley, listen to yourself. You're not being rational."

"Actually, I am. I have a key to Brandy's house. Unlike the detectives, I don't need permission or a search warrant based on some *feeling*. And we both know the detective won't obtain a search warrant when their prime suspect in today's murder is trying to make an excuse for her gun killing an innocent woman."

"You don't know it was your gun."

"I don't need to see all the evidence to feel the truth in it. A reporter just told me the shell casings at the scene were from the same type of ammo the department uses. When they pull those slugs out of Donna's body, they're going to see the striations from my gun — the gun I *didn't* report stolen until *after* Donna was killed. At least if I go to Brandy's house and invite the police in, a search warrant that no prosecutor is ever going to approve isn't necessary."

"That doesn't mean they're going to believe you any more than they would now." His voice sounded frustrated. Kind of like he wanted to yank her through the phone. She loved him all the more.

"No, it doesn't. But it gives them access to the evidence that will prove my innocence." She paused, waiting for him to argue. Knowing he wouldn't. "I love you."

"I love you, Kiley Gibbons. Please don't make me regret it."

CHAPTER
THIRTY-FOUR

Nothing was going right. In fact, Walt was pretty sure things couldn't get more fucked up. The detectives had asked funky questions. The kind police officers asked when they thought you'd gotten yourself in way too deep and you didn't know how to pull your sorry ass out. Now he understood why Kiley wanted to wait and call from Brandy's house.

As it was, he'd dropped the kids off at Rodriguez's and called Katie to help him, before making his team member promise not to open the door to *anyone*. Not a teammate, not a commander, not even the damn chief of police. No one was to get near his kids until he and Kiley were able to deliver all the answers to all of the questions.

Rodriguez promised easily enough, despite the stupid look on his face that said, "What do I do with this?" as he'd looked down at Gina pulling on his ear and Jamie running circles around him like a Jack Russell terrier.

Once the kids were safe, he headed back to Kiley's to the meet detectives. 'Cause she was going to be held, there was no doubt about it. The murder squad believed she had something to do with the murder. Hell, they probably thought he had something to do with the murder. But to use her own gun? A weapon issued and test fired and recorded with the department?

That was just stupid and Kiley wasn't dumb. Maybe if it had been a crime of passion it might be believable... a murder/suicide...

Fuck.

His fist pounded the steering wheel.

The calm he was known for was gone. Gauging the spaces in traffic, he made the luckiest U-turn of his life.

Horns blared as he accelerated and passed cars to the left and right. Traffic laws ceased to exist as he pushed his Challenger harder than ever before on city streets. If he didn't, he'd lose his ever-fucking mind, because Kiley was headed for more danger than either one of them had counted on. She was the next target for her own damned gun and she didn't even know it.

He dialed her number. It went to voice mail. He dialed it again ... and again. Every time, he got the recording of her sweet, perky voice. And every time, he died a little bit inside. All he could think about was hearing her voice in person as he watched her lips move, felt her breath tickling his cheek.

He'd never hated a recording so much in his life.

He gave up on calling and focused on driving. He was close. He would make it.

His phone rang from the passenger seat. The old man pulling out from a stop sign in an old Cadillac Deville should have scared the shit out of him — but nothing fazed him. Not now. He swerved and dodged, got back on track and answered his phone — praying it was Kiley.

"Kiley!"

"No, it's Jones from Homicide. I thought you were meeting us at Kiley's house."

Shit.

The homicide detectives were waiting for him at the wrong address.

The light at the next block yellowed and he focused on the traffic. One car stopped at each side of the intersection; a couple walked along the sidewalk.

Clear.

He floored it, giving the car the power it desired.

The detectives were waiting. Wondering. If he was wrong, he'd screw Kiley's plan. If he was right — he'd be saving her life. And having her alive in a holding cell until this mess got straightened out was a whole lot better than finding her bleeding out in the same damned spot her sister had nearly lost her life.

"Walt, listen, buddy—" Jones started.

He snorted. The detective was talking him down. Saving him from jumping off the cliff, but nothing Jones could say would stop him from taking the leap of faith he had in Kiley, in their relationship and in his instinct that she needed him now more than ever.

"Dana. Listen to me. Kiley's at 2836 Scarritt. I don't have time to go into details—" he slammed on the brakes for the next light he couldn't make "—but she's in danger. Someone's trying to kill her. I'm on my way, but if you have someone closer…" Traffic cleared before he came to a complete stop, and he blew the intersection with all the muscle the car had behind four hundred and seventy horsepower.

"I'll get some uniforms there. Are you armed?"

Fuck, no, he wasn't armed.

No gun in the glove box. No gun in the trunk. And no gun on his hip—because that was the last image he wanted the detectives to have as he met them at Kiley's house. He'd left his fucking sidearm at Rodriguez's. Locked in a fucking safe miles away.

"No." Two blocks and he'd be there.

"Walt—"

"I'm almost 10-23. Call an assist." He shoved his phone in his cargo pocket and unclicked his seat belt in one fluid move. An assist would send every officer within the area to their aid, and if he was right...

God, he hoped he was wrong...

Kiley needed them now.

Pulling the car over three houses from his target, he began running for the house while scanning the neighborhood the tactical unit had overtaken just a few days earlier. Reaching the front corner of the small structure, he knew the front door had been boarded up by the department. The lock had been obliterated. If Kiley still had a key to the house, the only place it could work would be the back door.

Skirting around the side of the house, he peeked in the front living room.

Vacant.

The next window, the bathroom, was too high. He moved past it to the rear bedroom — Jamie's. The shades were drawn but broken.

Empty.

The chain-link gate to the backyard stood open. He worked his way around and found the rear door closed. Bright yellow bows held back curtains on the window in the door — the color used by a woman who'd tried to bring happiness to her home. But failed.

The sight inside the small kitchen made him happy — and furious in one glance. Happy, because Kiley was alive. Pissed beyond what he thought was fucking possible, because she'd brought a knife to a gunfight.

Walt couldn't see his face. Couldn't identify the man threatening to kill the woman he loved, but recognized the weapon he brandished. It was definitely a department-issued Glock, with laser engravings of a KCPD badge on the side.

Luckily, for some reason, the gunman hadn't shot her and saw her knife as a threat — in a gunfight.

Being a fucking moron was going to be his downfall.

Kiley leaned against the counter, her hand steady as she kept distance between her and her assailant and talked to him calmly. Using that tone she used on the job while trying to appear relaxed. Her voice carried through an open window.

"Why'd you kill Donna?"

The asshole laughed. As if the woman's death was just a bad scene in a stupid horror flick. His demeanor telling Walt what he needed to know — he'd kill Kiley when he was ready.

"At first, it was like a reunion. Donna was my caseworker when I was a kid. When I saw her at the hospital, I knew this was my chance to get even with you. And she appreciated me coming forward with information for her background check — asked me all kinds of questions about you and your *boyfriend*."

It's fiancé, asshole.

"Then she asked me to come in and give a statement. When I got there, she said she couldn't use it — because of my background with the police. Said I was biased against you." His hand ran through his hair, pulling at it.

A mumbled voice next to Kiley made Walt realize someone else was in the room. Out of his line of sight.

What the hell?

"Shut up!" The gun jutted out toward the person to Kiley's left, and she moved to step in front of whoever it was. Shielding.

Protecting. Calmly talking to the gunman as he began to approach her.

"You don't want to do this, Tibbs."

Tibbs. Recruit Tibbs from the academy. *Son of a bitch.* The guy who'd laughed at her on the second day. Who'd hounded her — bullied her. Got fired for grabbing too many asses in the academy, including Kiley and Lee's. He was the one making phone calls to her. That's why they'd recognized the voice on the other end but couldn't identify it.

Keep him talking, baby.

Walt turned the doorknob with care and eased the door open, catching Kiley's eye as she looked over the man's shoulder. Fear was written all over her face, but it wasn't fear for herself. She feared for him.

He focused. Refused to allow his vision to tunnel in on Kiley's new fear — his safety. Rejected the need to concentrate on her once-steady hand that was now shaking as she fired off questions to cover the noise of his entry.

"Why did you have to kill her? Did she threaten to expose you? Threaten your job as a cameraman?"

"She didn't give me a choice. She said I needed to stop feeding reporters with lies. That I needed concrete evidence of your inability to be a good parent." His voice was taking on a chill that signaled he was gearing up to do the deed. "You stupid bitch, I was better than you and your sister combined."

Kiley refocused him. "But why Donna? She *cared* for you."

"She wouldn't listen to me, just like him," Tibb's nodded to the man duct taped to a kitchen chair, the man who threatened their chances of retaining custody of the kids. "They both stopped listening and started believing you were good enough to be a parent." His laughter bordered tears. "You're not who you pretend to be, women never are. I needed them to see I was right all along."

"But why is he here?" Kiley nodded toward Terry Caputo who wiggled in his chair desperately trying to get loose.

"He didn't believe me. This way the whole world will know they were wrong, and I'll be there to capture the entire story."

"But what about the kids?" Kiley seemed lost in his anger. "Who will take care of the kids if Terry and I are gone?"

Tibbs laughed, a pathetic sound of a man who didn't know the meaning of joy.

"Foster care is always an option."

Walt read her thrown-back shoulders, the lift of her chin, and the spark in her eyes the moment before her anger took over and her path changed from trying to talk Tibbs down, to taking him out. She moved toward the door, scooting Terry with her while her actions increased Tibbs' anger — forcing him to make a move that was going to get her killed.

"Stop moving!" Tibbs bellowed.

They stopped momentarily. Tibbs worked his way closer while Kiley stood her ground, determined to take out the asshole if he got within range.

"You were supposed to die with her this morning." Tibbs angled around the island that stood as a barrier between them.

"How did you get my gun?" she asked, her free hand behind her back, grasping Terry.

Laughter, no longer resembling even sick humor, spilled from Tibbs' chest. "You can thank him for that." He tried to lean around Kiley, pointing with his gun, but she maintained the shield, moving in front of the weapon.

Dammit, Kiley. Walt moved closer.

"He had the landlord let us in. Wanted to video the house as evidence in his custody battle with you and asked us to come along. All in an effort to show the police never planned on talking his brother out. I found your keys hanging on the hook — conveniently marked with your name. How many Kiley's could there be?"

Walt could hear the smirk in Tibbs' voice and silently made his way around the knocked-over chairs at the kitchen table.

"So you broke into my house, stole my gun, and used it to kill Donna?" Disbelief and horror dripped from her voice.

Sirens blared through the neighborhood. Dogs howled. Tibbs' voice ratcheted. "Move out of the way or I'll shoot him through you."

Kiley tried to maintain his attention. "Then it won't look like a murder/suicide and I'm not going to let you kill the kids' uncle. They need one of us."

The sirens drew closer. Tibbs' frantic gaze scanned the window, then found the open door.

He swung around, the gun following his eyes. Walt released the crazy fury roaring in his chest and plowed across the room as the gun rose for its target. He hit him with every ounce of force he could find; all of his anger directed at the arm holding the gun Tibbs had dared to point at Kiley. Forearm striking forearm. Meat striking bone.

A round exploded from the Glock. Gunpowder smoked in the air, the noise resonating through his ears, and his brain before the pistol hit the floor. Walt didn't stop.

His knee drove into Tibbs' thigh. His fist made contact with his throat as Tibbs attempted to retrieve the weapon.

Tibbs gasped, choked and staggered. The fight for the weapon turned into a fight for air as he grasped his neck.

Walt didn't let up. Grabbing his arm, he swept his feet out from under him. Tibbs' face connected with the counter as they went down to the floor. Bone crunched. Blood flowed. Air wheezed through Tibbs' chest as he sprawled on his stomach on the floor.

A uniform appeared, jumping into the mix and driving a knee into Tibbs' back. Walt yanked his arms behind his back, yelling the order, "Put your hands behind your back!"

Handcuffs clicked, but Walt didn't waste time.

"Kiley!" He jumped to his feet and found her on the floor on the opposite side of the island.

Covering Terrenzio Caputo with her body, her arm up displaying a deadly knife, ready to slice and dice anyone who came at the man. Protecting and shielding the man who wanted to take their kids.

Kiley's eyes swept his body the same way Walt's scanned hers. The knife dropped to the floor. He pulled her to her feet, making sure the bullet hadn't somehow made its way to her. And she did the same. Her small hands, shaking as badly as his, skimmed his body to make sure he was whole.

"Are you okay?" Her eyes held the concern of a wife for her husband.

His held the love that would see them through anything and everything, as a team.

"I couldn't be better."

Officers poured in through the door, filling the kitchen as Walt and Kiley turned toward the bound-up Terry lying on his side mumbling through the duct tape covering his mouth. Together they bent down and righted his chair. Kiley retrieved the knife she'd abandoned and began working to free his arms and legs as Walt slowly removed the piece of tape attached to his face.

Terry winced with pain.

"Sorry," Walt said. Although he wasn't sure he felt too much guilt.

Finally free, Terry stood on shaky legs as Walt steadied him until Terry nodded that it was okay to release him. "Thank you."

"Take it easy until the ambulance checks you out." Kiley warned.

Terry turned toward her, "You would've taken a bullet for me?"

Kiley gave him a sad smile and then grabbed Walt's arm before he had the chance to say, *No, asshole. I was not going to let her take a bullet for you.*

"The kids need their family to help them through this," she replied, as if sacrificing herself was okay.

Which it wasn't. And as soon as they were alone, Walt was definitely going to make sure she knew not to ever do such a foolish thing again.

"I don't think..." Terry shook his head, confusion and disbelief clouding his eyes. "I don't think I would have done the same for you. I don't know I would have done it for—"

She didn't let him finish. "Yes, you would have. You're not like your brother. The detectives let me see your background that Donna had started on you."

"But you're the one from the bar, a few years ago. Right?" Terry asked.

Kiley nodded.

"I treated you ... horribly."

Again, Kiley nodded. Not letting him escape his bad behavior, but forgiving him for it at the same time.

"And since then, you've stopped drinking. Gone back to school. Have a good job, married your high school sweetheart, and have a baby on the way. You'll make a good dad."

Walt saw her acceptance — Terry would make a good father to all three kids. He wanted to scream and yell. Terry couldn't have their kids. The tears welling in Kiley's eyes said the opposite.

"No, you're wrong," Terry responded. "I'll make a great dad and the best uncle your kids could ever have."

CHAPTER
THIRTY-FIVE

Gina wobbled as Jamie led her down the walk. Her small baby steps, improved from yesterday, would be even better tomorrow — thanks to the help of her adoring big brother. She smiled up at Jamie. The expression showcasing her four front teeth made Kiley want to weep with joy as a camera captured the moment.

Flower petals dribbled and plopped in piles from the basket in Jamie's other hand, marking their path. Midway to their destination, the entire basket toppled, drawing giggles and smiles with a few cringes from onlookers. Their matching outfits and the music coming from numerous speakers behind them expressed the significance of the occasion with its joyous message of unity.

In a few strides, Walt was there, helping the kids. Making them laugh and forget about spilt flowers. He swung a worried Jamie up onto his shoulders, and laughter filled the small gathering. Gina squeaked with delight, knowing she was next. She turned and reached for Kiley, her pudgy arms stretched out in front of her little body leaving Kiley no choice but to follow Walt's lead.

Lee scrambled to gather flowers. "Kiley, you're going to ruin—"

Kiley didn't listen to her twin. The flowers crunched under her feet as she picked up her daughter. She laughed at the way Gina pulled sections of her hair out of the carefully styled braid.

Then she almost … *almost* felt sorry for Lee as her husband, Mack, snuck up on his wife and tickled her ribs. Her sister actually *squealed*.

Big, bad Lee, sporting a dressier version of her combat boots, was dancing with her husband in the middle of the walkway. The two of them had the most awkward moves Kiley had ever seen.

Walt and Kiley followed their lead with squealing children on their shoulders as everyone else joined in the dance. Terry and his very pregnant wife moved slowly, watching for obstacles in their way. Rodriguez, who was now their regular babysitter, was solo and attempting to ignore the fact that one of his team mates was flirting with Katie.

Kiley smiled, she knew what it was like to resist the inevitable.

TAC members and detectives. Family and co-workers. Social workers and even neighbors they'd never met until that morning were all pitching in. Each one knowing the story of domestic violence and the strength it took to overcome it and break the cycle once and for all. Everyone gathered together, armed with music, good cheer, paint brushes and flowers, lawn mowers and trimmers for one purpose — to help a woman victimized for years.

The front door to 5308 Wornall Road opened, and the dancing stopped as a timid woman, with one arm wrapped in a sling and the other wrapped around her daughter's shoulder, looked at her visitors. Kiley stepped forward, pulling Walt up the stairs with her as they balanced two giggling children on their shoulders.

"Hi, Stacy." Kiley smiled warmly, knowing it would take baby steps, just like Gina's, for Stacy to get back on the road to recovery. "I'd like you to meet my husband, Walt, and our two kids, Jamie and Gina."

Kiley leaned back to make sure Stacey and her daughter saw just how many people had come to help them. "This is everyone else. We're here to help you get back on your feet."

A hint of tears welled in Stacy's eyes and her teenaged daughter blinked. Kiley found herself unable to talk as she witnessed the first glimmer of hope on their faces.

Walt filled in for her. "We're here for a fresh start, are you ready to join us?"

About the Author

Three career paths resonated for Kym during her early childhood: a detective, an investigative reporter, and…a nun. Being a nun, however, dropped by the wayside when she became aware of boys—they were the spice of life she couldn't deny.

In high school her path was forged when she took her first job at a dry cleaners and met every cop in town, especially the lone female police officer in patrol. From that point on there was no stopping Kym's pursuit of a career in law enforcement—even if she had to duct tape rolls of coins to her waist to meet the weight requirements to be hired.

Kym followed her dream and became a detective that fulfilled her desire to be an investigative reporter, with one extra perk—a badge. Promoted to sergeant Kym spent the majority of her career in SVU. She retired from the job reluctantly when her husband drug her kicking and screaming to another state, but writing continued to call her name, at least in her head.

Handled By Officer is her first book (which has been rewritten so many times, she can't count) and her only book to be written in third person. If you'd like to visit her on the web, she can be found at www.kymroberts.com or on Facebook or Twitter as kymroberts911.

Other books available now by Kym Roberts:
Dead On Arrival (A Malia Fern Mystery)
Dead Man's Carve (A Tickled to Death Mystery)

Dead On Arrival
A Malia Fern Mystery
*Catch the Wave of a wild new paranormal mystery series that will
leave you locked in the middle of the impact zone!*

Bikinis and board shorts are all in a day's work for surf
instructor Malia Fern. Life is good on the island of Kaua'i, even
if her social calendar is lacking and a big surf company is droppin'
in to steal her customers. When Malia stumbles upon the body of
tourist who speaks to her from his sandy grave, life as she knows
it disappears in the outgoing tide.

She didn't expect to find herself investigating his death, she
has no experience, nor any desire to work in the family business
of law enforcement, but that's exactly what she's doing because the
victim keeps asking for help and a group of mystical Menehune
men need her protection. If she knew how to offer it, things would
be a whole lot easier.

To make matters worse, her love life is out of control. Makaio
Natua, the forbidden bad boy cop, is everything she wants and his
charming, security specialist cousin, Alapai Lincoln, is everything
she needs. What could be worse than meeting the two of them at
the same time? A curse designed to control her future.

With life turning wacky, Malia is determined to discover
if the victim's death was an accident, a dope deal gone bad, or
something more sinister than she could possibly imagine, because
this time her last big wipe out may leave her *Dead On Arrival*.

Dead Man's Carve
A Tickled to Death Mystery

"There's nothing wooden about Dead Man's Carve. Roberts mingles a sparkling, unique voice with a great old-fashioned mystery."

Wendy Lyn Watson
Mysteries a la Mode
Pet Boutique Mysteries (as Annie Knox)

Rilee Dust isn't your typical wood carver, she's young and making a go of it in the small village of Tickle Creek, Oregon. She's also the only one in town who isn't determined to get rid her strip club neighbor. Everyone else, however, is ready to evict the *Girls, Girls, Girls.*

When a dog adopts her and turns her life upside down, Rilee's not so sure it's a good thing. Especially when he leads her to a moose, a man and a dead body. Because the moose kicked her butt, the man saved her life and the dead body is one of her customers.

Now Rilee's smack dab in the middle of all the small town politics with a killer on the loose who has an ax to grind. And Rilee just may be the next victim to have her name carved in stone.

Author's Note

Domestic Violence continues to plague our society at alarming rates. Children are brought into the vicious cycle that is unfortunately passed down from one generation to the next, whether it be as a victim or as an abuser.

The most dangerous time for any victim is when s/he tries to escape their abuser. If you know someone in need of assistance, contact your local police department or:

The National Domestic Violence Hotline:
1-(800) 799-SAFE (7233)
1-(800) 787-3224 (TTY)
Or chat live on the web @ www.thehotline.org

National Center for Missing and Exploited Children:
1-(800) THE-LOST (843-5678)
www.missingkids.com/home

RAINN (Rape, Abuse & Incest National Network):
The National Sexual Assault Hotline:
1-(800) 656-HOPE (4673)
www.rainn.org

Lee's story was the original HBO, but after numerous changes for different editors, Lee became a secondary character in the story. Of course, you never know when her combat boots will kick down my door and make her a Person of Interest.

Stay safe and go home, *HBO*.

Kym Roberts